DEAR LIFE

DEAR LIFE

Stories

Alice Munro

A DOUGLAS GIBSON BOOK

McCLELLAND & STEWART

Published in Canada by McClelland & Stewart Doubleday Canada, a division of Random House of Canada Limited, and in the United States by Alfred A. Knopf, a division of Random House, Inc., New York.

Library and Archives Canada Cataloguing in Publication

Munro, Alice, 1931-
Dear life / Alice Munro.
Short stories.
ISBN 978-0-7710-6486-9

I. Title.

PS8576.U57D43 2012   C813'.54   C2012-900978-4

Most of the stories contained in this work were previously published in the following: "In Sight of the Lake" and "Night" in *Granta*; "Pride" and "Train" in *Harper's*; "To Reach Japan" in *Narrative*; "Amundsen," "Corrie," "Dear Life," "Gravel," "Haven," and "Leaving Maverly" in *The New Yorker*; and "Dolly" in *Tin House*.

The lines on page 259 are from "Leanin' on the Old Top Rail" by Nick Kenny and Charles Kenny. Every effort has been made to contact the appropriate copyright holders. The publisher would be happy to amend credit lines as necessary in subsequent printings.

Typeset in Monotype Dante
Printed and bound in the United States of America

A Douglas Gibson Book

McClelland & Stewart,
a division of Random House of Canada Limited
One Toronto Street, Suite 300
Toronto, Ontario
M5C 2V6
www.mcclelland.com

1   2   3   4   5   16   15   14   13   12

CONTENTS

DEAR LIFE

TO REACH JAPAN

ONCE Peter had brought her suitcase on board the train he seemed eager to get himself out of the way. But not to leave. He explained to her that he was just uneasy that the train should start to move. Out on the platform looking up at their window, he stood waving. Smiling, waving. The smile for Katy was wide open, sunny, without a doubt in the world, as if he believed that she would continue to be a marvel to him, and he to her, forever. The smile for his wife seemed hopeful and trusting, with some sort of determination about it. Something that could not easily be put into words and indeed might never be. If Greta had mentioned such a thing he would have said, Don't be ridiculous. And she would have agreed with him, thinking that it was unnatural for people who saw each other daily, constantly, to have to go through explanations of any kind.

When Peter was a baby, his mother had carried him across some mountains whose name Greta kept forgetting, in order to get out of Soviet Czechoslovakia into Western Europe. There were other people of course. Peter's father had intended to be with them but he had been sent to a sanatorium just before the date for the secret departure. He was to follow them when he could, but he died instead.

"I've read stories like that," Greta said, when Peter first told her about this. She explained how in the stories the baby would start to cry and invariably had to be smothered or strangled so that the noise did not endanger the whole illegal party.

Peter said he had never heard such a story and would not say what his mother would have done in such circumstances.

What she did do was get to British Columbia, where she improved her English and got a job teaching what was then called Business Practice to high school students. She brought up Peter on her own and sent him to university, and now he was an engineer. When she came to their apartment, and later to their house, she always sat in the front room, never coming into the kitchen unless Greta invited her. That was her way. She carried not noticing to an extreme. Not noticing, not intruding, not suggesting, though in every single household skill or art she left her daughter-in-law far behind.

Also, she got rid of the apartment where Peter had been brought up and moved into a smaller one with no bedroom, just room for a foldout couch. So Peter can't go home to Mother? Greta teased her, but she seemed startled. Jokes pained her. Maybe it was a problem of language. But English was her usual language now and indeed the only language Peter knew. He had learned Business Practice—though not from his mother—when Greta was learning *Paradise Lost*. She avoided anything useful like the plague. It seemed he did the opposite.

With the glass between them, and Katy never allowing the waving to slow down, they indulged in looks of comic or indeed insane goodwill. She thought how nice-looking he was, and how he seemed to be so unaware of it. He wore a brush cut, in the style of the time—particularly if you were anything like an engineer—and his light-coloured skin was never flushed like hers, never blotchy from the sun, but evenly tanned whatever the season.

His opinions were something like his complexion. When they went to see a movie, he never wanted to talk about it afterwards. He would say that it was good, or pretty good, or okay. He didn't see the point in going further. He watched television, he read a book in somewhat the same way. He had patience with such things. The people who put them together were probably doing the best they could. Greta used to argue, rashly asking whether he would say the same thing about a bridge. The people who did it did their best but their best was not good enough so it fell down.

Instead of arguing, he just laughed.

It was not the same thing, he said.

No?

No.

Greta should have realized that this attitude—hands off, tolerant—was a blessing for her, because she was a poet, and there were things in her poems that were in no way cheerful or easy to explain.

(Peter's mother and the people he worked with—those who knew about it—still said poetess. She had trained him not to. Otherwise, no training necessary. The relatives she had left behind in her life, and the people she knew now in her role as a housewife and mother, did not have to be trained because they knew nothing about this peculiarity.)

It would become hard to explain, later on in her life, just what was okay in that time and what was not. You might say, well, feminism was not. But then you would have to explain that feminism was not even a word people used. Then you would get all tied up saying that having any serious idea, let alone ambition, or maybe even reading a real book, could be seen as suspect, having something to do with your child's getting pneumonia, and a political remark at an office party might have cost your husband his promotion. It would not have mattered which political party either. It was a woman's shooting off her mouth that did it.

People would laugh and say, Oh surely you are joking, and you would have to say, Well, but not that much. Then she would say, One thing, though, was that if you were writing poetry it was somewhat safer to be a woman than a man. That was where the word poetess came in handy, like a web of spun sugar. Peter would not have felt that way, she said, but remember he had been born in Europe. He would have understood, though, how the men he worked with were supposed to feel about such things.

That summer Peter was going to spend a month or maybe longer in charge of a job that was being done at Lund, far up, in fact as far as you could go north, on the mainland. There was no accommodation for Katy and Greta.

But Greta had kept in touch with a girl she used to work

with in the Vancouver library, who was married now and living in Toronto. She and her husband were going to spend a month in Europe that summer—he was a teacher—and she had written Greta wondering if Greta and her family would do them a favour—she was very polite—by occupying the house in Toronto for part of that time, not letting it stand empty. And Greta had written back telling her about Peter's job but taking up the offer for Katy and herself.

That was why they were now waving and waving from the platform and from the train.

There was a magazine then, called *The Echo Answers,* published irregularly in Toronto. Greta had found it in the library and sent them some poems. Two of the poems had been published, and the result was that when the editor of the magazine came to Vancouver, last fall, she had been invited to a party, with other writers, to meet him. The party was at the house of a writer whose name had been familiar to her, it seemed, for her whole life. It was held in the late afternoon, when Peter was still at work, so she hired a sitter and set off on the North Vancouver bus across Lions Gate Bridge and through Stanley Park. Then she had to wait in front of the Hudson's Bay for a long ride out to the university campus, which was where the writer lived. Let off at the bus's last turning, she found the street and walked along peering at house numbers. She was wearing high heels which slowed her down considerably. Also her most sophisticated black dress, zipped up at the back and skimming the waist and always a little too tight at the hips. It made her look somewhat ridiculous, she thought, as she stumbled slightly, along the curving streets with no sidewalks, the only person about in the waning afternoon. Modern houses, picture windows, as in any up-and-coming suburb, not at all the kind of neighbourhood she had expected. She was beginning to wonder if she had got the street wrong, and was not unhappy to think that. She could go back to the bus stop where there was a bench. She could slip off her shoes and settle down for the long solitary ride home.

But when she saw the cars parked, saw the number, it was too late to turn around. Noise seeped out around the closed door and she had to ring the bell twice.

She was greeted by a woman who seemed to have been expecting somebody else. Greeted was the wrong word—the woman opened the door and Greta said that this must be where they were having the party.

"What does it look like?" the woman said, and leaned on the doorframe. The way was barred till she—Greta—said, "May I come in?" and then there was a movement that seemed to cause considerable pain. She didn't ask Greta to follow her but Greta did anyway.

Nobody spoke to her or noticed her but in a short time a teenage girl thrust out a tray on which there were glasses of what looked like pink lemonade. Greta took one, and drank it down at a thirsty gulp, then took another. She thanked the girl, and tried to start a conversation about the long hot walk, but the girl was not interested and turned away, doing her job.

Greta moved on. She kept smiling. Nobody looked at her with any recognition or pleasure and why should they? People's eyes slid round her and then they went on with their conversations. They laughed. Everybody but Greta was equipped with friends, jokes, half-secrets, everybody appeared to have found somebody to welcome them. Except for the teenagers who kept sullenly relentlessly passing their pink drinks.

She didn't give up, though. The drink was helping her and she resolved to have another as soon as the tray came around. She watched for a conversational group that seemed to have a hole in it, where she might insert herself. She seemed to have found one when she heard the names of movies mentioned. European movies, such as were beginning to be shown in Vancouver at that time. She heard the name of one that she and Peter had gone to see. *The Four Hundred Blows.* "Oh, I saw that." She said this loudly and enthusiastically, and they all looked at her and one, a spokesperson evidently, said, *"Really?"*

Greta was drunk, of course. Pimm's No. 1 and pink grapefruit juice downed in a hurry. She didn't take this snub to heart as she might have done in a normal way. Just drifted on, knowing she had somehow lost her bearings but getting a feeling that there was a giddy atmosphere of permission in the room, and it didn't matter about not making friends, she could just wander around and pass her own judgments.

There was a knot of people in an archway who were important. She saw among them the host, the writer whose name and face she had known for such a long time. His conversation was loud and hectic and there seemed to be danger around him and a couple of other men, as if they would as soon fire off an insult as look at you. Their wives, she came to believe, made up the circle she had tried to crash into.

The woman who had answered the door was not one of

either group, being a writer herself. Greta saw her turn when her name was called. It was the name of a contributor to the magazine in which she herself had been published. On these grounds, might it not be possible to go up and introduce herself? An equal, in spite of the coolness at the door?

But now the woman had her head lolling on the shoulder of the man who had called her name, and they would not welcome an interruption.

This reflection made Greta sit down, and since there were no chairs she sat on the floor. She had a thought. She thought that when she went with Peter to an engineers' party, the atmosphere was pleasant though the talk was boring. That was because everybody had their importance fixed and settled at least for the time being. Here nobody was safe. Judgment might be passed behind backs, even on the known and published. An air of cleverness or nerves obtained, no matter who you were.

And here she had been desperate for anybody to throw her any old bone of conversation at all.

When she got her theory of the unpleasantness worked out she felt relieved and didn't much care if anybody talked to her or not. She took her shoes off and the relief was immense. She sat with her back against a wall and her legs stuck out on one of the lesser of the party's thoroughfares. She didn't want to risk spilling her drink on the rug so she finished it in a hurry.

A man stood over her. He said, "How did you get here?"

She pitied his dull clumping feet. She pitied anybody who had to stand up.

She said that she had been invited.

"Yes. But did you come in your car?"

II

"I walked." But that was not enough, and in a while she managed to offer up the rest of it.

"I came on a bus, then I walked."

One of the men who had been in the special circle was now behind the man in the shoes. He said, "Excellent idea." He actually seemed ready to talk to her.

The first man didn't care for this one so much. He had retrieved Greta's shoes, but she refused them, explaining that they hurt too much.

"Carry them. Or I will. Can you get up?"

She looked for the more important man to help her, but he wasn't there. Now she remembered what he'd written. A play about Doukhobors that had caused a big row because the Doukhobors were going to have to be naked. Of course they weren't real Doukhobors, they were actors. And they were not allowed to be naked after all.

She tried explaining this to the man who helped her up, but he was plainly not interested. She asked what he wrote. He said he was not that kind of writer, he was a journalist. Visiting in this house with his son and daughter, grandchildren of the hosts. They—the children—had been passing out the drinks.

"Lethal," he said, referring to the drinks. "Criminal."

Now they were outside. She walked in her stocking feet across the grass, barely avoiding a puddle.

"Somebody has thrown up there," she told her escort.

"Indeed," he said, and settled her into a car. The outside air had altered her mood, from an unsettled elation to something within reach of embarrassment, even shame.

"North Vancouver," he said. She must have told him that. "Okay? We'll proceed. The Lions Gate."

She hoped he wouldn't ask what she was doing at the party. If she had to say she was a poet, her present situation, her overindulgence, would be taken as drearily typical. It wasn't dark out, but it was evening. They seemed to be headed in the right direction, along some water then over a bridge. The Burrard Street Bridge. Then more traffic, she kept opening her eyes to trees passing by, then shutting them again without meaning to. She knew when the car stopped that it was too soon for them to be home. That is, at her home.

Those great leafy trees above them. You could not see any stars. But some shine on the water, between wherever they were and the city lights.

"Just sit and consider," he said.

She was enraptured by the word.

"Consider."

"How you're going to walk into the house, for instance. Can you manage dignified? Don't overdo it. Nonchalant? I presume you have a husband."

"I will have to thank you first for driving me home," she said. "So you will have to tell me your name."

He said that he had already told her that. Possibly twice. But once again, okay. Harris Bennett. Bennett. He was the son-in-law of the people who had given the party. Those were his children, passing out the drinks. He and they were visiting from Toronto. Was she satisfied?

"Do they have a mother?"

"Indeed they do. But she is in a hospital."

"I'm sorry."

"No need. It's quite a nice hospital. It's for mental problems. Or you might say emotional problems."

She hurried on to tell him that her husband was named Peter and that he was an engineer and that they had a daughter named Katy.

"Well that's very nice," he said, and started to back out.

On Lions Gate Bridge he said, "Excuse me for sounding how I did. I was thinking whether I would or wouldn't kiss you and I decided I wouldn't."

She thought he was saying that there was something about her that didn't quite measure up to being kissed. The mortification was like being slapped clean back into sobriety.

"Now when we get over the bridge do we go right on Marine Drive?" he continued. "I'll rely on you to tell me."

During the coming fall and winter and spring there was hardly a day when she didn't think of him. It was like having the very same dream the minute you fell asleep. She would lean her head against the back pillow of the sofa, thinking that she lay in his arms. You would not think that she'd remember his face but it would spring up in detail, the face of a creased and rather tired-looking, satirical, indoor sort of man. Nor was his body lacking, it was presented as reasonably worn but competent, and uniquely desirable.

She nearly wept with longing. Yet all this fantasy disappeared, went into hibernation when Peter came home. Daily affections sprang to the fore then, reliable as ever.

The dream was in fact a lot like the Vancouver weather—a dismal sort of longing, a rainy dreamy sadness, a weight that shifted round the heart.

So what about the rejection of kissing, that might seem an ungallant blow?

She simply cancelled it out. Forgot about it entirely.

And what about her poetry? Not a line, not a word. Not a hint that she had ever cared for it.

Of course she gave these fits houseroom mostly when Katy was napping. Sometimes she spoke his name out loud, she embraced idiocy. This followed by a scorching shame in which she despised herself. Idiocy indeed. Idiot.

Then a jolt came, the prospect then certainty of the job at Lund, the offer of the house in Toronto. A clear break in the weather, an access of boldness.

She found herself writing a letter. It didn't begin in any conventional way. No Dear Harris. No Remember me.

> *Writing this letter is like putting a note in a bottle—*
> *And hoping*
> *It will reach Japan.*

Nearest thing to a poem in some time.

She had no idea of an address. She was bold and foolish enough to phone the people who had given the party. But when the woman answered her mouth went dry and felt as big as a tundra and she had to hang up. Then she carted Katy over to the public library and found a Toronto phone book. There were lots of Bennetts but not a single Harris or H. Bennett.

She had a shocking idea then, to look in the obituaries. She couldn't stop herself. She waited till the man reading the library copy was finished. She did not see the Toronto paper usually because you had to go over the bridge to get it, and Peter always brought home the *Vancouver Sun*. Rustling through its pages finally she found his name at the top of a column. So he was not dead. A newspaper columnist. Naturally he would not want to be bothered with people calling him by name, at home.

He wrote about politics. His writing seemed intelligent but she did not care anything about it.

She sent her letter to him there, at the newspaper. She could not be sure that he opened his own mail and she thought that putting Private on the envelope was asking for trouble, so she wrote only the day of her arrival and the time of the train, after the bit about the bottle. No name. She thought that whoever opened the envelope might think of an elderly relative given to whimsical turns of phrase. Nothing to implicate him, even supposing such peculiar mail did get sent home and his wife opened it, being now out of the hospital.

Katy had evidently not understood that Peter's being outside on the platform meant that he would not be travelling with them. When they began to move and he didn't, and when with gathering speed they left him altogether behind, she took the desertion hard. But she settled down in a while, telling Greta that he would be there in the morning.

When that time came Greta was apprehensive, but Katy made no mention at all of the absence. Greta asked her if she was hungry and she said yes, then explained to her mother—as Greta had explained to her before they ever got on the train—that they now had to take off their pyjamas and look for their breakfast in another room.

"What do you want for breakfast?"

"Crisp peas." That meant Rice Krispies.

"We'll see if they have them."

They did.

"Now will we go and find Daddy?"

There was a play area for children but it was quite small. A boy and a girl—a brother and sister, by the looks of their matching bunny-rabbit outfits—had taken it over. Their game consisted of running small vehicles at each other then deflecting them at the last moment. CRASH BANG CRASH.

"This is Katy," Greta said. "I'm her mom. What are your names?"

The crashing took on more vehemence but they didn't look up.

"Daddy isn't here," said Katy.

Greta decided that they had better go back and get Katy's Christopher Robin book and take it up to the dome car and read it. They wouldn't be likely to bother anybody because breakfast wasn't over and the important mountain scenery hadn't started.

The problem was that once she finished Christopher Robin, Katy wanted it started again, immediately. During the first reading she had been quiet, but now she began chiming in with ends of lines. Next time she chanted word for word though still not ready to try it by herself. Greta could imagine this being an annoyance to people once the dome car filled up. Children Katy's age had no problem with monotony. In fact they embraced it, diving into it and wrapping the familiar words round their tongues as if they were a candy that could last forever.

A boy and a girl came up the stairs and sat down across from Greta and Katy. They said good morning with considerable cheer and Greta responded. Katy rather disapproved of her acknowledging them and continued to recite softly with her eyes on the book.

From across the aisle came the boy's voice, almost as quiet as hers:

They're changing guard at Buckingham Palace—
Christopher Robin went down with Alice.

After he finished that one he started another. " 'I do not like them, Sam-I-am.' "

Greta laughed but Katy didn't. Greta could see that she was a bit scandalized. She understood silly words coming out of a book but not coming out of somebody's mouth without a book.

"Sorry," said the boy to Greta. "We're preschoolers. That's our literature." He leaned across and spoke seriously and softly to Katy.

"That's a nice book, isn't it?"

"He means we work with preschoolers," the girl said to Greta. "Sometimes we do get confused though."

The boy went on talking to Katy.

"I maybe could guess your name now. What is it? Is it Rufus? Is it Rover?"

Katy bit her lips but then could not resist a severe reply.

"I'm not a dog," she said.

"No. I shouldn't have been so stupid. I'm a boy and my name's Greg. This girl's name is Laurie."

"He was teasing you," said Laurie. "Should I give him a swat?"

Katy considered this, then said, "No."

" 'Alice is marrying one of the guard,' " Greg continued. " 'A soldier's life is terrible hard, says Alice.' "

Katy chimed in softly on the second Alice.

Laurie told Greta that they had been going around to kindergartens, doing skits. This was called reading readiness work. They were actors, really. She was going to get off at Jasper, where she had a summer job waitressing and doing some comic bits. Not reading readiness exactly. Adult entertainment, was what it was called.

"Christ," she said. She laughed. "Take what you can get."

Greg was loose, and stopping off in Saskatoon. His family was there.

They were both quite beautiful, Greta thought. Tall, limber, almost unnaturally lean, he with crinkly dark hair, she black-haired and sleek as a Madonna. When she mentioned their similarity a bit later on, they said they had sometimes taken advantage of it, when it came to living arrangements. It made things no end easier, but they had to remember to ask for two beds and make sure both got mussed up overnight.

And now, they told her, now they didn't need to worry. Nothing to be scandalized about. They were breaking up, after three years together. They had been chaste for months, at least with each other.

"Now no more Buckingham Palace," said Greg to Katy. "I have to do my exercises."

Greta thought this meant that he had to go downstairs or at least into the aisle for some calisthenics, but instead he and Laurie threw their heads back, stretched their throats, and began to warble and caw and do strange singsongs. Katy was delighted, taking all this as an offering, a show for her benefit. She behaved as a proper audience, too—quite still until it ended, then breaking out in laughter.

Some people who had meant to come up the stairs had stopped at the bottom, less charmed than Katy and not knowing what to make of things.

"Sorry," said Greg, with no explanation but a note of intimate friendliness. He held out a hand to Katy.

"Let's see if there's a playroom."

Laurie and Greta followed them. Greta was hoping that he wasn't one of those adults who make friends with children mostly to test their own charms, then grow bored and grumpy when they realize how tireless a child's affections can be.

By lunchtime or sooner, she knew that she didn't need to worry. What had happened wasn't that Katy's attentions were wearing Greg out, but that various other children had joined the competition and he was giving no sign of being worn out at all.

He didn't set up a competition. He managed things so that he turned the attention first drawn to himself into the children's awareness of each other, and then into games that were lively or even wild, but not bad-tempered. Tantrums didn't occur. Spoils vanished. There simply was not time—so much more interesting stuff was going on. It was a miracle, how much ease with wildness was managed in such a small space. And the energy expended promised naps in the afternoon.

"He's remarkable," Greta said to Laurie.

"He's mostly just there," Laurie said. "He doesn't save

himself up. You know? A lot of actors do. Actors in particular. Dead offstage."

Greta thought, That's what I do. I save myself up, most of the time. Careful with Katy, careful with Peter.

In the decade that they had already entered but that she at least had not taken much notice of, there was going to be a lot of attention paid to this sort of thing. Being there was to mean something it didn't use to mean. Going with the flow. Giving. Some people were giving, other people were not very giving. Barriers between the inside and outside of your head were to be trampled down. Authenticity required it. Things like Greta's poems, things that did not flow right out, were suspect, even scorned. Of course she went right on doing as she did, fussing and probing, secretly tough as nails on the counterculture. But at the moment, her child surrendered to Greg, and to whatever he did; she was entirely grateful.

In the afternoon, as Greta had predicted, the children went to sleep. Their mothers too in some cases. Others played cards. Greg and Greta waved to Laurie when she got off at Jasper. She blew kisses from the platform. An older man appeared, took her suitcase, kissed her fondly, looked towards the train and waved to Greg. Greg waved to him.

"Her present squeeze," he said.

More waves as the train got going, then he and Greta took Katy back to the compartment, where she fell asleep between them, asleep in the very middle of a jump. They opened the compartment curtain to get more air, now that there was no danger of the child's falling out.

"Awesome to have a child," Greg said. That was another word new at the time, or at least new to Greta.

"It happens," she said.

"You're so calm. Next you'll say, 'That's life.' "

"I will not," Greta said, and outstared him till he shook his head and laughed.

He told her that he had got into acting by way of his religion. His family belonged to some Christian sect Greta had never heard of. This sect was not numerous but very rich, or at least some of them were. They had built a church with a theatre in it in a town on the prairie. That was where he started to act before he was ten years old. They did parables from the Bible but also present day, about the awful things that happened to people who didn't believe what they did. His family was very proud of him and of course so he was of himself. He wouldn't dream of telling them all that went on when the rich converts came to renew their vows and get revitalized in their holiness. Anyway he really liked getting all the approval and he liked the acting.

Till one day he just got the idea that he could do the acting and not go through all that church stuff. He tried to be polite about it, but they said it was the Devil getting hold. He said ha-ha I know who it was getting hold.

Bye-bye.

"I don't want you to think it was all bad. I still believe in praying and everything. But I never could tell my family what went on. Anything halfway true would just kill them. Don't you know people like that?"

She told him that when she and Peter first moved to Vancouver her grandmother, who lived in Ontario, had got in touch with a minister of a church there. He came to call and she, Greta, was very snooty to him. He said he would pray for her, and she as good as said, don't bother. Her grandmother was dying at the time. Greta felt ashamed and mad about being ashamed whenever she thought about it.

Peter didn't understand all that. His mother never went to church though one reason she had carried him through the mountains was presumably so they could be Catholics. He said Catholics probably had an advantage, you could hedge your bets right until you were dying.

This was the first time she had thought of Peter in a while.

The fact was that she and Greg were drinking while all this anguished but also somewhat comforting talk went on. He had produced a bottle of ouzo. She was fairly cautious with it, as she had been with any alcohol she'd had since the writers' party, but some effect was there. Enough that they began to stroke each other's hands and then to engage in some kissing and fondling. All of which had to go on beside the body of the sleeping child.

"We better stop this," Greta said. "Otherwise it will become deplorable."

"It isn't us," said Greg. "It's some other people."

"Tell them to stop, then. Do you know their names?"

"Wait a minute. Reg. Reg and Dorothy."

Greta said, "Cut that out, Reg. What about my innocent child?"

"We could go to my berth. It's not far along."

"I haven't got any—"

"I have."

"Not on you?"

"Certainly not. What kind of a beast do you think I am?"

So they arranged whatever clothing had been disarranged, slipped out of the compartment, carefully fastened every button of the berth where Katy was sleeping, and with a certain fancy nonchalance made their way from Greta's car to his. This was hardly necessary—they met no one. The people who were not in the dome car taking pictures of the everlasting mountains were in the bar car, or dozing.

In Greg's untidy quarters they took up where they had left off. There was no room for two people to lie down properly but they managed to roll over each other. At first no end of stifled laughter, then the great shocks of pleasure, with no place to look but into each other's wide eyes. Biting each other to hold in some ferocious noise.

"Nice," said Greg. "All right."

"I've got to get back."

"So soon?"

"Katy might wake up and I'm not there."

"Okay. Okay. I should get ready for Saskatoon anyway. What if we'd got there just in the middle of it? Hello Mom. Hello Daddy. Excuse me just a minute here while I—Wa—hoo!"

She got herself decent and left him. Actually she didn't much care who met her. She was weak, shocked, but buoyant, like some gladiator—she actually thought this out and smiled at it—after a session in the arena.

Anyway, she didn't meet a soul.

The bottom fastener of the curtain was undone. She was sure she remembered fastening it. Though even with it open Katy could hardly get out and surely wouldn't try. One time when Greta had left for a minute to go to the toilet, she had explained thoroughly that Katy must never try to follow, and Katy had said, "I wouldn't," as if even to suggest that was treating her like a baby.

Greta took hold of the curtains to open them all the

way, and when she had done so she saw that Katy was not there.

She went crazy. She yanked up the pillow, as if a child of Katy's size could have managed to cover herself with it. She pounded her hands on the blanket as if Katy could have been hiding underneath it. She got control of herself and tried to think where the train had stopped, or whether it had been stopped, during the time she had been with Greg. While it was stopped, if it had been stopped, could a kidnapper have got on the train and somehow made off with Katy?

She stood in the aisle, trying to think what she had to do to stop the train.

Then she thought, she made herself think, that nothing like that could have happened. Don't be ridiculous. Katy must have wakened and found her not there and gone looking for her. All by herself, she had gone looking.

Right around here, she must be right around here. The doors at either end of the coach were far too heavy for her to open.

Greta could barely move. Her whole body, her mind, emptied. This could not have happened. Go back, go back, to before she went with Greg. Stop there. Stop.

Across the aisle was a seat unoccupied for the time being. A woman's sweater and some magazine left to claim it. Farther along, a seat with the fasteners all done up, as hers—theirs—had been. She pulled them apart with one grab. The old man who was sleeping there turned over on his back but never woke up. There was no way he could be hiding anybody.

What idiocy.

A new fear then. Supposing Katy had made her way to one or the other end of the car and had actually managed to get a door open. Or followed a person who had opened it ahead of her. Between the cars there was a short walkway where you were actually walking over the place where the cars joined up. There you could feel the train's motion in a sudden and alarming way. A heavy door behind you and another in front, and on either side of the walkway clanging metal plates. These covered the steps that were let down when the train was stopped.

You always hurried through these passages, where the banging and swaying reminded you how things were put together in a way that seemed not so inevitable after all. Almost casual, yet in too much of a hurry, that banging and swaying.

The door at the end was heavy even for Greta. Or she was drained by her fear. She pushed mightily with her shoulder.

And there, between the cars, on one of those continually noisy sheets of metal—there sat Katy. Eyes wide open and mouth slightly open, amazed and alone. Not crying at all, but when she saw her mother she started.

Greta grabbed her and hoisted her onto her hip and stumbled back against the door that she had just opened.

All of the cars had names, to commemorate battles or explorations or illustrious Canadians. The name of their car was Connaught. She would never forget that.

Katy was not hurt at all. Her clothes hadn't caught as they might have on the shifting sharp edges of the metal plates.

"I went to look for you," she said.

When? Just a moment ago, or right after Greta had left her?

Surely not. Somebody would have spotted her there, picked her up, sounded an alarm.

The day was sunny but not really warm. Her face and hands were quite cold.

"I thought you were on the stairs," she said.

Greta covered her with the blanket in their berth, and it was then that she herself began to shake, as if she had a fever. She felt sick, and actually tasted vomit in her throat. Katy said, "Don't push me," and squirmed away.

"You smell a bad smell," she said.

Greta took her arms away and lay on her back.

This was so terrible, her thoughts of what might have happened so terrible. The child was still stiff with protest, keeping away from her.

Someone would have found Katy, surely. Some decent person, not an evil person, would have spotted her there and carried her to where it was safe. Greta would have heard the dismaying announcement, news that a child had been found alone on the train. A child who gave her name as Katy. She would have rushed from where she was at the moment, having got herself as decent as she could, she would have rushed to claim her child and lied, saying that she had just gone to the ladies' room. She would have been frightened, but she would have been spared the picture she had now, of Katy sitting in that noisy space, helpless between the cars. Not crying, not complaining, as if she was just to sit there forever and there was to be no explanation offered to her, no hope. Her eyes had been oddly without expression and her mouth just hanging open, in the moment before the fact of rescue struck her and she could begin to cry. Only then could she retrieve her world, her right to suffer and complain.

Now she said she wasn't sleepy, she wanted to get up. She asked where Greg was. Greta said that he was having a nap, he was tired.

She and Greta went to the dome car, to spend the rest of the afternoon. They had it mostly to themselves. The people taking pictures must have worn themselves out on the Rocky Mountains. And as Greg had commented, the prairies left them flat.

The train stopped for a short time in Saskatoon and several people got off. Greg was among them. Greta saw him greeted by a couple who must have been his parents. Also by a woman in a wheelchair, probably a grandmother, and then by several younger people who were hanging about, cheerful and embarrassed. None of them looked like members of a sect, or like people who were strict and disagreeable in any way.

But how could you spot that for sure in anybody?

Greg turned from them and scanned the windows of the train. She waved from the dome car and he caught sight of her and waved back.

"There's Greg," she said to Katy. "See down there. He's waving. Can you wave back?"

But Katy found it too difficult to look for him. Or else she did not try. She turned away with a proper and slightly offended air, and Greg, after one last antic wave, turned too. Greta wondered if the child could be punishing him for desertion, refusing to miss or even acknowledge him.

All right, if this is the way it's going to be, forget it.

"Greg waved to you," Greta said, as the train pulled away.

"I know."

While Katy slept beside her in the bunk that night Greta wrote a letter to Peter. A long letter that she intended to be funny, about all the different sorts of people to be found on the train. The preference most of them had for seeing through their camera, rather than looking at the real thing, and so on. Katy's generally agreeable behaviour. Nothing about the loss, of course, or the scare. She posted the letter when the prairies were far behind and the black spruce went on forever, and they were stopped for some reason in the little lost town of Hornepayne.

All of her waking time for these hundreds of miles had been devoted to Katy. She knew that such devotion on her part had never shown itself before. It was true that she had cared for the child, dressed her, fed her, talked to her, during those hours when they were together and Peter was at work. But Greta had other things to do around the house then, and her attention had been spasmodic, her tenderness often tactical.

And not just because of the housework. Other thoughts had crowded the child out. Even before the useless, exhausting, idiotic preoccupation with the man in Toronto, there was the other work, the work of poetry that it seemed she had been doing in her head for most of her life. That struck her now as another traitorous business—to Katy, to Peter, to life. And now, because of the picture in her head of Katy alone, Katy sitting there amid the metal clatter between the cars—that was something else she, Katy's mother, was going to have to give up.

A sin. She had given her attention elsewhere. Determined, foraging attention to something other than the child. A sin.

They arrived in Toronto in the middle of the morning. The day was dark. There was summer thunder and lightning. Katy had never seen such commotion on the West Coast, but Greta told her there was nothing to be afraid of and it seemed she wasn't. Or of the still greater, electrically lit darkness they encountered in the tunnel where the train stopped.

She said, "Night."

Greta said, No, no, they just had to walk to the end of the tunnel, now that they **were off** the train. Then up some steps, or maybe there would **be an** escalator, and then they would be in a big building **and then** outside, where they would get a taxi. A taxi was a car, that was all, and it would take them to their house. Their new house, where they would live for a while. They would live there for a while and then they would go back to Daddy.

They walked up a ramp, and there was an escalator. Katy halted, so Greta did too, till people got by them. Then Greta picked Katy up and set her on her hip, and managed the suitcase with the other arm, stooping and bumping it on the moving steps. At the top she put the child down and they were able to hold hands again, in the bright lofty light of Union Station.

There the people who had been walking in front of them began to peel off, to be claimed by those who were waiting, and who called out their names, or who simply walked up and took hold of their suitcases.

As someone now took hold of theirs. Took hold of it, took hold of Greta, and kissed her for the first time, in a determined and celebratory way.

Harris.

First a shock, then a tumbling in Greta's insides, an immense settling.

She was trying to hang on to Katy but at this moment the child pulled away and got her hand free.

She didn't try to escape. She just stood waiting for whatever had to come next.

AMUNDSEN

O n the bench outside the station I sat and waited. The station had been open when the train arrived but now it was locked. Another woman sat at the end of the bench, holding between her knees a string bag full of parcels wrapped in oiled paper. Meat—raw meat. You could smell it.

Across the tracks was the electric train, empty, waiting.

No other passengers showed up and after a while the stationmaster stuck his head out and called, "San." At first I thought he was calling a man's name, Sam. And another man wearing some kind of official outfit did come around the end of the building. He crossed the tracks and boarded the electric car. The woman with the parcels stood up and followed him, so I did the same. There was a burst of shouting from across the street and the doors of a dark-shingled flat-roofed building opened, letting loose several men who were jamming caps on their heads and banging lunch buckets against their thighs. By the noise they were making you would think the car was going to run away from them at any minute. But when they settled on board nothing happened. The car sat while they counted each other and said who was missing and told the driver he couldn't go yet. Then somebody remembered that it was the missing man's day off. The car started, though you couldn't tell if the driver had been listening to any of this, or cared.

All the men got off at a sawmill in the bush—it would not have been more than a ten-minute walk—and shortly after that the lake came into view, covered with snow. A long white wooden building in front of it. The woman readjusted her meat packages and stood up and I followed. The driver again called, "San," and the doors opened. A couple of women were waiting to get on. They greeted the woman with the meat and she said it was a raw day.

All avoided looking at me as I climbed down behind the meat woman.

There was no one to wait for at this end, apparently. The doors banged together and the train started back.

Then there was silence, the air like ice. Brittle-looking birch trees with black marks on their white bark, and some kind of small untidy evergreens rolled up like sleepy bears. The frozen lake not level but mounded along the shore, as if the waves had turned to ice in the act of falling. And the building beyond with its deliberate rows of windows, and its glassed-in porches at either end. Everything austere and northerly, black-and-white under the high dome of clouds.

But the birch bark not white after all as you got closer. Greyish yellow, greyish blue, grey.

So still, so immense an enchantment.

"Where you heading?" the meat woman called to me. "Visiting hours over at three."

"I'm not a visitor," I said. "I'm the teacher."

"Well they won't let you in the front door anyway," said the woman with some satisfaction. "You better head along with me. Didn't you bring a suitcase?"

"The stationmaster said he'd bring it later."

"The way you were just standing there looked like you were lost."

I said that I had stopped because it was so beautiful.

"Some might think so. Less they were too sick or too busy."

Nothing more was said until we entered the kitchen at one end of the building. Already I was in need of its warmth. I did not get a chance to look around me because attention was drawn to my boots.

"You better get those off before they track the floor."

I wrestled off the boots—there was no chair to sit down on—and set them on the mat where the woman had put hers.

"Pick them up and bring them with you, I don't know where they'll be putting you. You better keep your coat on, too, there's no heating in the cloakroom."

No heat, no light, except what came through a little window I could not reach. It was like being punished at school. Sent-to-the-cloakroom. Yes. The same smell of winter clothing that never really dried out, of boots soaked through to dirty socks, unwashed feet.

I climbed up on a bench but still could not see out. On the shelf where caps and scarves were thrown I found a bag with some figs and dates in it. Somebody must have stolen them and stashed them here to take home. All of a sudden I was hungry. Nothing to eat since morning, except for a dry cheese sandwich on the Ontario Northland. I considered the ethics of stealing from a thief. But the figs would catch in my teeth, to betray me.

I got myself down just in time. Somebody was entering the cloakroom. Not any of the kitchen help but a schoolgirl in a bulky winter coat, with a scarf over her hair. She came in with a rush—books thrown on the bench so they scattered on the floor, scarf snatched so her hair sprung out in a bush, and at the same time, it seemed, boots kicked loose one after the other and sent skittering across the cloakroom floor. Nobody had got hold of her, apparently, to make her take them off at the kitchen door.

"Hey, I wasn't trying to hit you," the girl said. "It's so dark in here after outside you don't know what you're doing. Aren't you freezing? Are you waiting for somebody to get off work?"

"I'm waiting to see Dr. Fox."

"Well you won't have to wait long, I just rode from town with him. You're not sick, are you? If you're sick you can't come here, you have to see him in town."

"I'm the teacher."

"Are you? Are you from Toronto?"

"Yes."

There was a certain pause, perhaps of respect.

But no. An examination of my coat.

"That's really nice. What's that fur on the collar?"

"Persian lamb. Actually it's imitation."

"Could have fooled me. I don't know what they put you in here for, it'll freeze your butt off. Excuse me. You want to see the doctor, I can show you. I know where everything is,

I've lived here practically since I was born. My mother runs the kitchen. My name is Mary. What's yours?"

"Vivi. Vivien."

"If you are a teacher shouldn't it be Miss? Miss what?"

"Miss Hyde."

"Tan your hide," she said. "Sorry, I just thought that up. I'd like if you could be my teacher but I have to go to school in town. It's the stupid rules. Because I have not got TB."

She was leading me while she talked, through the door at the far end of the cloakroom, then along a regular hospital corridor. Waxed linoleum. Dull green paint, an antiseptic smell.

"Now you're here maybe I'll get Reddy to let me switch."

"Who is Reddy?"

"Reddy Fox. It's out of a book. Me and Anabel just started calling him that."

"Who is Anabel?"

"Nobody now. She's dead."

"Oh, I'm sorry."

"Not your fault. It happens around here. I'm in high school this year. Anabel never really got to go to school at all. When I was just in public school Reddy got the town teacher to let me stay home a lot, so I could keep her company."

She stopped at a half-opened door and whistled.

"Hey. I brought the teacher."

A man's voice said, "Okay Mary. Enough out of you for one day."

"Okay. I heard you."

She sauntered away and left me facing a spare man of ordinary height, whose reddish fair hair was cut very short and glistened in the artificial light from the hallway.

"You've met Mary," he said. "She has a lot to say for herself.

She won't be in your class so you won't have to undergo that every day. People either take to her or they don't."

He struck me as between ten and fifteen years older than myself and at first he talked to me just in the way an older man would do. A preoccupied future employer. He asked about my trip, about the arrangements for my suitcase. He wanted to know how I would like living up here in the woods, after Toronto, whether I would be bored.

Not in the least, I said, and added that it was beautiful.

"It's like—it's like being inside a Russian novel."

He looked at me attentively for the first time.

"Is it really? Which Russian novel?"

His eyes were a light, bright greyish blue. One eyebrow had risen, like a little peaked cap.

It was not that I hadn't read Russian novels. I had read some all through and some partway. But because of that eyebrow, and his amused but confrontational expression, I could not remember any title except *War and Peace*. I did not want to say that because it was what anybody would remember.

"*War and Peace.*"

"Well, it's only the Peace we've got here, I'd say. But if it was the War you were hankering after I suppose you would have joined one of those women's outfits and got yourself overseas."

I was angry and humiliated because I had not really been showing off. Or not only showing off. I had wanted to say what a wonderful effect this scenery had on me.

He was evidently the sort of person who posed questions that were traps for you to fall into.

"I guess I was really expecting some sort of old lady teacher come out of the woodwork," he said, in some slight

apology. "As if everybody of reasonable age and qualifications would have got back into the system these days. You
didn't study to be a teacher, did you? Just what were you
planning to do once you got your B.A.?"

"Work on my M.A.," I said shortly.

"So what changed your mind?"

"I thought I should earn some money."

"Sensible idea. Though I'm afraid you won't earn much
here. Sorry to pry. I just wanted to make sure you were not
going to run off and leave us in the lurch. Not planning to
get married, are you?"

"No."

"All right. All right. You're off the hook now. Didn't dis-
courage you, did I?"

I had turned my head away.

"No."

"Go down the hall to Matron's office and she'll tell you
all you need to know. You'll eat your meals with the nurses.
She'll let you know where you sleep. Just try not to get a cold.
I don't suppose you have any experience with tuberculosis?"

"Well I've read—"

"I know. I know. You've read *The Magic Mountain.*"
Another trap sprung, and he seemed restored. "Things have
moved on a bit from that, I hope. Here, I've got some things
I've written out about the kids here and what I was thinking
you might try to do with them. Sometimes I'd rather express
myself in writing. Matron will give you the lowdown."

I had not been there a week before all the events of the first
day seemed unique and unlikely. The kitchen, the kitchen

cloakroom where the workers kept their clothes and concealed their thefts, were rooms I hadn't seen again and probably wouldn't see. The doctor's office was similarly out of bounds, Matron's room being the proper place for all inquiries, complaints, and ordinary rearrangements. Matron herself was short and stout, pink-faced, with rimless glasses and heavy breathing. Whatever you asked for seemed to astonish her, and cause difficulties, but eventually it was seen to or provided. Sometimes she ate in the nurses' dining room, where she was served a special junket, and cast a pall. Mostly she kept to her own quarters.

Besides Matron there were three registered nurses, not one of them within thirty years of my age. They had come out of retirement to serve, doing their wartime duty. Then there were the nurses' aides, who were my age or even younger, mostly married or engaged or working on being engaged, generally to men in the forces. They talked all the time if Matron and the nurses weren't there. They didn't have the least interest in me. They didn't want to know what Toronto was like, though some of them knew people who had gone there on their honeymoons, and they did not care how my teaching was going or what I had done before I came to work at the San. It wasn't that they were rude—they passed me the butter (it was called butter but it was really orange-streaked margarine, coloured in the kitchen as was the only legal way in those days) and they warned me off the shepherd's pie which they said had groundhog in it. It was just that whatever happened in places they didn't know or to people they didn't know or in times they didn't know had to be discounted. It got in their way and under their skin. They turned off the radio news every chance they got and tried to get music.

"Dance with a dolly with a hole in her stockin' . . ."

Both nurses and aides disliked the CBC which I had been brought up to believe was bringing culture to the hinterlands. Yet they were in awe of Dr. Fox partly because he had read so many books.

They also said that there was nobody like him to tear a strip off you if he felt like it.

I couldn't figure out if they felt there was a connection between reading a lot of books and tearing a strip off.

Usual notions of pedagogy out of place here. Some of these children will reenter the world or system and some will not. Better not a lot of stress. That is testing memorizing classifying nonsense.

Disregard whole grade business entirely. Those who need to can catch up later on or do without. Actually very simple skills, set of facts, etc., necessary for Going into the World. What about Superior Children so-called? Disgusting term. If they are smart in questionable academic way they can easily catch up.

Forget rivers of South America, likewise Magna Carta.

Drawing Music Stories preferred.

Games Okay but watch for overexcitement or too much competitiveness.

Challenge to keep between stress and boredom. Boredom curse of hospitalization.

If Matron can't supply what you need sometimes Janitor will have it stashed away somewhere.

Bon Voyage.

The numbers of children who showed up varied. Fifteen, or down to half a dozen. Mornings only, from nine o'clock till noon, including rest times. Children were kept away if their temperature had risen or if they were undergoing tests. When they were present they were quiet and tractable but not particularly interested. They had caught on right away that this was a pretend school where they were free of all requirements to learn anything, just as they were free of times-tables and memory work. This freedom didn't make them uppity, it didn't make them bored in any troublesome way, just docile and dreamy. They sang rounds softly. They played X's and O's. There was a shadow of defeat over the improvised classroom.

I decided to take the doctor at his word. Or some of his words, such as the ones about boredom being the enemy.

In the janitor's cubbyhole I had seen a world globe. I asked to have it brought out. I started on simple geography. The oceans, the continents, the climates. Why not the winds and the currents? The countries and the cities? The Tropic of Cancer and the Tropic of Capricorn? Why not, after all, the rivers of South America?

Some children had learned such things before, but they had nearly forgotten. The world beyond the lake and the forest had dropped away. I thought they cheered up, as if making friends again, with whatever they used to know. I didn't dump everything on them at once, of course. And I had to go easy with the ones who had never learned such things in their lives because of getting sick too soon.

But that was all right. It could be a game. I separated them into teams, got them calling out answers while I darted here and there with the pointer. I was careful not to let the excitement go on too long. But one day the doctor walked in, fresh from morning surgery, and I was caught. I could not stop things cold, but I tried to dampen the competition. He sat down, looking somewhat tired and withdrawn. He made no objection. After a few moments he began to join in the game, calling out quite ridiculous answers, names not just mistaken but imaginary. Then gradually he let his voice die down. Down, down, first to a mumble, then to a whisper, then till nothing could be heard at all. Nothing. In this way, with this absurdity, he took control of the room. The whole class took to mouthing, in order to imitate him. Their eyes were fixed on his lips.

Suddenly he let out a low growl that had them all laughing.

"Why the deuce is everybody looking at me? Is that what your teacher teaches you? To stare at people who aren't bothering anybody?"

Most laughed, but some couldn't stop watching him even for that. They were hungry for further antics.

"Go on. Go off and misbehave yourselves somewhere else."

He apologized to me for breaking up the class. I began to explain to him my reasons for making this more like real school.

"Though I do agree with you about stress—" I said earnestly. "I agree with what you said in your instructions. I just thought—"

"What instructions? Oh, that was just some bits and pieces that went through my head. I never meant them to be set in stone."

"I mean as long as they are not too sick—"

"I'm sure you're right, I don't suppose it matters."

"Otherwise they seemed sort of listless."

"There's not any need to make a song and dance about it," he said, and walked away.

Then turned to make a barely halfhearted apology.

"We can have a talk about it some other time."

That time, I thought, would never come. He evidently thought me a bother and a fool.

I discovered at lunch, from the aides, that somebody had not survived an operation that morning. So my anger did not turn out to be justified, and for that reason I had to feel more of a fool.

Every afternoon was free. My pupils went down for long naps and I sometimes felt like doing the same. My room was cold—every part of the building seemed cold, far colder than the apartment on Avenue Road, even though my grandparents kept the radiators turned low there, to be patriotic. And the covers were thin—surely people with tuberculosis needed something cozier.

I of course did not have tuberculosis. Maybe they skimped on provisions for people like me.

I was drowsy but couldn't sleep. Overhead there was the rumble of bed-carts being wheeled to the open porches for the icy afternoon exposure.

The building, the trees, the lake, could never again be the same to me as they were on that first day, when I was caught by their mystery and authority. On that day I had believed myself invisible. Now it seemed as if that was never true.

There's the teacher. What's she up to?

She's looking at the lake.

What for?

Nothing better to do.

Some people are lucky.

———

Once in a while I skipped lunch, even though it was part of my salary. I went in to Amundsen, where I ate in a coffee shop. The coffee was Postum and the best bet for a sandwich was tinned salmon, if they had any. The chicken salad had to be looked over well for bits of skin and gristle. Nevertheless I felt more at ease there, as if nobody would know who I was.

About that I was probably mistaken.

The coffee shop didn't have a ladies' room, so you had to go next door to the hotel, then past the open door of the beer parlour, always dark and noisy and letting out a smell of beer and whisky, a blast of cigarette and cigar smoke fit to knock you down. Nevertheless I felt easy enough there. The loggers, the men from the sawmill, would never yelp at you the way the soldiers and the airmen in Toronto did. They were deep down in a world of men, bawling out their own stories, not here to look for women. Possibly more eager in fact to get away from that company now or forever.

The doctor had an office on the main street. Just a small one-storey building so he must live elsewhere. I had picked up from the aides that there was no wife. On the only side street I found the house that might possibly belong to him— a stucco-covered house with a dormer window over the front door, books stacked on the sill of that window. There was a bleak but orderly look to the place, a suggestion of minimal but precise comfort, that a lone man—a regulated lone man—might contrive.

The school at the end of that only residential street was two storeys high. The downstairs served students up to grade eight, the upstairs to grade twelve. One afternoon I spotted Mary there, taking part in a snowball fight. It seemed to be girls against boys. When she saw me, Mary cried out loudly, "Hey, Teach," and gave the balls in both hands a random toss, then sauntered across the street. "See you tomorrow," she called over her shoulder, more or less as a warning that nobody was to follow.

"You on your way home?" she said. "Me too. I used to ride with Reddy, but he's got too late leaving. What do you do, take the tram?"

I said yes, and Mary said, "Oh I can show you the other way and you can save your money. The bush road."

She took me up a narrow but passable track looking down on the town, then running through the woods and past the sawmill.

"This is the way Reddy goes," she said. "It's higher up but shorter when you turn down at the San."

We passed the sawmill, and beneath us, some ugly cuts in the woods and a few shacks, apparently inhabited because they had woodpiles and clotheslines and rising smoke. From one of them a big wolfish dog ran out with a great display of barking and snarling.

"You shut your face," yelled Mary. In no time she had packed and flung a snowball which caught the animal between the eyes. It whirled around and she had another snowball ready to catch it in the rump. A woman in an apron came out and yelled, "You could of killed him."

"Good riddance to bad rubbish."

"I'll get my old man after you."

"That'll be the day. Your old man can't hit a shithouse."

The dog followed at a distance, with some insincere threatening.

"I can take care of any dog, don't worry," Mary said. "I bet I could take care of a bear if we ran into one."

"Don't bears tend to hibernate at this time of year?"

I had been quite scared by the dog but affected carelessness.

"Yeah, but you never know. One came out early and it got into the garbage down at the San. My mom turned around and there it was. Reddy got his gun and shot it.

"Reddy used to take me and Anabel out on the sled, and sometimes other kids too and he had a special whistle that scared off bears. It was pitched too high for the ears of humans."

"Really. Did you see it?"

"It wasn't that kind. I meant one he could do with his mouth."

I thought of the performance in the classroom.

"I don't know, maybe that was just to keep Anabel from getting scared he said that. She couldn't ride, he had to pull her on a toboggan. I'd go right behind her and sometimes I'd jump on the toboggan and he'd say what's the matter with this thing, it weighs a tonne. Then he'd try to turn around quick and catch me, but he never did. And he'd ask Anabel what makes it so heavy what did you have to eat for breakfast, but she never told. If there was other kids I wouldn't do it. It was best when just me and Anabel went. She was the best friend I ever will have."

"What about those girls at the school? Aren't they friends?"

"I just hang around with them when there's nobody else. They're nothing.

"Anabel and me had our birthdays in the same month. June. Our eleventh birthday Reddy took us down the lake in a boat. He taught us swimming. Well, me. He always had to hold Anabel though, she couldn't really learn. Once he went swimming way out by himself and we filled his shoes up with sand. And then our twelfth birthday we couldn't go anywhere like that, but we went to his house and had a cake. She couldn't eat even a little piece of it, so he took us in his car and we threw pieces out the window and fed the seagulls. They were fighting and screaming like mad. We were laughing ourselves crazy and he had to stop and hold Anabel so she wouldn't have a hemorrhage.

"And after that," she said, "after that I wasn't allowed to see her anymore. My mom never wanted me anyway to hang around with kids that had TB. But Reddy talked her into it, he said he'd stop it when he had to. So he did and I got mad. But she wouldn't have been any fun anymore she was too sick. I'd show you her grave but there isn't anything to mark it yet. Reddy and me are going to make something when he gets time. If we'd've gone straight along on the road instead of turning down where we did we would have come to her graveyard. It's just for people that don't have anybody to come and take them home."

By this time we were down on level ground approaching the San.

She said, "Oh I almost forgot," and brought out a fistful of tickets.

"For Valentine's Day. We're putting on this play at the school and it's called *Pinafore*. I got all these to sell and you can be my first sale. I'm in it."

I was right about the house in Amundsen being where the doctor lived. He took me there for supper. The invitation seemed to come rather on the spur of the moment when he met me in the hall. Perhaps he had an uneasy memory of saying we would get together to talk about teaching ideas.

The evening he proposed was the one for which I had bought a ticket for *Pinafore*. I told him that and he said, "Well I did too. It doesn't mean we have to show up."

"I sort of feel as if I'd promised her."

"Well. Now you can sort of unpromise her. It will be dreadful, believe me."

I did as he told me, though I did not see Mary, to tell her. I was waiting where he had instructed me to be, on the open porch outside the front door. I was wearing my best dress of dark green crepe with the little pearl buttons and the real lace collar, and had rammed my feet into suede high-heeled shoes inside my snow boots. I waited past the time mentioned—worried, first, that Matron would come out of her office and spot me, and second, that he would have forgotten all about it.

But then he came along, buttoning up his overcoat, and apologized.

"Always a few bits and bobs to clear up," he said, and led me under the bright stars around the building to his car. "Are you steady?" he said, and when I said yes—though I wondered about the suede shoes—he did not offer his arm.

His car was old and shabby as most cars were in those days. It didn't have a heater. When he said we were going to his house I was relieved. I could not see how we would manage with the crowd at the hotel and I had hoped not to make do with the sandwiches at the café.

In the house, he told me not to take off my coat until the place was warmed up a bit. He got busy at once making a fire in the woodstove.

"I'm your janitor and your cook and your server," he said.

"It'll soon be comfortable here and the meal won't take me long. Don't offer to help, I prefer to work alone. Where would you like to wait? If you want to you could look over the books in the front room. It shouldn't be too unbearable in there with your coat on. The house is heated with stoves throughout and I don't heat up a room if it isn't in use. The light switch is just inside the door. You don't mind if I listen to the news? It's a habit I've got into."

I went into the front room, feeling as if I had more or less been ordered to, leaving the kitchen door open. He came and closed it, saying, "Just until we get a bit of warmth in the kitchen," and went back to the sombrely dramatic, almost religious voice of the CBC, giving out the news of this last year of the war. I had not been able to hear that voice since I left my grandparents' apartment and I rather wished that I could have stayed in the kitchen. But there were quantities of books to look at. Not just on bookshelves but on tables and chairs and windowsills and piled on the floor. After I had examined several of them I concluded that he favoured buying books in batches and probably belonged to several book clubs. The Harvard Classics. The Histories of Will and Ariel Durant—the very same that could be found on my grandfather's shelves. Fiction and poetry seemed in short supply, though there were a few surprising children's classics.

Books on the American Civil War, the South African War, the Napoleonic Wars, the Peloponnesian Wars, the campaigns of Julius Caesar. *Explorations of the Amazon and the Arctic. Shackleton Caught in the Ice. Franklin's Doom, the Donner Party and the Lost Tribes, Buried Cities of Central Africa, Newton and Alchemy, Secrets of the Hindu Kush.* Books suggesting someone anxious to know, to possess great scattered lumps of knowledge. Perhaps not someone whose tastes were firm and exacting.

So when he had asked me, "Which Russian novel?" it was possible that he had not had so firm a platform as I had thought.

When he called, "Ready," and I opened the door, I was armed with this new skepticism.

I said, "Who do you agree with, Naphta or Settembrini?"

"I beg your pardon?"

"In *The Magic Mountain*. Do you like Naphta best or Settembrini?"

"To be honest, I've always thought they were a pair of windbags. You?"

"Settembrini is more humane but Naphta is more interesting."

"They tell you that in school?"

"I never read it in school," I said coolly.

He gave me a quick look, the eyebrow raised.

"Pardon me. If there's anything in there that interests you, feel free. Feel free to come down here and read in your time off. There's an electric heater I could set up, since I imagine you are not experienced with woodstoves. Shall we think about that? I can rustle you up an extra key."

"Thank you."

Pork chops for supper, mashed potatoes, canned peas. Dessert was an apple pie from the bakery, which would have been better if he had thought to heat it up.

He asked me about my life in Toronto, my university courses, my grandparents. He said that he supposed I had been brought up on the straight and narrow.

"My grandfather is a liberal clergyman sort of in the Paul Tillich mode."

"And you? Liberal little Christian granddaughter?"

"No."

"*Touché.* Do you think I'm rude?"

"That depends. If you are interviewing me as an employer, no."

"So I'll go on. Do you have a boyfriend?"

"Yes."

"In the forces I suppose."

I said, In the Navy. That struck me as a good choice, accounting for my never knowing where he was and not getting regular letters. I could manage that he did not get shore leave.

The doctor got up and fetched the tea.

"What sort of boat is he on?"

"Corvette." Another good choice. After a while I could have him torpedoed, as was always happening to corvettes.

"Brave fellow. Milk or sugar in your tea?"

"Neither one thanks."

"That's good because I haven't got any. You know it shows when you're lying, you get hot in the face."

If I hadn't got hot before I did then. My flush rose from my feet up and sweat trickled down under my arms. I hoped the dress would not be ruined.

"I always go hot when I drink tea."

"Oh I see."

Things could not get any worse so I resolved to face him down. I changed the subject on him, asking about how he operated on people. Did he remove lungs, as I had heard?

He could have answered that with more teasing, more superiority—possibly his notion of flirtation—and I believed that if he had done so I would have put on my coat and walked out into the cold. And perhaps he knew that. He began to talk about thoracoplasty, and explain that it was, however, not so easy on the patient as collapsing and deflating a lung. Which interestingly enough even Hippocrates had known about. Of course removal of the lobe had also become popular recently.

"But don't you lose some?" I said.

He must have thought it was time to joke again.

"But of course. Running off and hiding in the bush, we don't know where they get to— Jumping in the lake— Or did you mean don't they die? There's cases of things not working. Yes."

But great things were coming, he said. The surgery he went in for was going to become as obsolete as bloodletting. A new drug was on the way. Streptomycin. Already used in trial. Some problems, naturally there would be problems. Toxicity of the nervous system. But there would be a way found to deal with that.

"Put the sawbones like me out of business."

He washed the dishes, I dried. He put a dish towel round my waist to protect my dress. When the ends were efficiently tied he laid his hand against my upper back. Such firm pressure, fingers separated—he might almost have been taking stock of my body in a professional way. When I went to bed that night I could still feel that pressure. I felt it develop its intensity from the little finger to the hard thumb. I enjoyed it. That was more important really than the kiss placed on my forehead later, the moment before I got out of his car. A dry-lipped kiss, brief and formal, set upon me with hasty authority.

———

The key to his house showed up on the floor of my room, slipped under the door when I wasn't there. But after all I couldn't use it. If anybody else had made me this offer I would have jumped at the chance. Especially if it included a heater. But in this case his past and future presence would be drawing all ordinary comfort out of the situation and replacing it with a pleasure that was tight and nerve-racking rather than expansive. I would not be able to stop shivering even when it wasn't cold, and I doubted whether I could have read a word.

I thought that Mary would probably appear, to scold me for missing *Pinafore*. I thought of saying that I had not been well. I'd had a cold. But then I remembered that colds in this place were a serious business, involving masks and disinfectant, banishment. And soon I understood that there was no hope of hiding my visit to the doctor's house, in any case. It was a secret from nobody, not even, surely, from the nurses who said nothing, either because they were too lofty and discreet or because such carryings-on had ceased to interest them. But the aides teased me.

"Enjoy your supper the other night?"

Their tone was friendly, they seemed to approve. It looked as if my particular oddity had joined up with the doctor's familiar and respected oddity, and that was all to the good. My stock had risen. Now, whatever else I was, I at least might turn out to be a woman with a man.

Mary did not put in an appearance all week.

———

"Next Saturday," were the words that had been said, just before he administered the kiss. So I waited again on the front porch and this time he was not late. We drove to the house and I went into the front room while he got the fire going. There I noticed the dusty electric heater.

"Didn't take me up on my offer," he said. "Did you think I didn't mean it? I always mean what I say."

I said that I hadn't wanted to come into town for fear of meeting Mary.

"Because of missing her concert."

"That's if you're going to arrange your life to suit Mary," he said.

The menu was much the same as before. Pork chops, mashed potatoes, corn niblets instead of peas. This time he let me help in the kitchen, even asking me to set the table.

"You may as well learn where things are. It's all fairly logical, I believe."

This meant that I could watch him working at the stove. His easy concentration, economical movements, setting up in me a procession of sparks and chills.

We had just begun the meal when there was a knock at the door. He got up and drew the bolt and in burst Mary.

She was carrying a cardboard box which she set on the table. Then she threw off her coat and displayed herself in a red-and-yellow costume.

"Happy late Valentine's Day," she said. "You never came to see me in the concert so I brought the concert to you. And I brought you a present in the box."

Her excellent balance allowed her to stand on one foot while she kicked off first one boot, then the other. She pushed them out of her way and began to prance around the table, singing at the same time in a plaintive but vigorous young voice.

> *I'm called Little Buttercup,*
> *Poor Little Buttercup,*
> *Though I can never tell why.*
> *But still I'm called Buttercup*
> *Poor Little Buttercup*
> *Dear Little Buttercup I—*

The doctor had got up even before she began to sing. He was standing at the stove, busy scraping at the frying pan that had held the pork chops.

I applauded. I said, "What a gorgeous costume."

It was indeed. Red skirt, bright yellow petticoat, fluttering white apron, embroidered bodice.

"My mom made it."

"Even the embroidery?"

"Sure. She stayed up till four o'clock to get it done the night before."

There was further whirling and stomping to show it off. The dishes tinkled on the shelves. I applauded some more. Both of us wanted only one thing. We wanted the doctor to turn around and stop ignoring us. For him to say, even grudgingly, one polite word.

"And lookit what else," Mary said. "For a Valentine." She tore open the cardboard box and there were Valentine cookies, all cut in heart shapes and plastered with thick red icing.

"How splendid," I said, and Mary resumed her prancing.

> *I am the Captain of the* Pinafore.
> *And a right good captain, too!*

You're very, very good, and be it understood,
I command a right good crew.

The doctor turned at last and she saluted him.
"All right," he said. "That's enough."
She ignored him.

Then give three cheers, and one cheer more
For the hardy captain of the Pinafore—

"I said, that's enough."
" 'For the gallant captain of the *Pinafore*—' "
"Mary. We are eating supper. And you are not invited. Do you understand that? Not invited."
She was quiet at last. But only for a moment.
"Well pooh on you then. You're not very nice."
"And you could just as well do without any of those cookies. You could quit eating cookies altogether. You're on the way to getting as plump as a young pig."
Mary's face was swollen as if she would start to cry but instead she said, "Look who's talking. You got one eye crooked to the other."
"That's enough."
"Well you have."
The doctor picked up her boots and set them down in front of her.
"Put these on."
She did so, with her eyes full of tears and her nose running. She snuffled mightily. He brought her coat and did not help her as she flailed her way into it and found the buttons.
"That's right. Now—how did you get here?"
She refused to answer.

"Walked, did you? Where's your mother?"

"Euchre."

"Well I can drive you home. So you won't get any chance to fling yourself in a snowbank and freeze to death out of self-pity."

I did not say a word. Mary did not look at me once. The moment was too full of shock for good-byes.

When I heard the car start I began clearing the table. We had not got to dessert, which was apple pie again. Perhaps he did not know of any other kind, or perhaps it was all the bakery made.

I picked up one of the heart-shaped cookies and ate it. The icing was horribly sweet. No berry or cherry flavour, just sugar and red food colouring. I ate another and another.

I knew that I should have said good-bye at least. I should have said thank you. But it wouldn't have mattered. I told myself it wouldn't have mattered. The show had not been for me. Or perhaps only a small part of it had been for me.

He had been brutal. It shocked me, that he had been so brutal. To one so much in need. But he had done it for me, in a way. So that his time with me should not be taken away. This thought flattered me and I was ashamed that it flattered me. I did not know what I would say to him when he got back.

He did not want me to say anything. He took me to bed. Had this been in the cards all along, or was it almost as much of a surprise to him as it was to me? My state of virginity at least did not appear to be a surprise—he provided a towel as well as a condom—and he persisted, going as easily as he could. My passion could have been the surprise to us both. Imagination, as it turned out, might be as good a preparation as experience.

"I do intend to marry you," he said.

Before he took me home he tossed all the cookies, all those red hearts, out in the snow to feed the winter birds.

So it was settled. Our sudden engagement—he was a little wary of the word—was a private settled fact. I was not to write a word to my grandparents. The wedding would take place whenever he could get a couple of consecutive days off. A bare-bones wedding, he said. I was to understand that the idea of a ceremony, carried on in the presence of others, whose ideas he did not respect, and who would inflict on us all that snickering and simpering, was more than he was prepared to put up with.

Nor was he in favour of diamond rings. I told him that I had never wanted one, which was true, because I had never thought about it. He said that was good, he had known that I was not that idiotic conventional sort of girl.

It was better to stop having supper together, not just because of the talk but because it was hard to get enough meat for two people on one ration card. My card was not available, having been handed over to the kitchen authorities—to Mary's mother—as soon as I began to eat at the San.

Better not to call attention.

Of course everybody suspected something. The elderly nurses turned cordial and even Matron gave me a pained smile. I did preen in a modest way, almost without meaning to. I took to folding myself in, with a velvet stillness, eyes rather cast down. It did not quite occur to me that these older women were watching to see what turn this intimacy might take and that they were ready to turn righteous if the doctor should decide to drop me.

It was the aides who were wholeheartedly on my side, and teased that they saw wedding bells in my tea leaves.

The month of March was grim and busy behind the hospital doors. It was always the worst month for trouble to strike, the aides said. For some reason people took it into their heads to die then, after making it through the attacks of winter. If a child did not show up for class I would not know if there had been a major turn for the worse or just a bedding-down with a suspicion of a cold. I had got hold of a moveable blackboard and had written the children's names all around the edges of it. Now I never even had to wipe off the names of the children whose absences were to be prolonged. Other children did it for me, without a mention. They understood the etiquette which I had still to learn.

Time was found, however, for the doctor to make some arrangements. He slipped a note under the door of my room, saying to be ready by the first week of April. Unless there was some real crisis, he could manage a couple of days then.

We are going to Huntsville.

Going to Huntsville—our code for getting married.

We have begun the day that I am sure I will remember all my life. I have my green crepe dry-cleaned and rolled up carefully in my overnight bag. My grandmother once taught me the trick of tight rolling, so much better than folding to prevent wrinkles. I suppose I will have to change my clothes in a ladies' toilet somewhere. I am watching to see if there are any early wildflowers along the road, that I could pick to make a bouquet. Would he agree to my having a bouquet? But it's too early even for marsh marigolds. Along the empty curving road nothing is to be seen but skinny black spruce trees and islands of spreading juniper and bogs. And in the road cuts a chaotic jumble of the rocks that have become familiar to me here—bloodstained iron and slanting shelves of granite.

The car radio is on and playing triumphal music, because the Allies are getting closer and closer to Berlin. The doctor—Alister—says that they are delaying to let the Russians in first. He says they'll be sorry.

Now that we are away from Amundsen I find that I can call him Alister. This is the longest drive we have ever taken together and I am aroused by his male unawareness of me—which I know now can quickly shift to its opposite—and by his casual skill as a driver. I find it exciting that he is a surgeon though I would never admit that. Right now I believe I could lie down for him in any bog or mucky hole, or feel my spine crushed against any roadside rock, should he require an upright encounter. I know too that I must keep these feelings to myself.

I turn my mind to the future. Once we get to Huntsville I expect that we will find a minister and stand side by side in a living room which will have some of the modest gentility of my grandparents' apartment, of the living rooms I have known all my life. I recall times when my grandfather would be sought out for wedding purposes even after his retirement. My grandmother would rub a little rouge on her cheeks and take out the dark blue lace jacket that she kept for being a witness on such occasions.

But I discover there are other ways to get married, and another aversion of my bridegroom's that I hadn't grasped. He won't have anything to do with a minister. In the Town Hall in Huntsville we fill out forms that swear to our single state and make an appointment to be married by a justice of the peace later in the day.

Time for lunch. Alister stops outside a restaurant that could be a first cousin to the coffee shop in Amundsen.

"This'll do?"

But on looking into my face he does change his mind.

"No?" he says. "Okay."

We end up eating lunch in the chilly front room of one of the genteel houses that advertise chicken dinners. The plates are icy cold, there are no other diners, there is no radio music but only the clink of our cutlery as we try to separate parts of the stringy chicken. I am sure he is thinking that we might have done better in the restaurant he suggested in the first place.

Nonetheless I have the courage to ask about the ladies' room, and there, in cold air even more discouraging than that of the front room, I shake out my green dress and put it on, repaint my mouth and fix my hair.

When I come out Alister stands up to greet me and smiles and squeezes my hand and says I look pretty.

We walk stiffly back to the car, holding hands. He opens the car door for me, goes around and gets in, settles himself and turns the key in the ignition, then turns it off.

The car is parked in front of a hardware store. Shovels for snow removal are on sale at half price. There is still a sign in the window that says skates can be sharpened inside.

Across the street there is a wooden house painted an oily

yellow. Its front steps have become unsafe and two boards forming an X have been nailed across them.

The truck parked in front of Alister's car is a prewar model, with a runningboard and a fringe of rust on its fenders. A man in overalls comes out of the hardware store and gets into it. After some engine complaint, then some rattling and bouncing in place, it is driven away. Now a delivery truck with the store's name on it tries to park in the space left vacant. There is not quite enough room. The driver gets out and comes and raps on Alister's window. Alister is surprised—if he had not been talking so earnestly he would have noticed the problem. He rolls down the window and the man asks if we are parked there because we intend to buy something in the store. If not, could we please move along?

"Just leaving," says Alister, the man sitting beside me who was going to marry me but now is not going to marry me. "We were just leaving."

We. He has said we. For a moment I cling to that word. Then I think it's the last time. The last time I'll be included in his we.

It's not the "we" that matters, that is not what tells me the truth. It's his male-to-male tone to the driver, his calm and reasonable apology. I could wish now to go back to what he was saying before, when he did not even notice the van trying to park. What he was saying then had been terrible but his tight grip on the wheel, his grip and his abstraction and his voice had pain in them. No matter what he said and meant, he spoke out of the same deep place then, that he spoke from when he was in bed with me. But it is not so now, after he has spoken to another man. He rolls up the window and gives his attention to the car, to backing it out of its tight spot and moving it so as not to come in contact with the van.

And a moment later I would be glad even to go back to that time, when he craned his head to see behind him. Better that than driving—as he is driving now—down the main street of Huntsville, as if there is no more to be said or managed.

I can't do it, he has said.

He has said that he can't go through with this.

He can't explain it.

Only that it's a mistake.

I think that I will never be able to look at curly S's like those on the Skates Sharpened sign, without hearing his voice. Or at rough boards knocked into an X like those across the steps of the yellow house opposite the store.

"I'm going to drive you to the station now. I'll buy your ticket to Toronto. I'm pretty sure there's a train to Toronto late in the afternoon. I'll think up some very plausible story and I'll get somebody to pack up your things. You'll need to give me your Toronto address, I don't think I've kept it. Oh, and I'll write you a reference. You've done a good job. You wouldn't have finished out a term anyway—I hadn't told you yet but the children are going to be moved. All kinds of big changes going on."

A new tone in his voice, almost jaunty. A knockabout tone of relief. He is trying to hold that in, not let relief out till I am gone.

I watch the streets. It's something like being driven to the place of execution. Not yet. A little while yet. Not yet do I hear his voice for the last time. Not yet.

He doesn't have to ask the way. I wonder out loud if he has put girls on the train before.

"Don't be like that," he says.

Every turn is like a shearing-off of what's left of my life.

There is a train to Toronto at five o'clock. He has told me to wait in the car, while he goes in to check. He comes out with the ticket in his hand and what I think is a lighter step. He must have realized this because as he approaches the car he becomes more sedate.

"It's nice and warm in the station. There's a special ladies' waiting room."

He has opened the car door for me.

"Or would you rather I waited and saw you off? Maybe there's a place where we can get a decent piece of pie. That was a horrible dinner."

This makes me stir myself. I get out and walk ahead of him into the station. He points out the ladies' waiting room. He raises his eyebrow at me and tries to make a final joke.

"Maybe someday you'll count this one of the luckiest days of your life."

I choose a bench in the ladies' waiting room that has a view of the station's front doors. That is to be able to see him if he comes back. He will tell me that this is all a joke. Or a test, as in some medieval drama.

Or perhaps he has had a change of mind. Driving down the highway seeing the pale spring sunlight on the rocks that we so lately looked at together. Struck by a realization of his folly he turns in the middle of the road and comes speeding back.

It is an hour at least before the Toronto train comes into the station, but it seems hardly any time at all. And even now fantasies are running through my mind. I board the train as if there are chains on my ankles. I press my face to the window to look along the platform as the whistle blows for our departure. Even now it might not be too late for me to jump from the train. Jump free and run through the station to the street where he would just have parked the car and is running up the steps thinking not too late, pray not too late.

Myself running to meet him, not too late.

And what is the commotion, shouting, hollering, not one but a gaggle of latecomers pounding between the seats. High school girls in athletic outfits, hooting at the trouble they have caused. The conductor displeased and hurrying them along as they scramble for their seats.

One of them, and perhaps the loudest, is Mary.

I turn my head and do not look at them again.

But here she is, crying out my name and wanting to know where I have been.

To visit with a friend, I tell her.

She plunks herself down beside me and tells me that they have been playing basketball against Huntsville. It was a riot. They lost.

"We lost, didn't we?" she calls out in apparent delight, and the others groan and giggle. She mentions the score which is indeed quite shameful.

"You're all dressed up," she says. But she doesn't much care, she seems to take my explanation without real interest.

She barely notices when I say that I am going on to Toronto to visit my grandparents. Except to remark that they must be really old. Not a word about Alister. Not even a bad word.

She would not have forgotten. Just tidied up the scene and put it away, in a closet with her former selves. Or maybe she really is a person who can deal recklessly with humiliation.

I am grateful to her now, even if I was not able to feel such a thing at the time. Left all to myself, what might I have done when we got to Amundsen? What jumping up and leaving the train and running to his house and demanding to know why, why. What shame on me forever. As it was, the stop there gave the team barely time to get themselves collected and to rap on the windows alerting the people who had come to pick them up, while being warned by the conductor that if they don't get a move on they will be riding to Toronto.

For years I thought I might run into him. I lived, and still live, in Toronto. It seemed to me that everybody ended up in Toronto at least for a little while. Of course that hardly means that you will get to see that person, provided that you should in any way want to.

It finally happened. Crossing a crowded street where you could not even slow down. Going in opposite directions. Staring, at the same time, a bare shock on our time-damaged faces.

He called out, "How are you?" and I answered, "Fine." Then added for good measure, "Happy."

At the moment this was only generally true. I was having some kind of dragged-out row with my husband, about our paying a debt run up by one of his children. I had gone that afternoon to a show at an art gallery, to get myself into a more comfortable frame of mind.

He called back to me once more:

"Good for you."

It still seemed as if we could make our way out of that crowd, that in a moment we would be together. But just as certain that we would carry on in the way we were going. And so we did. No breathless cry, no hand on my shoulder when I reached the sidewalk. Just that flash, that I had seen in an instant, when one of his eyes opened wider. It was the left eye, always the left, as I remembered. And it always looked so strange, alert and wondering, as if some whole impossibility had occurred to him, one that almost made him laugh.

For me, it was the same as when I left Amundsen, the train dragging me still dazed and full of disbelief.

Nothing changes really about love.

LEAVING MAVERLEY

I N the old days when there was a movie theatre in every town there was one in this town, too, in Maverley, and it was called the Capital, as such theatres often were. Morgan Holly was the owner and the projectionist. He didn't like dealing with the public—he preferred to sit in his upstairs cubbyhole managing the story on the screen—so naturally he was annoyed when the girl who took the tickets told him that she was going to have to quit, because she was having a baby. He might have expected this—she had been married for half a year, and in those days you were supposed to get out of the public eye before you began to show—but he so disliked change and the idea of people having private lives that he was taken by surprise.

Fortunately, she came up with somebody who might

replace her. A girl who lived on her street had mentioned that she would like to have an evening job. She was not able to work in the daytime, because she had to help her mother look after the younger children. She was smart enough to manage, though shy.

Morgan said that that was fine—he didn't hire a ticket taker to gab with the customers.

So the girl came. Her name was Leah, and Morgan's first and last question for her was to ask what kind of name that was. She said that it was out of the Bible. He noticed then that she did not have any makeup on and that her hair was slicked unbecomingly tight to her head and held there with bobby pins. He had a moment's worry about whether she was really sixteen and could legally hold a job, but close up he saw that it was likely the truth. He told her that she would need to work one show, starting at eight o'clock, on weeknights and two shows, starting at seven, on Saturday nights. After closing, she would be responsible for counting the take and locking it away.

There was only one problem. She said that she would be able to walk herself home on weeknights but it would not be allowed on Saturday nights and her father could not come for her then, because he himself had a night job at the mill.

Morgan said that he did not know what there was to be scared of in a place like this, and was about to tell her to get lost, when he remembered the night policeman who often broke his rounds to watch a little of the movie. Perhaps he could be charged with getting Leah home.

She said that she would ask her father.

Her father agreed, but he had to be satisfied on other accounts. Leah was not to look at the screen or listen to any of the dialogue. The religion that the family belonged to did not allow it. Morgan said that he did not hire his ticket takers to give them a free peek at the show. As for the dialogue, he lied and said that the theatre was soundproofed.

Ray Elliot, the night policeman, had taken the job so that he would be able to help his wife manage for at least some part of the daytime. He could get by with about five hours' sleep in the morning and then a nap in the late afternoon. Often, the nap did not materialize, because of some chore that had to be done or just because he and his wife—her name was Isabel—got to talking. They had no children and could get talking anytime about anything. He brought her the news of the town, which often made her laugh, and she told him about the books she was reading.

Ray had joined up for the war as soon as he was eighteen. He chose the Air Force, which promised, as was said, the most adventure and the quickest death. He had been a mid-upper gunner—a position that Isabel could never get straight in her head—and he had survived. Close to the end of the war, he'd been transferred to a new crew, and within a couple of weeks his old crew, the men he'd flown with so many times, were shot down and lost. He came home with a vague idea that he had to do something meaningful with the life that had so inexplicably been left to him, but he didn't know what.

First, he had to finish high school. In the town where he had grown up, a special school had been set up for veterans who were doing just that and hoping to go on to university, courtesy of the grateful citizens. The teacher of English

Language and Literature was Isabel. She was thirty years old and married. Her husband, too, was a veteran, who considerably outranked the students in her English class. She was planning to put in this one year of teaching out of general patriotism, and then she was going to retire and start a family. She discussed this openly with her students, who said, just out of her earshot, that some guys got all the luck.

Ray disliked hearing that kind of talk, and the reason was that he had fallen in love with her. And she with him, which seemed infinitely more surprising. It was preposterous to everybody except themselves. There was a divorce—a scandal to her well-connected family and a shock to her husband, who had wanted to marry her since they were children. Ray had an easier time of it than she did, because he had little family to speak of, and those he did have announced that they supposed they wouldn't be good enough for him now that he was marrying so high up, and they would just stay out of his way in the future. If they expected any denial or reassurance in response to this, they did not get it. Okay with him was what he more or less said. Time to make a fresh start. Isabel said that she could go on teaching until Ray had finished university and got established in whatever it was that he wanted to do.

But the plan had to change. She was not well. At first, they thought it was nerves. The upheaval. The foolish fuss.

Then the pains came. Pain whenever she took a deep breath. Pain under the breastbone and in her left shoulder. She ignored it. She joked about God punishing her for her amorous adventure and said that he, God, was wasting his time when she didn't even believe in him.

She had something called pericarditis. It was serious and

she had ignored it to her peril. It was something she would not be cured of but could manage, with difficulty. She could never teach again. Any infection would be dangerous, and where is infection more rampant than in a schoolroom? It was Ray who now had to support her, and he took a job as a policeman in this small town called Maverley, just over the Grey-Bruce border. He didn't mind the work and she didn't mind, after a while, her semiseclusion.

There was one thing they didn't talk about. Each of them wondered whether the other minded not being able to have children. It occurred to Ray that that disappointment might have something to do with Isabel's wanting to hear all about the girl he had to walk home on Saturday nights.

"That is deplorable," she said when she heard about the ban on movies, and she was even more upset when he told her that the girl had been kept out of high school to help at home.

"And you say she's intelligent."

Ray did not remember having said that. He had said that she was weirdly shy, so that during their walks he had to rack his brains for a subject of conversation. Some questions he thought of wouldn't do. Such as, What is your favourite subject at school? That would have had to go into the past tense and it would not matter now whether she'd liked anything. Or, What did she want to do when she was grown up? She was grown up now, for all intents and purposes, and she had her work cut out for her, whether she wanted it or not. Also the question of whether she liked this town, and did she miss wherever it was that she used to live—pointless. And they had already gone through, without elaboration, the names and ages of the younger children in her family.

When he inquired after a dog or a cat, she reported that she didn't have any.

She did come up with a question for him eventually. She asked what it was that people had been laughing about in the movie that night.

He didn't think he should remind her that she wasn't supposed to have heard anything. But he could not remember what might have been funny. So he said that it must have been some stupid thing—you could never tell what would make the audience laugh. He said that he didn't get too involved in the movies, seeing them as he did, in bits and pieces. He seldom followed the plots.

"Plots," she said.

He had to tell her what that meant—that there were stories being told. And from that time on there was no problem making conversation. Nor did he need to warn her that it might not be wise to repeat any of it at home. She understood. He was called upon not to tell any specific story—which he could hardly have done anyway—but to explain that the stories were often about crooks and innocent people and that the crooks generally managed well enough at first by committing their crimes and hoodwinking people singing in nightclubs (which were like dance halls) or sometimes, God knows why, singing on mountaintops or in some other unlikely outdoor scenery, holding up the action. Sometimes the movies were in colour. With magnificent costumes if the story was set in the past. Dressed-up actors making a big show of killing one another. Glycerin tears running down ladies' cheeks. Jungle animals brought in from zoos, probably, and teased to act ferocious. People getting up from being murdered in various ways the moment the camera was off them. Alive and well, though you had just seen them shot or on the executioner's block with their heads rolling in a basket.

"You should take it easy," Isabel said. "You could give her nightmares."

Ray said he'd be surprised. And certainly the girl had an air of figuring things out, rather than being alarmed or confused. For instance, she never asked what the executioner's block was or seemed surprised at the thought of heads on it. There was something in her, he told Isabel, something that made her want to absorb whatever you said to her, instead of just being thrilled or mystified by it. Some way in which he thought she had already shut herself off from her family. Not to be contemptuous of them, or unkind. She was just rock-bottom thoughtful.

But then he said what made him sorrier than he knew why.

"She hasn't got much to look forward to, one way or the other."

"Well, we could snatch her away," Isabel said.

Then he warned her. Be serious.

"Don't even think about it."

Shortly before Christmas (though the cold had not really set in yet), Morgan came to the police station around midnight one night in the middle of the week to say that Leah was missing.

She had sold the tickets as usual and closed the window and put the money where it was supposed to go and set off for home, so far as he knew. He himself had shut things up when the show was done, but when he got outside this woman he didn't know had appeared, asking what had become of Leah. This was the mother—Leah's mother. The father was still at his job at the mill, and Morgan had suggested that the girl might have taken it into her head to go and see him at work. The mother didn't seem to know what he was talking about, so he said that they could go to the mill and see if the girl was there, and she—the mother—cried and begged him not to do any such thing. So Morgan gave her a ride home, thinking that the girl might have turned up by now, but no luck, and then he thought he had better go and inform Ray.

He didn't relish the thought of having to break the news to the father.

Ray said that they should go to the mill at once—there was a slim chance she might be there. But of course when they located the father he hadn't seen anything of her, and he got into a rage about his wife's going out like that when she did not have permission to leave the house.

Ray asked about friends and was not surprised to learn that Leah didn't have any. Then he let Morgan go home and went himself to the house, where the mother was very much in the distracted state that Morgan had described. The children were still up, or some of them were, and they, too, proved to be speechless. They trembled either from fright and their misgivings about the stranger in the house or from the cold, which Ray noticed was definitely on the rise, even indoors. Maybe the father had rules about the heat as well.

Leah had been wearing her winter coat—he got that much out of them. He knew the baggy brown checked garment and thought that it would keep her warm for a while, at least. Between the time that Morgan had first shown up and now, snow had begun to fall fairly heavily.

When his shift was over, Ray went home and told Isabel what had happened. Then he went out again and she didn't try to stop him.

An hour later, he was back with no results, and the news that the roads were likely to be closed for the first big snowstorm of the winter.

By morning, that was in fact the case; the town was boxed in for the first time that year and the main street was the only one that the snowplows tried to keep open. Nearly all the stores were closed, and in the part of town where Leah's family lived the power had gone out and there was nothing that could be done about it, with the wind arching and bowing the trees until it looked as if they were trying to sweep the ground.

The day-shift policeman had an idea that had not occurred to Ray. He was a member of the United Church and he was aware—or his wife was aware—that Leah did ironing every week for the minister's wife. He and Ray went to the parsonage to see if anybody there knew anything that could account for the girl's disappearance, but there was no information to be had, and after that brief stirring of hope the trail seemed even more hopeless than before.

Ray was a little surprised that the girl had taken on another job and not mentioned it. Even though, compared with the theatre, it hardly seemed like much of a foray into the world.

He tried to sleep in the afternoon and did manage an

hour or so. Isabel attempted to get a conversation going at supper but nothing lasted. Ray's talk kept circling back to the visit to the minister, and how the wife had been helpful and concerned, as much as she could be, but how he—the minister—had not exactly behaved as you might think a minister should. He had answered the door impatiently, as if he had been interrupted while writing his sermon or something. He'd called to his wife and when she came she'd had to remind him who the girl was. Remember the girl who comes to help out with the ironing? Leah? Then he'd said that he hoped there would be some news soon, while trying to inch the door shut against the wind.

"Well, what else could he have done?" Isabel said. "Prayed?"

Ray thought that it wouldn't have hurt.

"It would just have embarrassed everybody and exposed the futility," Isabel said. Then she added that he was probably a very up-to-date minister who went in more for the symbolic.

Some sort of search had to be carried out, never mind the weather. Back sheds and an old horse barn unused for years had to be pried open and ransacked in case she had taken shelter there. Nothing came to light. The local radio station was alerted and broadcast a description.

If Leah had been hitchhiking, Ray thought, she might have been picked up before the storm got started, which could be good or bad.

The broadcast said that she was a little under average height—Ray would have said a little over—and that she had straight medium-brown hair. He would have said very dark brown, close to black.

· 77 ·

Her father did not take part in the search; nor did any of her brothers. Of course, the boys were younger than she was and would never have got out of the house without the father's consent anyway. When Ray went around to the house on foot and made it through to the door, it was hardly opened, and the father didn't waste any time telling him that the girl was most likely a runaway. Her punishment was out of his hands and in God's now. There was no invitation to Ray to come in and thaw himself out. Perhaps there was still no heat in the house.

The storm did die down, around the middle of the next day. The snowplows got out and cleared the town streets. The county plows took over the highway. The drivers were told to keep their eyes open for a body frozen in the drifts.

The day after that, the mail truck came through and there was a letter. It was addressed not to anyone in Leah's family but to the minister and his wife. It was from Leah, to report that she had got married. The bridegroom was the minister's son, who was a saxophone player in a jazz band. He had added the words "Surprise Surprise" at the bottom of the page. Or so it was reported, though Isabel asked how anybody could know that, unless they were in the habit of steaming envelopes open at the post office.

The sax player hadn't lived in this town when he was a child. His father had been posted elsewhere then. And he had visited very rarely. Most people could not even have told you what he looked like. He never attended church. He had brought a woman home a couple of years ago. Very made-up and dressy. It was said that she was his wife, but apparently she hadn't been.

How often had the girl been in the minister's house, doing

the ironing, when the sax player was there? Some people had worked it out. It would have been one time only. This was what Ray heard at the police station, where gossip could flourish as well as it did among women.

Isabel thought it was a great story. And not the elopers' fault. They had not ordered the snowstorm, after all.

It turned out that she herself had some slight knowledge of the sax player. She had run into him at the post office once, when he happened to be home and she was having one of her spells of being well enough to go out. She had sent away for a record but it hadn't come. He had asked her what it was and she had told him. Something she could not remember now. He'd told her then about his own involvement with a different kind of music. Something had already made her sure that he wasn't a local. The way he leaned into her and the way he smelled strongly of Juicy Fruit gum. He didn't mention the parsonage, but somebody else told her of the connection, after he had wished her good-bye and good luck.

Just a little bit flirtatious, or sure of his welcome. Some nonsense about letting him come and listen to the record if it ever arrived. She hoped she was meant to take that as a joke.

She teased Ray, wondering if it was on account of his descriptions of the wide world via the movies that the girl had got the idea.

Ray did not reveal and could hardly believe the desolation he had felt during the time when the girl was missing. He was, of course, greatly relieved when he found out what had happened.

Still, she was gone. In a not entirely unusual or unhopeful

way, she was gone. Absurdly, he felt offended. As if she could have shown some inkling, at least, that there was another part of her life.

Her parents and all the other children were soon gone as well, and it seemed that nobody knew where.

The minister and his wife did not leave town when he retired.

They were able to keep the same house and it was often still referred to as the parsonage, although it was not really that anymore. The new minister's young wife had taken issue with some features of the place, and the church authorities, rather than fix it up, had decided to build a new house so that she could not complain anymore. The old parsonage was then sold cheaply to the old minister. It had room for the musician son and his wife when they came to visit with their children.

There were two, their names appearing in the newspaper when they were born. A boy and then a girl. They came occasionally to visit, usually with Leah only; the father was busy with his dances or whatever. Neither Ray nor Isabel had run into them at those times.

Isabel was better; she was almost normal. She cooked so well that they both put on weight and she had to stop, or at least do the fancier things less often. She got together with some other women in the town to read and discuss Great Books. A few had not understood what this would really be like and dropped out, but aside from them it was a startling success. Isabel laughed about the fuss there would be in Heaven as they tackled poor old Dante.

Then there was some fainting or near-fainting, but she would not go to the doctor till Ray got angry with her and she claimed it was his temper that had made her sick. She apologized and they made up, but her heart took such a plunge that they had to hire a woman who was called a practical nurse to stay with her when Ray could not be there. Fortunately, there was some money—hers from an inheritance and his from a slight raise—which materialized, even though by choice he kept on with the night shift.

One summer morning, on his way home, he checked at the post office to see if the mail was ready. Sometimes they had got it sorted by this time; sometimes they hadn't. This morning they hadn't.

And now on the sidewalk, coming towards him in the bright early light of the day, was Leah. She was pushing a stroller, with a little girl about two years old inside it, kicking her legs against the metal footrest. Another child was taking things more soberly, holding on to his mother's skirt. Or to what was really a long orangey pair of trousers. She was wearing with them a loose white top, something like an undervest. Her hair had more shine than it used to have, and her smile, which he had never actually seen before, seemed positively to shower him with delight.

She could almost have been one of Isabel's new friends, who were mostly either younger or recently arrived in this town, though there were a few older, once more cautious residents, who had been swept up in this bright new era, their former viewpoints dismissed and their language altered, straining to be crisp and crude.

He had been feeling disappointed not to find any new magazines at the post office. Not that it mattered so much to Isabel now. She used to live for her magazines, which were all serious and thought-provoking but with witty cartoons that she laughed at. Even the ads for furs and jewels had made her laugh, and he hoped, still, that they would revive her. Now, at least, he'd have something to tell her about. Leah.

Leah greeted him with a new voice and pretended to be amazed that he had recognized her, since she had grown—as she put it—into practically an old lady. She introduced the little girl, who would not look up and kept a rhythm going on the metal footrest, and the boy, who looked into the distance and muttered. She teased the boy because he would not let go of her clothes.

"We're across the street now, honeybunch."

His name was David and the girl's was Shelley. Ray had not remembered those names from the paper. He had an idea that both were fashionable.

She said that they were staying with her in-laws.

Not visiting them. Staying with them. He didn't think of that till later and it might have meant nothing.

"We're just on our way to the post office."

He told her that he was coming from there, but they weren't through with the sorting yet.

"Oh too bad. We thought there might be a letter from Daddy, didn't we, David?"

The little boy had hold of her clothing again.

"Wait till they get them sorted," she said. "Maybe there'll be one then."

There was a feeling that she didn't quite want to part with Ray yet, and Ray did not want it either, but it was hard to think of anything else to say.

"I'm on my way to the drugstore," he said.

"Oh, are you?"

"I have to pick up a prescription for my wife."

"Oh I hope she's not sick."

Then he felt as if he had committed a betrayal and said rather shortly, "No. Nothing much."

She was looking past Ray now, and saying hello to somebody else in the same delighted voice with which she had greeted him some moments ago.

It was the United Church minister, the new, or fairly new, one, whose wife had demanded the up-to-date house.

She asked the two men if they knew each other and they said yes, they did. Both spoke in a tone that indicated not well, and that maybe showed some satisfaction that it should be so. Ray noticed that the man was not wearing his dog collar.

"Hasn't had to haul me in for any infractions yet," the minister said, perhaps thinking that he should have been jollier. He shook Ray's hand.

"This is so lucky," Leah said. "I've been wanting to ask you some questions and now here you are."

"Here I am," said the minister.

"I mean about Sunday School," Leah said. "I've been wondering. I've got these two little kids growing up and I've been wondering how soon and what's the procedure and everything."

"Oh yes," the minister said.

Ray could see that he was one of those who didn't particularly like doing their ministering in public. Didn't want the subject brought up, as it were, every time they took to the streets. But the minister hid his discomfort as well as he could and there must have been some compensation for him in talking to a girl who looked like Leah.

"We should discuss it," he said. "Make an appointment anytime."

Ray was saying that he had to be off.

"Good to run into you," he said to Leah, and gave a nod to the man of the cloth.

He went on, in possession of two new pieces of information. She was going to be here for some time, if she was trying to make arrangements for Sunday School. And she had not got out of her system all the religion that her upbringing had put into it.

He looked forward to running into her again, but that did not happen.

When he got home, he told Isabel about how the girl had changed, and she said, "It all sounds pretty commonplace, after all."

She seemed a little testy, perhaps because she had been waiting for him to get her coffee. Her helper was not due till nine o'clock and she was forbidden, after a scalding accident, to try to manage it herself.

It was downhill and several scares for them till Christmastime, and then Ray got a leave of absence. They took off for the city, where certain medical specialists were to be found. Isabel was admitted to the hospital immediately and Ray was able to get into one of the rooms provided for the use of relatives from out of town. Suddenly, he had no responsibilities except to visit Isabel for long hours each day and take note of how she was responding to various treatments. At first, he tried to distract her with lively talk of the past, or observations about the hospital and other patients he got glimpses of. He took walks almost every day, in spite of the weather, and he told her all about those as well. He brought a newspaper with him and read her the news. Finally, she said, "It's so good of you, darling, but I seem to be past it."

"Past what?" he countered, but she said, "Oh please," and after that he found himself silently reading some book from the hospital library. She said, "Don't worry if I close my eyes. I know you're there."

She had been moved some time ago from Acute Care into a room that held four women who were more or less in the same condition as she was, though one occasionally roused herself to holler at Ray, "Give us a kiss."

Then one day he came in and found another woman in Isabel's bed. For a moment, he thought she had died and nobody had told him. But the voluble patient in the kitty-corner bed cried out, "Upstairs." With some notion of jollity or triumph.

And that was what had happened. Isabel had failed to wake up that morning and had been moved to another floor, where it seemed they stashed the people who had no chance of improving—even less chance than those in the previous room—but were refusing to die.

"You might as well go home," they told him. They said that they would get in touch if there was any change.

That made sense. For one thing, he had used up all his time in the relatives' housing. And he had more than used up his time away from the police force in Maverley. All signs said that the right thing to do was to go back there.

Instead, he stayed in the city. He got a job with the hospital maintenance crew, cleaning and clearing and mopping. He found a furnished apartment, with just essentials in it, not far away.

He went home, but only briefly. As soon as he got there, he started making arrangements to sell the house and whatever was in it. He put the real-estate people in charge of that and got out of their way as quickly as he could; he did not want to explain anything to anybody. He did not care about anything that had happened in that place. All those years in the town, all he knew about it, seemed to just slip away from him.

He did hear something while he was there, a kind of scandal involving the United Church minister, who was trying to get his wife to divorce him, on the grounds of adultery. Committing adultery with a parishioner was bad enough, but it seemed that the minister, instead of keeping it as quiet as possible and slinking off to get rehabilitated or to serve in some forsaken parish in the hinterlands, had chosen to face the music from the pulpit. He had more than confessed. Everything had been a sham, he said. His mouthing of the Gospels and the commandments he didn't fully believe in, and most of all his preachings about love and sex, his conventional, timid, and evasive recommendations: a sham. He was now a man set free, free to tell them what a relief it was to celebrate the life of the body along with the life of the spirit. The woman who had done this for him, it seemed, was Leah. Her husband, the musician, Ray was told, had come back to get her sometime before, but she hadn't wanted to go with him. He'd blamed it on the minister, but he was a drunk—the husband was—so nobody had known whether to believe him or not. His mother must have believed him, though, because she had kicked Leah out and hung on to the children.

As far as Ray was concerned, this was all revolting chatter. Adulteries and drunks and scandals—who was right and who was wrong? Who could care? That girl had grown up to preen and bargain like the rest of them. The waste of time, the waste of life, by people all scrambling for excitement and paying no attention to anything that mattered.

Of course, when he had been able to talk to Isabel, everything had been different. Not that Isabel would have been looking for answers—rather, that she would have made him feel as if there were more to the subject than he had taken account of. Then she'd have ended up laughing.

He got along well enough at work. They asked him if he wanted to join a bowling team and he thanked them but said he didn't have time. He had plenty of time, actually, but had to spend it with Isabel. Watching for any change, any explanation. Not letting anything slip away.

"Her name is Isabel," he used to remind the nurses if they said, "Now, my lady," or "Okay, missus, over we go."

Then he got used to hearing them speak to her that way. So there were changes, after all. If not in Isabel, he could find them in himself.

For quite a while, he had been going to see her once a day. Then he made it every other day. Then twice a week.

Four years. He thought it must be close to a record. He asked those who cared for her if that was so and they said, "Well. Getting there." They had a habit of being vague about everything.

He had got over the persistent idea that she was thinking. He was no longer waiting for her to open her eyes. It was just that he could not go off and leave her there alone.

She had changed from a very thin woman not to a child

but to an ungainly and ill-assorted collection of bones, with a birdlike crest, ready to die every minute with the erratic shaping of her breath.

There were some large rooms used for rehabilitation and exercise, connected to the hospital. Usually he saw them only when they were empty, all the equipment put away and the lights turned off. But one night as he was leaving he took a different route through the building for some reason and saw a light left on.

And when he went to investigate he saw that somebody was still there. A woman. She was sitting astride one of the blown-up exercise balls, just resting there, or perhaps trying to remember where she was supposed to go next.

It was Leah. He didn't recognize her at first, but then he looked again and it was Leah. He wouldn't have gone in, maybe, if he'd seen who it was, but now he was halfway on his mission to turn off the light. She saw him.

She slid off her perch. She was wearing some sort of purposeful athletic outfit and had gained a fair amount of weight.

"I thought I might run into you sometime," she said. "How is Isabel?"

It was a bit of a surprise to hear her call Isabel by her first name, or to speak of her at all, as if she'd known her.

He told her briefly how Isabel was. No way to tell it now except briefly.

"Do you talk to her?" she said.

"Not so much anymore."

"Oh, you should. You shouldn't give up talking to them."

How did she come to think she knew so much about everything?

"You're not surprised to see me, are you? You must have heard?" she said.

He did not know how to answer this.

"Well," he said.

"It's been a while since I heard that you were here and all, so I guess I just thought you'd know about me being down here too."

He said no.

"I do recreation," she told him. "I mean for the cancer patients. If they're up to it, like."

He said he guessed that was a good idea.

"It's great. I mean for me too. I'm pretty much okay, but sometimes things get to me. I mean particularly at suppertime. That's when it can start to feel weird."

She saw that he didn't know what she was talking about and she was ready—maybe eager—to explain.

"I mean without the kids and all. You didn't know their father got them?"

"No," he said.

"Oh, well. It's because they thought his mother could look after them, really. He's in AA and all, but the judgment wouldn't have gone like that if it wasn't for her."

She snuffled and dashed away tears in an almost disregarding way.

"Don't be embarrassed—it isn't as bad as it looks. I just automatically cry. Crying isn't so bad for you, either, so long as you don't make a career of it."

The man in AA would be the sax player. But what about the minister and whatever had been going on there?

Just as if he had asked her aloud, she said, "Oh. Then. Carl. That stuff was such a big deal and everything? I should have had my head examined.

"Carl got married again," she continued. "That made him feel better. I mean because he'd sort of got past whatever it was he had on me. It was really kind of funny. He went and married another minister. You know how they let women be ministers now? Well, she's one. So he's like the minister's wife. I think that's a howl."

Dry-eyed now, smiling. He knew that there was more coming, but he could not guess what it might be.

"You must have been here quite a while. You got a place of your own?"

"Yes."

"You cook your own supper and everything?"

He said that that was the case.

"I could do that for you once in a while. Would that be a good idea?"

Her eyes had brightened, holding his.

He said maybe, but to tell the truth there wasn't room in his place for more than one person to move around at a time.

Then he said that he hadn't looked in on Isabel for a couple of days, and he must go and do it now.

She nodded just slightly in agreement. She did not appear hurt or discouraged.

"See you around."

"See you."

They had been looking all over for him. Isabel was finally gone. They said "gone," as if she had got up and left. When someone had checked her about an hour ago, she had been the same as ever, and now she was gone.

He had often wondered what difference it would make.

But the emptiness in place of her was astounding.

He looked at the nurse in wonder. She thought he was asking her what he had to do next and she began to tell him. Filling him in. He understood her fine, but was still preoccupied.

He'd thought that it had happened long before with Isabel, but it hadn't. Not until now.

She had existed and now she did not. Not at all, as if not ever. And people hurried around, as if this outrageous fact could be overcome by making sensible arrangements. He, too, obeyed the customs, signing where he was told to sign, arranging—as they said—for the remains.

What an excellent word—"remains." Like something left to dry out in sooty layers in a cupboard.

And before long he found himself outside, pretending that he had as ordinary and good a reason as anybody else to put one foot ahead of the other.

What he carried with him, all he carried with him, was a lack, something like a lack of air, of proper behaviour in his lungs, a difficulty that he supposed would go on forever.

The girl he'd been talking to, whom he'd once known—she had spoken of her children. The loss of her children. Getting used to that. A problem at suppertime.

An expert at losing, she might be called—himself a novice by comparison. And now he could not remember her name. Had lost her name, though he'd known it well. Losing, lost. A joke on him, if you wanted one.

He was going up his own steps when it came to him.

Leah.

A relief out of all proportion, to remember her.

GRAVEL

A T that time we were living beside a gravel pit. Not a large one, hollowed out by monster machinery, just a minor pit that a farmer must have made some money from years before. In fact, the pit was shallow enough to lead you to think that there might have been some other intention for it—foundations for a house, maybe, that never made it any further.

My mother was the one who insisted on calling attention to it. "We live by the old gravel pit out the service-station road," she'd tell people, and laugh, because she was so happy to have shed everything connected with the house, the street—the husband—with the life she'd had before.

I barely remember that life. That is, I remember some parts of it clearly, but without the links you need to form a proper picture. All that I retain in my head of the house in town is the wallpaper with teddy bears in my old room. In this new house, which was really a trailer, my sister, Caro, and I had narrow cots, stacked one above the other. When we first moved there, Caro talked to me a lot about our old house, trying to get me to remember this or that. It was when we were in bed that she talked like this, and generally the conversation ended with me failing to remember and her getting cross. Sometimes I thought I did remember, but out of contrariness or fear of getting things wrong I pretended not to.

It was summer when we moved to the trailer. We had our dog with us. Blitzee. "Blitzee loves it here," my mother said, and it was true. What dog wouldn't love to exchange a town street, even one with spacious lawns and big houses, for the wide-open countryside? She took to barking at every car that went past, as if she owned the road, and now and then she brought home a squirrel or a groundhog she'd killed. At first Caro was quite upset by this, and Neal would have a talk with her, explaining about a dog's nature and the chain of life in which some things had to eat other things.

"She gets her dog food," Caro argued, but Neal said, "Suppose she didn't? Suppose someday we all disappeared and she had to fend for herself?"

"I'm not going to," Caro said. "I'm not going to disappear, and I'm always going to look after her."

"You think so?" Neal said, and our mother stepped in to deflect him. Neal was always ready to get on the subject of the Americans and the atomic bomb, and our mother didn't think we were ready for that yet. She didn't know that when he brought it up I thought he was talking about an atomic bun. I knew that there was something wrong with this interpretation, but I wasn't about to ask questions and get laughed at.

Neal was an actor. In town there was a professional summer theatre, a new thing at the time, which some people were enthusiastic about and others worried about, fearing that it would bring in riffraff. My mother and father had been among those in favour, my mother more actively so, because she had more time. My father was an insurance agent and travelled a lot. My mother had got busy with various fund-raising schemes for the theatre and donated her services as an usher. She was good-looking and young enough to be mistaken for an actress. She'd begun to dress like an actress too, in shawls and long skirts and dangling necklaces. She'd let her hair go wild and stopped wearing makeup. Of course, I had not understood or even particularly noticed these changes at the time. My mother was my mother. But no doubt Caro had noticed. And my father must have. Though, from all that I know of his nature and his feelings for my mother, I think he may have been proud to see how good she looked in these liberating styles and how well she fit in with the theatre people. When he spoke about this time, later on, he said that he had always approved of the arts. I can imagine now how embarrassed my mother would have been, cringing and laughing to cover up her cringing, if he'd made this declaration in front of her theatre friends.

Well, then came a development that could have been foreseen and probably was, but not by my father. I don't know if it happened to any of the other volunteers. I do know, though I don't remember it, that my father wept and for a whole day followed my mother around the house, not letting her out of his sight and refusing to believe her. And, instead of telling him anything to make him feel better, she told him something that made him feel worse.

She told him that the baby was Neal's.

Was she sure?

Absolutely. She had been keeping track.

What happened then?

My father gave up weeping. He had to get back to work. My mother packed up our things and took us to live with Neal in the trailer he had found, out in the country. She said afterwards that she had wept too. But she said also that she had felt alive. Maybe for the first time in her life, truly alive. She felt as if she had been given a chance; she had started her life all over again. She'd walked out on her silver and her china and her decorating scheme and her flower garden and even on the books in her bookcase. She would live now, not read. She'd left her clothes hanging in the closet and her high-heeled shoes in their shoe trees. Her diamond ring and her wedding ring on the dresser. Her silk nightdresses in their drawer. She meant to go around naked at least some of the time in the country, as long as the weather stayed warm.

That didn't work out, because when she tried it Caro went and hid in her cot and even Neal said he wasn't crazy about the idea.

What did he think of all this? Neal. His philosophy, as he put it later, was to welcome whatever happened. Everything is a gift. We give and we take.

I am suspicious of people who talk like this, but I can't say that I have a right to be.

He was not really an actor. He had got into acting, he said, as an experiment. To see what he could find out about himself. In university, before he dropped out, he had performed as part of the Chorus in *Oedipus Rex*. He had liked that—the giving yourself over, blending with others. Then one day, on the street in Toronto, he ran into a friend who was on his way to try out for a summer job with a new small-town theatre company. He went along, having nothing better to do, and ended up getting the job, while the other fellow didn't. He would play Banquo. Sometimes they make Banquo's Ghost visible, sometimes not. This time they wanted a visible version and Neal was the right size. An excellent size. A solid ghost.

He had been thinking of wintering in our town anyway, before my mother sprang her surprise. He had already spotted the trailer. He had enough carpentry experience to pick up work renovating the theatre, which would see him through till spring. That was as far ahead as he liked to think.

Caro didn't even have to change schools. She was picked up by the school bus at the end of the short lane that ran alongside the gravel pit. She had to make friends with the country children, and perhaps explain some things to the town children who had been her friends the year before, but if she had any difficulty with that I never heard about it.

Blitzee was always waiting by the road for her to come home.

I didn't go to kindergarten, because my mother didn't have a car. But I didn't mind doing without other children. Caro, when she got home, was enough for me. And my mother was often in a playful mood. As soon as it snowed that winter she and I built a snowman and she asked, "Shall we call it Neal?" I said okay, and we stuck various things on it to make it funny. Then we decided that I would run out of the house when his car came and say, Here's Neal, here's Neal! but be pointing up at the snowman. Which I did, but Neal got out of the car mad and yelled that he could have run me over.

That was one of the few times that I saw him act like a father.

Those short winter days must have seemed strange to me—in town, the lights came on at dusk. But children get used to changes. Sometimes I wondered about our other house. I didn't exactly miss it or want to live there again— I just wondered where it had gone.

My mother's good times with Neal went on into the night. If I woke up and had to go to the bathroom, I'd call for her. She would come happily but not in any hurry, with some piece of cloth or a scarf wrapped around her—also a smell that I associated with candlelight and music. And love.

Something did happen that was not so reassuring, but I didn't try to make much sense of it at the time. Blitzee, our dog, was not very big, but she didn't seem small enough to fit under Caro's coat. I don't know how Caro managed to do it. Not once but twice. She hid the dog under her coat on the school bus, and then, instead of going straight to school, she took Blitzee back to our old house in town, which was less than a block away. That was where my father found the dog, on the winter porch, which was not locked, when he came home for his solitary lunch. There was great surprise that she had got there, found her way home like a dog in a story.

Caro made the biggest fuss, and claimed not to have seen the dog at all that morning. But then she made the mistake of trying it again, maybe a week later, and this time, though nobody on the bus or at school suspected her, our mother did.

I can't remember if our father brought Blitzee back to us. I can't imagine him in the trailer or at the door of the trailer or even on the road to it. Maybe Neal went to the house in town and picked her up. Not that that's any easier to imagine.

If I've made it sound as though Caro was unhappy or scheming all the time, that isn't the truth. As I've said, she did try to make me talk about things, at night in bed, but she wasn't constantly airing grievances. It wasn't her nature to be sulky. She was far too keen on making a good impression. She liked people to like her; she liked to stir up the air in a room with the promise of something you could even call merriment. She thought more about that than I did.

She was the one who most took after our mother, I think now.

There must have been some probing about what she'd done with the dog. I think I can remember some of it.

"I did it for a trick."

"Do you want to go and live with your father?"

I believe that was asked, and I believe she said no.

I didn't ask her anything. What she had done didn't seem strange to me. That's probably how it is with younger children—nothing that the strangely powerful older child does seems out of the ordinary.

Our mail was deposited in a tin box on a post, down by the road. My mother and I would walk there every day, unless it was particularly stormy, to see what had been left for us. We did this after I got up from my nap. Sometimes it was the only time we went outside all day. In the morning, we watched children's television shows—or she read while I watched. (She had not given up reading for very long.) We heated up some canned soup for lunch, then I went down for my nap while she read some more. She was quite big with the baby now and it stirred around in her stomach, so that I could feel it. Its name was going to be Brandy—already was Brandy—whether it was a boy or a girl.

One day when we were going down the lane for the mail, and were in fact not far from the box, my mother stopped and stood quite still.

"Quiet," she said to me, though I hadn't said a word and wasn't even playing the shuffling game with my boots in the snow.

"I was being quiet," I said.

"Shush. Turn around."

"But we didn't get the mail."

"Never mind. Just walk."

Then I noticed that Blitzee, who was always with us, just behind or ahead of us, wasn't there anymore. Another dog was, on the opposite side of the road, a few feet from the mailbox.

My mother phoned the theatre as soon as we got home and let in Blitzee, who was waiting for us. Nobody answered. She phoned the school and asked someone to tell the bus driver to drive Caro up to the door. It turned out that the driver couldn't do that, because it had snowed since Neal last plowed the lane, but he—the driver—did watch until she got to the house. There was no wolf to be seen by that time.

Neal was of the opinion that there never had been one. And if there had been, he said, it would have been no danger to us, weak as it was probably from hibernation.

Caro said that wolves did not hibernate. "We learned about them in school."

Our mother wanted Neal to get a gun.

"You think I'm going to get a gun and go and shoot a goddam poor mother wolf who has probably got a bunch of babies back in the bush and is just trying to protect them, the way you're trying to protect yours?" he said quietly.

Caro said, "Only two. They only have two at a time."

"Okay, okay. I'm talking to your mother."

"You don't know that," my mother said. "You don't know if it's got hungry cubs or anything."

I had never thought she'd talk to him like that.

He said, "Easy. Easy. Let's just think a bit. Guns are a terrible thing. If I went and got a gun, then what would I be saying? That Vietnam was okay? That I might as well have gone to Vietnam?"

"You're not an American."

"You're not going to rile me."

This is more or less what they said, and it ended up with Neal not having to get a gun. We never saw the wolf again, if it was a wolf. I think my mother stopped going to get the mail, but she may have become too big to be comfortable doing that anyway.

The snow dwindled magically. The trees were still bare of leaves and my mother made Caro wear her coat in the mornings, but she came home after school dragging it behind her.

My mother said that the baby had got to be twins, but the doctor said it wasn't.

"Great. Great," Neal said, all in favour of the twins idea. "What do doctors know."

The gravel pit had filled to its brim with melted snow and rain, so that Caro had to edge around it on her way to catch the school bus. It was a little lake, still and dazzling under the clear sky. Caro asked with not much hope if we could play in it.

Our mother said not to be crazy. "It must be twenty feet deep," she said.

Neal said, "Maybe ten."

Caro said, "Right around the edge it wouldn't be."

Our mother said yes it was. "It just drops off," she said. "It's not like going in at the beach, for fuck's sake. Just stay away from it."

She had started saying "fuck" quite a lot, perhaps more than Neal did, and in a more exasperated tone of voice.

"Should we keep the dog away from it, too?" she asked him.

Neal said that that wasn't a problem. "Dogs can swim."

A Saturday. Caro watched *The Friendly Giant* with me and made comments that spoiled it. Neal was lying on the couch, which unfolded into his and my mother's bed. He was smoking his kind of cigarettes, which could not be smoked at work so had to be made the most of on weekends. Caro sometimes bothered him, asking to try one. Once he had let her, but told her not to tell our mother.

I was there, though, so I told.

There was alarm, though not quite a row.

"You know he'd have those kids out of here like a shot," our mother said. "Never again."

"Never again," Neal said agreeably. "So what if he feeds them poison Rice Krispies crap?"

In the beginning, we hadn't seen our father at all. Then, after Christmas, a plan had been worked out for Saturdays. Our mother always asked afterwards if we had had a good time. I always said yes, and meant it, because I thought that if you went to a movie or to look at Lake Huron, or ate in a restaurant, that meant that you had had a good time. Caro said yes, too, but in a tone of voice that suggested that it was none of our mother's business. Then my father went on a winter holiday to Cuba (my mother remarked on this with some surprise and maybe approval) and came back with a lingering sort of flu that caused the visits to lapse. They were supposed to resume in the spring, but so far they hadn't.

After the television was turned off, Caro and I were sent outside to run around, as our mother said, and get some fresh air. We took the dog with us.

When we got outside, the first thing we did was loosen and let trail the scarves our mother had wrapped around our necks. (The fact was, though we may not have put the two things together, the deeper she got into her pregnancy the more she slipped back into behaving like an ordinary mother, at least when it was a matter of scarves we didn't need or regular meals. There was not so much champion-ing of wild ways as there had been in the fall.) Caro asked me what I wanted to do, and I said I didn't know. This was a formality on her part but the honest truth on mine. We let the dog lead us, anyway, and Blitzee's idea was to go and look at the gravel pit. The wind was whipping the water up into little waves, and very soon we got cold, so we wound our scarves back around our necks.

I don't know how much time we spent just wandering around the water's edge, knowing that we couldn't be seen from the trailer. After a while, I realized that I was being given instructions.

I was to go back to the trailer and tell Neal and our mother something.

That the dog had fallen into the water.

The dog had fallen into the water and Caro was afraid she'd be drowned.

Blitzee. Drownded.

Drowned.

But Blitzee wasn't in the water.

She could be. And Caro could jump in to save her.

I believe I still put up some argument, along the lines of she hasn't, you haven't, it could happen but it hasn't. I also remembered that Neal had said dogs didn't drown.

Caro instructed me to do as I was told.

Why?

I may have said that, or I may have just stood there not obeying and trying to work up another argument.

In my mind I can see her picking up Blitzee and tossing her, though Blitzee was trying to hang on to her coat. Then backing up, Caro backing up to take a run at the water. Running, jumping, all of a sudden hurling herself at the water. But I can't recall the sound of the splashes as they, one after the other, hit the water. Not a little splash or a big one. Perhaps I had turned towards the trailer by then—I must have done so.

When I dream of this, I am always running. And in my dreams I am running not towards the trailer but back towards the gravel pit. I can see Blitzee floundering around and Caro swimming towards her, swimming strongly, on the way to rescue her. I see her light-brown checked coat and her plaid scarf and her proud successful face and reddish hair darkened at the end of its curls by the water. All I have to do is watch and be happy—nothing required of me, after all.

What I really did was make my way up the little incline towards the trailer. And when I got there I sat down. Just as if there had been a porch or a bench, though in fact the trailer had neither of these things. I sat down and waited for the next thing to happen.

I know this because it's a fact. I don't know, however, what my plan was or what I was thinking. I was waiting, maybe, for the next act in Caro's drama. Or in the dog's.

I don't know if I sat there for five minutes. More? Less? It wasn't too cold.

I went to see a professional person about this once and she convinced me—for a time, she convinced me—that I must have tried the door of the trailer and found it locked. Locked because my mother and Neal were having sex and had locked it against interruptions. If I'd banged on the door they would have been angry. The counsellor was satisfied to bring me to this conclusion, and I was satisfied, too. For a while. But I no longer think that was true. I don't think they would have locked the door, because I know that once they didn't and Caro walked in and they laughed at the look on her face.

Maybe I remembered that Neal had said that dogs did not drown, which meant that Caro's rescue of Blitzee would not be necessary. Therefore she herself wouldn't be able to carry out her game. So many games, with Caro.

Did I think she could swim? At nine, many children can. And in fact it turned out that she'd had one lesson the summer before, but then we had moved to the trailer and she hadn't taken any more. She may have thought she could manage well enough. And I may indeed have thought that she could do anything she wanted to.

The counsellor did not suggest that I might have been sick of carrying out Caro's orders, but the thought did occur to me. It doesn't quite seem right, though. If I'd been older, maybe. At the time, I still expected her to fill my world.

How long did I sit there? Likely not long. And it's possible that I did knock. After a while. After a minute or two. In any case, my mother did, at some point, open the door, for no reason. A presentiment.

Next thing, I am inside. My mother is yelling at Neal and trying to make him understand something. He is getting to his feet and standing there speaking to her, touching her, with such mildness and gentleness and consolation. But that is not what my mother wants at all and she tears herself away from him and runs out the door. He shakes his head and looks down at his bare feet. His big helpless-looking toes.

I think he says something to me with a singsong sadness in his voice. Strange.

Beyond that I have no details.

My mother didn't throw herself into the water. She didn't go into labour from the shock. My brother, Brent, was not born until a week or ten days after the funeral, and he was a full-term infant. Where she was while she waited for the birth to happen I do not know. Perhaps she was kept in the hospital and sedated as much as possible under the circumstances.

I remember the day of the funeral quite well. A very pleasant and comfortable woman I didn't know—her name was Josie—took me on an expedition. We visited some swings and a sort of dollhouse that was large enough for me to go inside, and we ate a lunch of my favourite treats, but not enough to make me sick. Josie was somebody I got to know very well later on. She was a friend my father had made in Cuba, and after the divorce she became my stepmother, his second wife.

My mother recovered. She had to. There was Brent to look after and, most of the time, me. I believe I stayed with my father and Josie while she got settled in the house that she planned to live in for the rest of her life. I don't remember being there with Brent until he was big enough to sit up in his high chair.

My mother went back to her old duties at the theatre. At first she may have worked as she had before, as a volunteer usher, but by the time I was in school she had a real job, with pay, and year-round responsibilities. She was the business manager. The theatre survived, through various ups and downs, and is still going now.

Neal didn't believe in funerals, so he didn't attend Caro's. He never saw Brent. He wrote a letter—I found this out much later—saying that since he did not intend to act as a father it would be better for him to bow out at the start. I never mentioned him to Brent, because I thought it would upset my mother. Also because Brent showed so little sign of being like him—like Neal—and seemed, in fact, so much more like my father that I really wondered about what was going on around the time he was conceived. My father has never said anything about this and never would. He treats Brent just as he treats me, but he is the kind of man who would do that anyway.

He and Josie have not had any children of their own, but I don't think that bothers them. Josie is the only person who ever talks about Caro, and even she doesn't do it often. She does say that my father doesn't hold my mother responsible. He has also said that he must have been sort of a stick-in-the-mud when my mother wanted more excitement in her life. He needed a shaking-up, and he got one. There's no use being sorry about it. Without the shaking-up, he would never have found Josie and the two of them would not have been so happy now.

"Which two?" I might say, just to derail him, and he would staunchly say, "Josie. Josie, of course."

My mother cannot be made to recall any of those times, and I don't bother her with them. I know that she has driven down the lane we lived on, and found it quite changed, with the sort of trendy houses you see now, put up on unproductive land. She mentioned this with the slight scorn that such houses evoke in her. I went down the lane myself but did not tell anyone. All the eviscerating that is done in families these days strikes me as a mistake.

Even where the gravel pit was a house now stands, the ground beneath it levelled.

I have a partner, Ruthann, who is younger than I am but, I think, somewhat wiser. Or at least more optimistic about what she calls routing out my demons. I would never have got in touch with Neal if it had not been for her urging. Of course, for a long time I had no way, just as I had no thought, of getting in touch. It was he who finally wrote to me. A brief note of congratulations, he said, after seeing my picture in the *Alumni Gazette*. What he was doing looking through the *Alumni Gazette* I have no idea. I had received one of those academic honours that mean something in a restricted circle and little anywhere else.

He was living hardly fifty miles away from where I teach, which also happens to be where I went to university. I wondered if he had been there at that time. So close. Had he become a scholar?

At first I had no intention of replying to the note, but I told Ruthann and she said that I should think about writing back. So the upshot was that I sent him an e-mail, and arrangements were made. I was to meet him in his town, in the unthreatening surroundings of a university cafeteria. I told myself that if he looked unbearable—I did not quite know what I meant by this—I could just walk on through.

He was shorter than he used to be, as adults we remember from childhood usually are. His hair was thin, and trimmed close to his head. He got me a cup of tea. He was drinking tea himself.

What did he do for a living?

He said that he tutored students in preparation for exams. Also, he helped them write their essays. Sometimes, you might say, he wrote those essays. Of course, he charged.

"It's no way to get to be a millionaire, I can tell you."

He lived in a dump. Or a semi-respectable dump. He liked it. He looked for clothes at the Sally Ann. That was okay too.

"Suits my principles."

I did not congratulate him on any of this, but, to tell the truth, I doubt that he expected me to.

"Anyway, I don't think my lifestyle is so interesting. I think you might want to know how it happened."

I could not figure out how to speak.

"I was stoned," he said. "And, furthermore, I'm not a swimmer. Not many swimming pools around where I grew up. I'd have drowned too. Is that what you wanted to know?"

I said that he was not really the one that I was wondering about.

Then he became the third person I'd asked, "What do you think Caro had in mind?"

The counsellor had said that we couldn't know. "Likely she herself didn't know what she wanted. Attention? I don't think she meant to drown herself. Attention to how bad she was feeling?"

Ruthann had said, "To make your mother do what she wanted? Make her smarten up and see that she had to go back to your father?"

Neal said, "It doesn't matter. Maybe she thought she could paddle better than she could. Maybe she didn't know how heavy winter clothes can get. Or that there wasn't anybody in a position to help her."

He said to me, "Don't waste your time. You're not thinking what if you had hurried up and told, are you? Not trying to get in on the guilt?"

I said that I had considered what he was saying, but no.

"The thing is to be happy," he said. "No matter what. Just try that. You can. It gets to be easier and easier. It's nothing to do with circumstances. You wouldn't believe how good it is. Accept everything and then tragedy disappears. Or tragedy lightens, anyway, and you're just there, going along easy in the world."

Now, good-bye.

I see what he meant. It really is the right thing to do. But, in my mind, Caro keeps running at the water and throwing herself in, as if in triumph, and I'm still caught, waiting for her to explain to me, waiting for the splash.

HAVEN

Aᴸᴸ this happened in the seventies, though in that town and other small towns like it, the seventies were not as we picture them now, or as I had known them even in Vancouver. The boys' hair was longer than it had been, but not straggling down their backs, and there didn't seem to be an unusual amount of liberation or defiance in the air.

My uncle started off by teasing me about grace. About not saying grace. I was thirteen years old, living with him and my aunt for the year that my parents were in Africa. I had never bowed my head over a plate of food in my life.

"Lord bless this food to our use and us to thy service," Uncle Jasper said, while I held my fork in midair and refrained from chewing the meat and potatoes that were already in my mouth.

III

"Surprised?" he said, after "for Jesus' sake. Amen." He wanted to know if my parents said a different prayer, perhaps at the end of the meal.

"They don't say anything," I told him.

"Don't they really?" he said. These words were delivered with fake amazement. "You don't mean to tell me that? People who don't say the Lord's grace going over to Africa to minister to the heathen—think of that!"

In Ghana, where my parents were teaching school, they seemed not to have come across any heathens. Christianity bloomed disconcertingly all around them, even on signs on the backs of buses.

"My parents are Unitarians," I said, for some reason excluding myself.

Uncle Jasper shook his head and asked me to explain the word. Were they not believers in the God of Moses? Nor in the God of Abraham? Surely they must be Jews. No? Not Muhammadans, were they?

"It's mostly that every person has his own idea of God," I said, perhaps more firmly than he'd expected. I had two brothers in university and it didn't look as though they were going to turn out to be Unitarians, so I was used to intense religious—as well as atheistic—discussions around the dinner table.

"But they believe in doing good works and living a good life," I added.

A mistake. Not only did an incredulous expression come over my uncle's face—raised eyebrows, marvelling nod—but the words just out of my mouth sounded alien even to me, pompous and lacking in conviction.

I had not approved of my parents' going to Africa. I had

objected to being dumped—my word for it—with my aunt
and uncle. I may even have told them, my long-suffering parents, that their good works were a load of crap. In our house
we were allowed to express ourselves as we liked. Though I
don't think my parents themselves would ever have spoken
of "good works" or of "doing good."

My uncle was satisfied, for the moment. He said that we'd
have to drop the subject, as he himself needed to be back at
his practice doing his own good works by one o'clock.

It was probably then that my aunt picked up her fork and
began to eat. She would have waited until the bristling was
over. This may have been out of habit, rather than out of
alarm at my forwardness. She was used to holding back
until she was sure that my uncle had said all that he meant
to say. Even if I spoke to her directly, she would wait, looking at him to see if he wanted to do the answering. What
she did say was always cheerful, and she smiled just as soon
as she knew it was okay to smile, so it was hard to think of
her as being suppressed. Also hard to think of her as my
mother's sister, because she looked so much younger and
fresher and tidier, as well as being given to those radiant
smiles.

My mother would talk right over my father if she had
something she really wanted to say, and that was often the
case. My brothers, even the one who said he was thinking
of becoming a Muslim so that he could chastise women,
always listened to her as an equal authority.

"Dawn's life is devoted to her husband," my mother had
said, with an attempt at neutrality. Or, more drily, "Her life
revolves around that man."

This was something that was said at the time, and it was

not always meant as disparagement. But I had not seen before a woman of whom it seemed so true as Aunt Dawn.

Of course it would have been quite different, my mother said, if they'd had children.

Imagine that. Children. Getting in Uncle Jasper's way, whining for a corner of their mother's attention. Being sick, sulking, messing up the house, wanting food he didn't like.

Impossible. The house was his, the choice of menus his, the radio and television programs his. Even if he was at his practice next door, or out on a call, things had to be ready for his approval at any moment.

The slow realization that came to me was that such a regime could be quite agreeable. Bright sterling spoons and forks, polished dark floors, comforting linen sheets—all this household godliness was presided over by my aunt and arrived at by Bernice, the maid. Bernice cooked from scratch, ironed the dish towels. All the other doctors in town sent their linens to the Chinese laundry, while Bernice and Aunt Dawn herself hung ours out on the clothesline. White from the sun, fresh from the wind, sheets and bandages all superior and sweet-smelling. My uncle was of the opinion that the Chinks went too heavy on the starch.

"Chinese," my aunt said in a soft, teasing voice, as if she had to apologize to both my uncle and the laundrymen.

"Chinks," my uncle said boisterously.

Bernice was the only one who could say it quite naturally.

Gradually, I became less loyal to my home, with its intellectual seriousness and physical disorder. Of course it took all a woman's energy to keep up such a haven as this. You could not be typing out Unitarian manifestos, or running off to Africa. (At first I said, "My parents went to *work* in

Africa," every time a person in this house spoke of their running off. Then I got sick of making the correction.)

Haven was the word. "A woman's most important job is making a haven for her man."

Did Aunt Dawn actually say that? I don't think so. She shied away from statements. I probably read it in one of the housekeeping magazines I found in the house. Such as would have made my mother puke.

At first I explored the town. I found a heavy old bicycle in the back of the garage and took it out to ride without thinking of getting permission. Going downhill on a newly gravelled road above the harbour I lost control. One of my knees was badly scraped, and I had to visit my uncle at his practice attached to the house. He dealt expertly with the wound. He was all business then, matter-of-fact, with a mildness that was quite impersonal. No jokes. He said he couldn't remember where that bike had come from—it was a treacherous old monster, and if I was keen on bicycling we could see about getting me a decent one. When I got better acquainted with my new school and with the rules about what girls there did after they reached their teens, I realized that biking was out of the question, so nothing came of this. What surprised me was that my uncle himself had not brought up any question of propriety or what girls should or should not do. He seemed to have forgotten, in his office, that I was a person who needed straightening out on many matters, or who had to be urged, especially at the dinner table, to copy the behaviour of my aunt Dawn.

"You went riding up there all by yourself?" was what she

said when she heard about this. "What were you looking for? Never mind, you'll soon have some friends."

She was right, both about my acquiring a few friends and about the way that that would limit the things I could do.

Uncle Jasper was not just a doctor; he was *the* doctor. He had been the force behind the building of the town hospital, and had resisted its being named for him. He had grown up poor but smart and had taught school until he could afford medical training. He had delivered babies and operated on appendix cases in farmhouse kitchens after driving through snowstorms. Even in the fifties and sixties, such things had happened. He was relied on never to give up, to tackle cases of blood poisoning and pneumonia and to bring patients out alive in the days when the new drugs had not been heard of.

Yet in his office he seemed so easygoing, compared with the way he was at home. As if in the house a constant watch was needed but in the office no oversight was necessary, though you might have thought that the exact opposite would be the case. The nurse who worked there did not even treat him with any special deference—she was nothing like Aunt Dawn. She stuck her head around the door of the room where he was treating my scrape and said that she was going home early.

"You'll have to get the phone, Dr. Cassel. Remember, I told you?"

"Mmm-hmm," he said.

Of course she was old, maybe over fifty, and women of that age could take on a habit of authority.

But I couldn't imagine that Aunt Dawn ever would. She seemed fixed in rosy and timorous youth. Early in my stay, when I thought I had the right to wander anywhere, I had gone into my aunt and uncle's bedroom to look at a picture of her, on his bedside table.

The soft curves and dark wavy hair she had still. But there was an unbecoming red cap covering part of that hair and she was wearing a purple cape. When I went downstairs I asked her what that outfit was and she said, "What outfit? Oh. That was my nursing student's getup."

"You were a nurse?"

"Oh no." She laughed as if that would have been absurd effrontery. "I dropped out."

"Is that how you met Uncle Jasper?"

"Oh no. He'd been a doctor for years before that. I met him when I had a ruptured appendix. I was staying with a friend—I mean a friend's family up here—and I got really sick but I didn't know what it was. He diagnosed it and took it out." At this she blushed rather more than usual and said that perhaps I should not go into the bedroom unless I asked permission. Even I could understand that this meant never.

"So is your friend still here?"

"Oh you know. You don't have friends in the same way once you get married."

About the time I nosed out these facts I also discovered that Uncle Jasper was not altogether without family, as I had supposed. He had a sister. She, too, had been successful in the world, at least to my way of thinking. She was a musician, a violinist. Her name was Mona. Or that was the name she went by, though her proper, baptized name was Maud. Mona Cassel. My first knowledge of her existence came when I had lived in the town for about half the school year. When I was walking home from school one day I saw a poster in the window of the newspaper office, advertising a concert that was to be given at the Town Hall in a couple of weeks' time. Three musicians from Toronto. Mona Cassel was the tall, white-haired lady with the violin. When I got home I told Aunt Dawn about the coincidence of names and she said, "Oh yes. That would be your uncle's sister."

Then she said, "Just don't mention anything about it around here."

After a moment she seemed to feel obliged to say more.

"Your uncle doesn't go for that kind of music, you know. Symphony music."

And then more.

She said that the sister was a few years older than Uncle Jasper, and that something had happened when they were young. Some relatives had thought that this girl should be taken away and given a better chance, because she was so musical. So she was brought up in a different way and the brother and sister had nothing in common and that was really all that she—Aunt Dawn—knew about it. Except that my uncle would not like it that she had told me even that much.

"He doesn't like that music?" I said. "What kind of music does he like?"

"Sort of more old-fashioned, you could say. Definitely not classical, though."

"The Beatles?"

"Oh goodness."

"Not Lawrence Welk?"

"It's not up to us to discuss this, is it? I shouldn't have got going on it."

I disregarded her.

"So what do *you* like?"

"I like pretty much anything."

"You must like some things better than other things."

She wouldn't grant more than one of her little laughs. This was the nervous laugh, similar to but more concerned than, for example, the laugh with which she asked Uncle Jasper how he liked his supper. He nearly always gave approval, but with qualifications. All right, but a bit too spicy or a bit too bland. Perhaps a little over- or possibly undercooked. Once, he said, "I didn't," and refused to elaborate, and the laugh vanished into her tight lips and heroic self-control.

What could that dinner have been? I want to say curry, but maybe that's because my father didn't like curry, though he didn't make a fuss about it. My uncle got up and made himself a peanut butter sandwich, and the emphasis he put into this did amount to making a fuss. Whatever Aunt Dawn had served, it wouldn't have been a deliberate provocation. Maybe just something slightly unusual that had looked good in a magazine. And, as I recall, he had eaten it all before pronouncing his verdict. So he was propelled not by hunger but by the need to make a statement of pure and mighty disapproval.

It occurs to me now that something might have gone wrong at the hospital that day, somebody might have died who wasn't supposed to—perhaps the problem wasn't with food at all. But I don't think it occurred to Aunt Dawn—or, even if it did, she didn't let her suspicion show. She was all contrition.

At the time, Aunt Dawn had another problem, a problem that I wouldn't understand until later. She had the problem of the couple next door. They had moved in about the same time as I had. He was the county-school inspector, she a music teacher. They were perhaps the same age as Aunt Dawn, younger than Uncle Jasper. They had no children either, which left them free for sociability. And they were at that stage of taking on a new community, where every prospect looks bright and easy. In this spirit they had asked Aunt Dawn and Uncle Jasper around for drinks. The social life of my aunt and uncle was so restricted, and so well known around town to be restricted, that my aunt had no practice in saying no. And so they found themselves visiting, having drinks and chatting, and I can imagine that Uncle Jasper warmed to the occasion, though without forgiving my aunt's blunder in having accepted the invitation.

Now she was in a quandary. She understood that when people had invited you to their house and you had gone you were supposed to ask them back. Drinks for drinks, coffee for coffee. No need for a meal. But even what little was required she did not know how to do. My uncle had found no fault with the neighbours—he simply did not like having people in his house, on any account.

Then, with the news I had brought her, came the possibility of a solution to the problem. The trio from Toronto—including, of course, Mona—was performing at the Town Hall on one evening only. And it so happened that that was the very evening when Uncle Jasper had to be out of the house and had to stay out fairly late. It was the night of the County Physicians Annual General Meeting and Dinner. Not a banquet—wives were not invited.

The neighbours were planning to attend the concert. They would have had to, given her profession. But they agreed to drop in as soon as it was over, for coffee and snacks. And to meet—this was where my aunt overreached herself—to meet the members of the trio, who would also be dropping in for a few moments.

I don't know how much my aunt revealed to the neighbours about the relationship with Mona Cassel. If she had any sense, it was nothing. And sense was something she had plenty of, most of the time. She did, I'm sure, explain that the doctor could not be present on that evening, but she would never have gone so far as to tell them that the gathering was to be kept secret from him. And what about keeping it secret from Bernice, who went home at suppertime and would surely get a whiff of the preparations? I don't know. And, most important of all, I don't know how Aunt Dawn got the invitation through to the performers. Had she been in touch with Mona all along? I shouldn't think so. She surely didn't have it in her to deceive my uncle on a long-term basis.

I imagine she just got giddy and wrote a note, and took it to the hotel where the trio would be staying. She wouldn't have had a Toronto address.

Even going into the hotel, she must have wondered what eyes were on her, and prayed that she would get not the manager, who knew her husband, but the new young woman, who was some sort of foreigner and might not even know that she was the doctor's wife.

She would have indicated to the musicians that she did not expect them to stay for more than a little while. Concerts are tiring, and they would have to be on their way to another town early in the morning.

Why did she take the risk? Why not entertain the neighbours by herself? Hard to say. Maybe she felt unable to carry a conversation by herself. Maybe she wanted to preen a little in front of those neighbours. Maybe—though I can hardly believe this—she wanted to make some slight gesture of friendship or acceptance towards the sister-in-law, whom, as far as I know, she had never met.

She must have gone around dazed at her own connivance. Not to mention with various crossed fingers and good-luck prayers, during those days before, when there was a danger of Uncle Jasper's accidentally finding out. Meeting the music teacher on the street, for instance, and having her gush her thanks and expectations all over him.

The musicians were not so tired after the concert as you might have expected. Or so disheartened by the small size of the Town Hall crowd, which had probably not been a surprise. The enthusiasm of the next-door guests and the warmth of the living room (the Town Hall had been chilly), as well as the glow of the cherry-coloured velvet curtains that were a dull maroon in the daytime but looked festive after dark—all these things must have lifted their spirits. The dreariness outside provided a contrast, and the coffee warmed these exotic but weatherbeaten strangers. Not to mention the sherry that succeeded the coffee. Sherry or port in crystal glasses of the correct shape and size, and also little cakes topped with shredded coconut, diamond- or crescent-shaped shortbread, chocolate wafers. I myself had never seen the like. My parents gave the kind of parties where people ate chili out of clay pots.

Aunt Dawn wore a dress that was modestly cut, made of flesh-coloured crepe. It was the sort of dress an older woman might have worn and made look proper in a fussy way, but my aunt could not help looking as if she were taking part in some slightly risqué celebration. The neighbour wife was also dressed up, a bit more perhaps than the occasion warranted. The short, thick man who played the cello wore a black suit that was saved by a bow tie from making him look like an undertaker, and the pianist, who was his wife, wore a black dress that was too frilly for her wide figure. But Mona Cassel was shining like the moon, in a straight-cut gown of some silvery material. She was large-boned, with a big nose, like her brother's.

Aunt Dawn must have had the piano tuned, or they wouldn't have stuck with it. (And if it seems odd that there was a piano in the house at all, given my uncle's soon-to-be-revealed opinions on the subject of music, I can say only that every house of a certain style and period used to have one.)

The neighbour wife asked for *Eine Kleine Nachtmusik,* and I seconded her, showing off. The fact was I didn't know the music but only the title, from studying German at my old city school.

Then the neighbour husband asked for something, and it was played, and when it was finished he begged pardon from Aunt Dawn for having been so rude, jumping in with his favourite before the hostess had had a chance to ask for hers.

Aunt Dawn said, Oh no, not to bother about her, she liked everything. Then she disappeared in a towering blush. I don't know if she cared about the music at all, but it certainly looked as if she were excited about something. Perhaps just about being personally responsible for these moments, this spread of delight?

Could she have forgotten—how could she have forgotten? The meeting of the County Physicians, the Annual Dinner and the Election of Officers was normally over by ten thirty. It was now eleven o'clock.

Too late, too late, we both noticed the time.

The storm door is opening now, then the door into the front hall and, without the usual pause there to remove boots and winter coat or scarf, my uncle strides into the living room.

The musicians, in the middle of a piece, do not stop. The neighbours greet my uncle cheerfully but with voices lowered in deference to the playing. He looks twice his size with his coat unbuttoned and his scarf loose and his boots on. He glares, but not at anybody in particular, not even at his wife.

And she isn't looking at him. She has begun to gather up the plates on the table beside her, placing them one on top of the other and not even noticing that some still have the little cakes on them, which will be squashed to pieces.

Without haste and without halting, he walks through the double living room, then through the dining room and the swinging doors into the kitchen.

The pianist is sitting with her hands quiet on the keys, and the cello player has stopped. The violinist continues alone. I have no idea, even now, if that was the way the piece was supposed to go or if she was flouting him on purpose. She never looked up, as far as I can remember, to face this scowling man. Her large white head, similar to his but more weathered, trembles a little but may have been trembling all along.

He is back, with a plateful of pork and beans. He must have just opened a can and slopped the contents out cold on the plate. He hasn't bothered to take off his winter coat. And still without looking at anybody, but making a great clatter with his fork, he is eating as if alone, and hungry. You might think there had not been a bite of food offered at the Annual Meeting and Dinner.

I have never seen him eat like this. His table manners have always been lordly, but decent.

The music his sister is playing comes to an end, presumably at its own proper time. It's a little ahead of the pork and beans. The neighbours have got themselves into the front hall and wrapped themselves in their outdoor clothes and stuck their heads in once to express their profuse thanks, in the middle of their desperation to be out of here.

And now the musicians are leaving, though not in quite such a hurry. Instruments have to be properly packed up, after all; you don't just thrust them into their cases. The musicians manage things in what must be their usual way, methodically, and then they, too, disappear. I can't remember anything that was said, or whether Aunt Dawn pulled herself together enough to thank them or follow them to the door. I can't pay attention to them because Uncle Jasper has taken to talking, in a very loud voice, and the person he is talking to is me. I think I remember the violinist taking one look at him, just as he begins to talk. A look that he completely ignores or maybe doesn't even see. It's not an angry look, as you might expect, or even an amazed one. She is just terribly tired, and her face whiter perhaps than any you could imagine.

"Now, tell me," my uncle is saying, addressing me as if nobody else were there, "tell me, do your parents go in for this sort of thing? What I mean is, this kind of music? Concerts and the like? They ever pay money to sit down for a couple of hours and wear their bottoms out listening to something they wouldn't recognize half a day later? Pay money simply to perpetrate a fraud? You ever know them to do that?"

I said no, and it was the truth. I had never known them to go to a concert, though they were in favour of concerts in general.

"See? They've got too much sense, your parents. Too much sense to join all these people who are fussing and clapping and carrying on like it's just the wonder of the world. You know the kind of people I mean? They're lying. A load of horse manure. All in the hope of appearing high-class. Or more likely giving in to their wives' hope to appear high-class. Remember that when you get out in the world. Okay?"

I agreed to remember. I was not really surprised by what he was saying. A lot of people thought that way. Especially men. There was a quantity of things that men hated. Or had no use for, as they said. And that was exactly right. They had no use for it, so they hated it. Maybe it was the same way I felt about algebra—I doubted very much that I would ever find any use for it.

But I didn't go so far as to want it wiped off the face of the earth for that reason.

When I came down in the morning, Uncle Jasper had already left the house. Bernice was washing dishes in the kitchen and Aunt Dawn was putting away the crystal glasses in the china cabinet. She smiled at me, but her hands were not quite steady, so that the glasses gave a little warning clink.

"A man's home is his castle," she said.

"That's a pun," I said, to cheer her up. "Cassel."

She smiled again, but I don't think she even knew what I was talking about.

"When you write to your mother, in Ghana—" she said, "when you write to her, I don't think you should mention— I mean, I wonder if you should mention the little upset we had here last night. When she sees so many real troubles and people starving and that sort of thing, I mean, it would seem pretty trivial and self-centred of us."

I understood. I did not bother to say that so far there had been no reports of starvation in Ghana.

It was only in the first month, anyway, that I had sent my parents letters full of sarcastic descriptions and complaints. Now everything had become much too complicated to explain.

After our conversation about music, Uncle Jasper's attention to me became more respectful. He listened to my views on socialized health care as if they were my own and not derived from those of my parents. Once, he said that it was a pleasure to have an intelligent person to talk to across the table. My aunt said yes it was. She had said this only to be agreeable, and when my uncle laughed in a particular way she turned red. Life was hard for her, but by Valentine's Day she was forgiven, receiving a bloodstone pendant that made her smile and turn aside to shed a few tears of relief all at the same time.

Mona's candlelight pallor, her sharp bones, not quite softened by the silver dress, may have been signs of illness. Her death was noted in the local paper, that spring, along with a mention of the Town Hall concert. An obituary from a Toronto paper was reprinted, with a brief outline of a career that seemed to have been adequate to support her, if not brilliant. Uncle Jasper expressed surprise—not at her death but at the fact that she was not going to be buried in Toronto. The funeral and interment were to be at the Church of the Hosannas, which was a few miles north of this town, out in the country. It had been the family church when Uncle Jasper and Mona / Maud were small and it was Anglican. Uncle Jasper and Aunt Dawn went to the United Church now, as most well-to-do people in town did. United Church people were firm in their faith but did not think that you had to turn up every Sunday, and did not believe that God objected to your having a drink now and then. (Bernice, the maid, attended another church, and played the organ there. Its congregation was small and strange—they left pamphlets on doorsteps around town, with lists of people who were going to Hell. Not local people, but well-known ones, like Pierre Trudeau.)

"The Church of the Hosannas isn't even open for services anymore," Uncle Jasper said. "What is the sense of bringing her way up here? I wouldn't think it would even be allowed."

But it turned out that the church was opened regularly. People who had known it in their youth liked to use it for funerals, and sometimes their children got married there. It was well kept up inside, owing to a sizable bequest, and the heating was up-to-date.

Aunt Dawn and I drove there in her car. Uncle Jasper was busy until the last minute.

I had never been to a funeral. My parents would not have thought that a child needed to experience such a thing, even though in their circle—as I seem to remember—it was referred to as a celebration of life.

Aunt Dawn was not dressed in black, as I'd expected. She was wearing a suit of a soft lilac colour and a Persian lamb jacket with a matching Persian lamb pillbox hat. She looked very pretty and seemed to be in good spirits that she could hardly subdue.

A thorn had been removed. A thorn had been removed from Uncle Jasper's side, and that could not help but make her happy.

Some of my ideas had changed during the time I had been living with my aunt and uncle. For instance, I was no longer so uncritical about people like Mona. Or about Mona herself, and her music and her career. I did not believe that she was—or had been—a freak, but I could understand how some people might think so. It wasn't just her big bones and her big white nose, and the violin and the somewhat silly way you had to hold it—it was the music itself and her devotion to it. Devotion to anything, if you were female, could make you ridiculous.

I don't mean that I was won over to Uncle Jasper's way of thinking entirely—just that it did not seem so alien to me as it once had. Creeping past my aunt and uncle's closed bedroom door early on a Sunday morning, on my way to help myself to one of the cinnamon scones Aunt Dawn made every Saturday night, I had heard sounds such as I had never heard from my parents or from anyone else—a sort of pleasurable growling and squealing in which there was a complicity and an abandonment that disturbed and darkly undermined me.

"I wouldn't think many Toronto people would drive way up here," Aunt Dawn said. "The Gibsons aren't going to be able to make it, even. He's got a meeting and she can't reschedule her students."

The Gibsons were the people next door. Their friendship had continued but in a lower key, one that didn't include visits to each other's houses.

A girl at school had said to me, "Wait till they make you do the Last Look. I had to look at my grandma and I fainted."

I had not heard about the Last Look, but I figured out what it must be. I decided that I would slit my eyes and just pretend.

"As long as the church doesn't have that musty smell," Aunt Dawn said. "That gets into your uncle's sinuses."

No musty smell. No dispiriting damp seeping out of the stone walls and floor. Someone must have got up early in the morning and come to turn the heat on.

The pews were almost full.

"Quite a few of your uncle's patients have made it out here," Aunt Dawn said softly. "That's nice. There isn't any other doctor in town they would do this for."

The organist was playing a piece I knew quite well. A girl who was a friend of mine, in Vancouver, had played it for an Easter concert. "Jesu, Joy of Man's Desiring."

The woman at the organ was the pianist who had played in the abortive little concert at the house. The cellist was sitting in one of the choir seats close by. Probably he would be playing later.

After we had been settled listening for a bit there was a discreet commotion at the back of the church. I did not turn to look because I had just noticed the dark polished wooden box sitting crossways just below the altar. The coffin. Some people called it the casket. It was closed. Unless they opened it up at some point, I did not have to worry about the Last Look. Even so, I pictured Mona inside it. Her big bony nose sticking up, her flesh fallen away, her eyes stuck shut. I made myself fix that image uppermost in my mind, until I felt strong enough for it not to make me sick.

Aunt Dawn, like me, did not turn to see what was happening behind us.

The source of the mild disturbance was coming up the aisle and it revealed itself to be Uncle Jasper. He did not stop at the pew where Aunt Dawn and I had kept a seat for him. He went right by, at a respectful yet businesslike pace, and he had somebody with him.

The maid, Bernice. She was dressed up. A navy blue suit and a matching hat with a little nest of flowers in it. She wasn't looking at us or at anybody. Her face was flushed and her lips tight.

Neither was Aunt Dawn looking at anybody. She had busied herself, at this moment, with leafing through the hymnbook that she had taken out of the pocket of the seat in front of her.

Uncle Jasper didn't stop at the coffin; he was leading Bernice to the organ. There was a strange surprised sort of thump in the music. Then a drone, a loss, a silence, except for people in the pews shuffling and straining to see what was going on.

Now the pianist who had presided at the organ and the cellist were gone. There must have been a side door up there for them to escape through. Uncle Jasper had seated Bernice in the woman's place.

As Bernice began to play, my uncle moved forward and

made a gesture to the congregation. Rise and sing, this gesture said, and a few people did. Then more. Then all.

They rustled around in their hymnbooks, but most of them were able to start singing even before they could find the words: "The Old Rugged Cross."

Uncle Jasper's job is done. He can come back and occupy the place we have kept for him.

Except for one problem. A thing he has not reckoned on.

This is an Anglican Church. In the United Church that Uncle Jasper is used to, the members of the choir enter through a door behind the pulpit, and settle themselves before the minister appears, so that they can look out at the congregation in a comfortable here-we-are-all-together sort of way. Then comes the minister, a signal that things can get started. But in the Anglican Church the choir members come up the aisle from the back of the church, singing and making a serious but anonymous show of themselves. They lift their eyes from their books only to gaze ahead at the altar and they appear slightly transformed, removed from their everyday identities and not quite aware of their relatives or neighbours or anybody else in the congregation.

They are coming up the aisle now, singing "The Old Rugged Cross," just like everybody else—Uncle Jasper must have talked to them before things started. Possibly he made it out to be a favourite of the deceased.

The problem is one of space and bodies. With the choir in the aisle, there is no way for Uncle Jasper to get back to our pew. He is stranded.

There is one thing to be done and done quickly, so he does it. The choir has not yet reached the very front pew, so he squeezes in there. The people standing with him are surprised but they make room for him. That is, they make what room they can. By chance, they are heavy people and he is a broad, though lean, man.

> *I will cherish the Old Rugged Cross*
> *Till my trophies at last I lay down.*
> *I will cling to the Old Rugged Cross*
> *And exchange it someday for a crown.*

That is what my uncle sings, as heartily as he can in the space he's been given. He cannot turn to face the altar but has to face outward into the profiles of the moving choir. He can't help looking a little trapped there. Everything has gone okay but, just the same, not quite as he imagined it. Even after the singing is over, he stays in that spot, sitting squeezed in as tightly as he can be with those people. Perhaps he thinks it would be anticlimactic now to get up and walk back down the aisle to join us.

Aunt Dawn has not participated in the singing, because she never found the right place in the hymnbook. It seems that she could not just trail along, the way I did.

Or perhaps she caught the shadow of disappointment on Uncle Jasper's face before he was even aware of it himself.

Or perhaps she realized that, for the first time, she didn't care. For the life of her, couldn't care.

"Let us pray," says the minister.

PRIDE

SOME people get everything wrong. How can I explain? I mean, there are those who can have everything against them—three strikes, twenty strikes, for that matter—and they turn out fine. Make mistakes early on—dirty their pants in grade two, for instance—and then live out their lives in a town like ours where nothing is forgotten (any town, that is, any town is a place like that) and they manage, they prove themselves hearty and jovial, claiming and meaning that they would not for the world want to live in any place but this.

With other people, it's different. They don't move away but you wish they had. For their own sake, you could say. Whatever hole they started digging for themselves when they were young—not by any means as obvious as the dirty pants either—they keep right on at it, digging away, even exaggerating if there is a chance that it might not be noticed.

Things have changed, of course. There are counsellors at the ready. Kindness and understanding. Life is harder for some, we're told. Not their fault, even if the blows are purely imaginary. Felt just as keenly by the recipient, or the non-recipient, as the case may be.

But good use can be made of everything, if you are willing.

Oneida didn't go to school with the rest of us, anyway. I mean that nothing could have happened there, to set her up for life. She went to a girls' school, a private school, that I can't remember the name of, if I ever knew it. Even in the summers she was not around much. I believe the family had a place on Lake Simcoe. They had lots of money—so much, in fact, that they weren't in a category with anybody else in town, even the well-to-do ones.

Oneida was an unusual name—it still is—and it did not catch on here. Indian, I found out later. Likely her mother's choice. The mother died when she, Oneida, was in her teens. Her father, I believe, called her Ida.

I had all the papers once, heaps of papers for the town history I was working on. But gaps even there. There was no satisfactory explanation of how the money disappeared. However, there was no need. Word of mouth would do the trick thoroughly enough back then. What isn't taken account of is how all the mouths get lost, given time.

Ida's father ran the bank. Even in those days bankers came and went, I suppose to keep them from ever getting too cozy with the customers. But the Jantzens had been having their way in town for too long for any regulations to matter, or that was how it seemed. Horace Jantzen had certainly the look of a man born to be in power. A heavy white beard, even though according to photographs, beards were out of style by the First World War, a good height and stomach and a ponderous expression.

In the hard times of the thirties people were still coming up with ideas. Jails were opened up to shelter the men who followed the railway tracks, but even some of them, you can be sure, were nursing a notion bound to make them a million dollars.

A million dollars in those days was a million dollars.

It wasn't any railway tramp, however, who got into the bank to talk to Horace Jantzen. Who knows if it was a single person or a cohort. Maybe a stranger or some friends of friends. Well dressed and plausible looking, you may be sure. Horace set store by appearances and he wasn't a fool, though maybe not as quick as he should have been to smell a rat.

The idea was the resurrection of the steam-driven car, such as had been around at the turn of the century. Horace Jantzen may have had one himself and had a fondness for them. This new model would be an improved version, of course, and have the advantages of being economical and not making a racket.

I'm not acquainted with the details, having been in high school at the time. But I can imagine the leak of talk and the scoffing and enthusiasm and the news getting through of some entrepreneurs from Toronto or Windsor or Kitchener getting ready to set up locally. Some hotshots, people would say. And others would ask if they had the backing.

They did indeed, because the bank had put up the loan.

It was Jantzen's decision and there was some confusion whether he had put in his own money. He may have done so, but it came out later that he had also dipped improperly into bank funds, thinking no doubt that he could pay it back with nobody the wiser. Maybe the laws were not so tight then. There were actually men hired and the old livery stable was cleared out to be their place of operations. And here my memory grows shaky, because I graduated from high school, and I had to think about earning a living if that was possible. My impediment, even with the lip stitched up, ruled out anything that involved a lot of talking, so I settled for bookkeeping, and that meant going out of town to apprentice to an outfit in Goderich. By the time I got back home the steam-car operation was spoken of with scorn by the people who had been against it and not at all by those who had promoted it. The visitors to town who had been all for it had disappeared.

The bank had lost a lot of money.

There was talk not of cheating but of mismanagement. Somebody had to be punished. Any ordinary manager would have been out on his ear, but given that it was Horace Jantzen, this was avoided. What happened to him was almost worse. He was switched to the job of bank manager in the little village of Hawksburg, about six miles up the highway. Prior to this there had been no manager there at all, because they didn't need one. There had just been a head cashier and an underling cashier, both women.

Surely he could have refused, but pride, as it was thought, chose otherwise. Pride chose that he be driven every morning those six miles to sit behind a partial wall of cheap varnished boards, no proper office at all. There he sat and did nothing until it came time for him to be driven home.

The person who drove him was his daughter. Sometime in these years of driving she made the transition from Ida to Oneida. At last she had something to do. She didn't keep house, though, because they couldn't let Mrs. Birch go. That was one way of putting it. Another might be that they'd never paid Mrs. Birch enough to keep her out of the poor-house, if letting her go had ever been considered.

If I picture Oneida and her father on these journeys to and from Hawksburg, I see him riding in the backseat, and her in front, like a chauffeur. It may have been that he was too bulky to ride up beside her. Or maybe the beard needed space. I don't see Oneida looking downtrodden or unhappy at the arrangement, nor her father looking actually unhappy. Dignity was what he had, and plenty of it. She had something different. When she went into a store or even walked on the street, there seemed to be a little space cleared around her, made ready for whatever she might want or greetings she might spread. She seemed then a bit flustered but gracious, ready to laugh a little at herself or the situation. Of course she had her good bones and bright looks, all that fair dazzle of skin and hair. So it might seem strange that I could feel sorry for her, the way she was all on the surface of things, trusting.

Imagine me, sorry.

The war was on, and it seemed things changed overnight. Tramps no longer followed the trains. Jobs opened up, and the young men were not searching for jobs or hitching rides but appearing everywhere in their dull blue or khaki uniforms. My mother said it was lucky for me that I was how

I was, and I believed she was right but told her not to say that outside the house. I was home from Goderich, finished with my apprenticing, and I got work right away doing the books at Krebs's department store. Of course it might have been said, and probably was, that I got the job because of my mother working there in dry goods, but there was also the coincidence of Kenny Krebs, the young manager, going off to join the Air Force and being killed on a training flight.

There was shock like that and yet a welcome energy everywhere, and people going around with money in their pockets. I felt cut off from men of my own age, but my being cut off in a way was nothing so new. And there were others in the same boat. Farmers' sons were exempt from service to look after the crops and the animals. I knew some who took the exemption even though there was a hired man. I knew that if anybody asked me why I was not in service it would be a joke. And I was ready with the response that I had to look after the books. Krebs's books and soon others. Had to look after the figures. It wasn't quite accepted yet that women could do that. Even by the end of the war, when they'd been doing some of it for a while. For truly reliable service it was still believed you needed a man.

I've asked myself sometimes, Why should a harelip, decently if not quite cleverly tidied up, and a voice that sounded somewhat peculiar but was capable of being understood, have been considered enough to keep me home? I must have got my notice, I must have gone to the doctor to get an exemption. I simply don't remember. Was it that I was so used to being exempted from one thing or another that I took it, like a lot of other things, completely for granted?

I may have told my mother to be quiet on certain matters, but what she said did not usually carry much weight with me. Invariably she looked on the bright side. Other things I knew but not from her. I knew that because of me she was afraid to have any more children and had lost a man who was once interested in her when she told him that. But it didn't occur to me to feel sorry for either of us. I didn't miss a father dead before I could have seen him, or any girlfriend I could have had if I'd looked different, or the brief swagger of walking off to war.

My mother and I had things we liked to eat for supper, and radio programs we liked to listen to, and always the BBC overseas news before we went to bed. My mother's eyes would glisten when the king spoke, or Winston Churchill. I took her to see the movie *Mrs. Miniver,* and she was affected by that as well. Drama filled our lives, the fictional kind and the real kind. The evacuation from Dunkirk, the brave behaviour of the royal family, the bombing of London night after night and Big Ben still ringing to announce its sombre news. Ships lost at sea and then, most dreadfully, a civilian boat, a ferry, sunk between Canada and Newfoundland, that close to our own shores.

That night I could not sleep and walked the streets of the town. I had to think of the people gone to the bottom of the sea. Old women, nearly old women like my mother, hanging on to their knitting. Some kid bothered by a toothache. Other people who had spent their last half hour before drowning complaining of seasickness. I had a very strange feeling that was part horror and part—as near as I can describe it—a kind of chilly exhilaration. The blowing away of everything, the equality—I have to say it—the equality, all of a sudden, of people like me and worse than me and people like them.

Of course this feeling vanished when I got used to seeing

things, later in the war. Naked healthy buttocks, thin old buttocks, all of them being herded into the gas chambers.

Or if it didn't quite vanish, I did learn to bat it down.

I must have run into Oneida during those years, and kept track of her life. I would have had to. Her father died right before VE-day, mixing up the funeral with the celebrations in an awkward way. The same for my mother's, which occurred the following summer, just when everybody heard about the atomic bomb. My mother did die more startlingly and publicly, at work, just after she said, "I'm going to have to sit down."

Oneida's father had hardly been seen or heard of during the last year of his life. The charade of Hawksburg was over, but Oneida seemed busier than ever. Or maybe you just got the feeling then that everybody you met was busy, what with keeping track of ration books and posting letters to the front and telling about letters they had got in return.

And in Oneida's case there was the care of that big house, which she now had to run alone.

She stopped me on the street one day and said she would like to have my advice about selling it. The house. I said that I wasn't really the person she should be talking to. She said maybe not but she knew me. Of course she didn't know me any more than she knew anybody else in town, but she persisted, and came to my house to talk further. She admired the paint job I had done, along with rearranging the furniture, and she remarked that the change must have helped to keep me from missing my mother.

True, but most people would not have come right out and said that.

I wasn't used to entertaining, so I didn't offer any refreshments, just gave her some serious and cautionary advice about selling and kept reminding her that I was no expert.

Then she went ahead and ignored everything I had said. She sold it at the first offer and did that mainly because the buyer went on about how he loved the place and looked forward to raising his family there. He was the last person in town I would have trusted, children or no children, and the price was pitiful. I had to tell her so. I said the children would make a shambles of it, and she said that was what children were for. All banging around, the very opposite of her own childhood. As a matter of fact, they never got a chance to, because the buyer proceeded to pull it down and put up an apartment building, four storeys high, with an elevator, and turned the grounds into a parking lot. The first genuine building of this sort the town had ever seen. She came to see me in a state of shock when all this began and wanted to know if she could do something—have it declared a heritage building, or sue the buyer for breaking his never-written word, or whatever. She was amazed that a person could do such a thing. A person who went regularly to church.

"I wouldn't have done it," she said, "and I'm only good enough to go at Christmas."

Then she shook her head and burst out laughing.

"Such a fool," she said. "I should have listened to you, shouldn't I?"

She was living in half of a decent rented house at this time but complained that all she could see was the house across the street.

As if that wasn't all most people get to see, I didn't say.

Then when all the apartments were finished what did she do but move back into one of them, on the top floor. I know for a fact she did not get a reduced rent, or even ask for one. She had let go of her bad feelings for the owner and was full of praise for the view and the laundry room in the basement where she paid in coin every time she did her washing.

"I'm learning to be economical," she said. "Instead of just throwing something in when I feel like it."

"After all, it's people like him who make the world go round," she said of her shyster. She invited me to come and see her view, but I made excuses.

This was the beginning of a time, however, when she and I saw a good deal of each other. She had got into the habit of dropping by to talk about her housing woes and decisions, and she kept on doing so even when she was satisfied. I had bought a television set—something she had not done, because she said she was afraid of becoming an addict.

I didn't worry about that, being out most of the day. And there were a lot of good programs in those years. Her tastes mainly coincided with mine. We were fans of public television and particularly of English comedies. Some of these we watched over and over. Situations appealed to us, rather than just the telling of jokes. I was embarrassed at the beginning by the British frankness, even smuttiness, but Oneida enjoyed that as much as anything else. We would groan when a series started all over again from the beginning, but we invariably got sucked in and watched it. We even watched the colour fading. Nowadays I sometimes come across one of those old series all brightened up fresh as new, and I switch the channel, it makes me feel so sad.

I had learned early on to be a decent cook, and since some of the best things on television came on soon after supper, I would make us a meal and she would bring dessert from the bakeshop. I invested in a couple of those folding tables and we would eat watching the news, then afterwards our programs. My mother had always insisted on our eating at the table because she thought that was the only way to be decent, but Oneida seemed to have no prohibitions in that regard.

It might be after ten when she left. She wouldn't have minded walking, but I didn't like the idea, so I would get out my car and drive her. She had never bought another car after getting rid of the one she used to drive her father in. She never minded being seen walking all over town, though people laughed about it. That was before the days of walking and exercising becoming fashionable.

We never went anywhere together. There were times when I didn't see her, because she was going out of town, or maybe not going away but entertaining people who were outsiders here. I did not get to meet them.

No. That makes it seem as if I felt snubbed. I didn't. Meeting new people was an ordeal for me, and she must have understood that. And the custom we had of eating together, spending the evenings in front of the television together—that was so easygoing and flexible that it seemed there could never be any difficulty. Many people must have known about it, but because it was me they took little notice. It was known that I did her income tax too, but why not? It was what I knew how to do, and nobody would expect her to know how.

I don't know if it was known that she never paid me. I would have asked for a nominal sum just to make things proper, but the subject did not come up. Not that she was tightfisted. She just didn't think of it.

If I had to mention her name for some reason, it sometimes slipped out as Ida. She would tease me a little if I did that to her face. She would point out how I always preferred to call people by their old school nicknames if I had the opportunity. I had not noticed this myself.

"Nobody minds," she said. "It's just you."

This made me slightly huffy, though I did my best to conceal it. What right had she to be commenting about how people would feel about something concerning what I did or didn't do? The implication was that I somehow preferred to hang on to my childhood, so that I wanted to stay there and make everybody else stay with me.

That made it too simple. All my school years had been spent, as I saw it, in getting used to what I was like—what my face was like—and what other people were like in regard to it. I suppose it was a triumph of a minor sort to have managed that, to know I could survive here and make my living and not continually be having to break new people in. But as for wanting to put us all back in grade four, no thank you.

And who was Oneida to have opinions? It didn't seem to me that she was settled yet. Actually, now that the big house was gone, a good deal of her was gone with it. The town was changing, and her place in it was changing, and she hardly knew it. Of course there had always been changes, but in the time before the war it was the change of people moving out, looking for something better somewhere else. In the fifties and sixties and seventies it was changed by new kinds of people moving in. You would think Oneida would have acknowledged that when she went to live in the apartment building. But she hadn't altogether caught on. There was still that strange hesitation and lightness about her, as if she were waiting for life to begin.

She went away on trips of course, and maybe she thought it would begin there. No such luck.

During those years when the new shopping mall was built on the south edge of town, and Krebs's folded (no problem for me, I had enough to do without them), there seemed to be more and more people from town taking winter holidays, and that meant going to Mexico or the West Indies or someplace we never used to have anything to do with. The result, in my opinion, was to bring back diseases we never used to have anything to do with either. For a while, this happened. There would be Disease of the Year, with a special name on it. Maybe these are still going around, but nobody notices them so much anymore. Or it could be that people my age have got beyond noticing. You can be sure you're not going to be carried off by anything dramatic, or it would have happened by now.

One evening I got up at the end of a television show to make us a cup of tea before Oneida was to go home. I walked towards the kitchen and suddenly I felt terrible. I stumbled and went down on my knees, then onto the floor. Oneida grabbed me and got me up into a chair and the blackout passed. I told her I sometimes had spells and not to worry. This was a lie, and I don't know why I told it, but she didn't believe me anyway. She got me into the downstairs room where I slept, and she took off my shoes. Then somehow together, and with a bit of protest on my part, we got me out of my clothes and into pyjamas. I could only realize things by fits and starts. I told her to get a taxi and go home, but she didn't pay any attention.

She slept that night on the living-room couch, and upon

exploring the house the next day she settled into my mother's bedroom. She must have gone back to her apartment in the daytime for such things as she needed, and maybe also to the mall for such groceries as she thought would round out my supplies. She also talked to the doctor and got a prescription from the drugstore that I swallowed whenever she held it to my lips.

I was in and out of consciousness and sick and feverish for the better part of a week. Occasionally I told her that I was feeling recovered, and that I could manage by myself, but this was nonsense. Mostly I just obeyed her and came to depend on her in the matter-of-fact way that you would on a nurse in a hospital. She was not as skilled at dealing with a fevered body as a nurse might be, and sometimes if I had the energy I would complain like a six-year-old. She would apologize then and not take offence. In between telling her I was better, and she should think about getting back to her own place, I was selfish enough to be calling her name for no reason but to reassure myself that she was there.

Then I was well enough to worry about her catching whatever it was that I had.

"You should have a mask on."

"Don't worry," she said. "If I was going to get it I think I'd have got it by now."

When I first really felt better I was too lazy to acknowledge the fact that I had spells of feeling like a small child again.

But of course she was not my mother, and I had to wake up one morning and realize that. I had to think about all the things she had done for me, and that embarrassed me considerably. As it would any man, but me especially because of remembering how I looked. I had more or less forgotten that, and now it seemed to me that she had not been embarrassed, that she had been able to do things so matter-of-factly because I was a neuter to her, or an unfortunate child.

I was polite now, and worked in, between my expressions of gratitude, my by now very genuine wish that she would go home.

She got that message, she wasn't offended. She must have been tired out from all the broken sleep and unaccustomed care. She did a last bit of shopping for what I'd need and took my temperature for the final time and went off, as I thought, in the satisfied mood of somebody who has finished a job well done. Just before doing that she had waited in the front room to see if I could get my clothes on without assistance and had been satisfied that I could. She was barely out of the house when I got some accounts out and set into doing the work I had been doing on the day I fell sick.

My mind was slower, but accurate, and that was a great relief to me.

She left me alone until the day—or evening, rather—when we were accustomed to watch television. Then she arrived with a can of soup. Not enough to make a meal in itself, and not something she had made, but nevertheless a contribution to a meal. And she was early, to make time for that. She opened it, too, without questioning me. She knew her way around my kitchen. She heated it and got out the soup bowls and we ate together. Her behaviour seemed to remind me that I had been a sick man needing immediate nourishment. And that was true, in a way. That day at noon I had been unable, for shakiness, to use the can opener myself.

There were two shows we watched, back-to-back. But on that evening we never got to see the second one. She could not wait until the second one had its turn before starting a conversation that was very unsettling to me.

The gist of it was that she was prepared to move in.

For one thing, she said, she was not happy living in her apartment. That had been a big mistake. She liked houses. But that did not mean that she regretted leaving the house that she was born in. She would have gone batty living in that house by herself. The mistake was simply in thinking that an apartment could be the answer. She had never been happy in that place and never could be. What made her realize this was the time she had spent in my house. When I was sick. She should have realized it long ago. Long ago, when she was a little girl and looked at certain houses, she would wish that she was living there.

Another thing she said was that we were not entirely capable of looking after ourselves. What if I had got sick and been all alone? What if such a thing should happen again? Or should happen to her?

We had a certain feeling for each other, she said. We had a feeling which was not just the usual thing. We could live together like brother and sister and look after each other like brother and sister and it would be the most natural thing in the world. Everybody would accept it as so. How could they not?

All the time she was speaking I felt terrible. Angry, scared, appalled. The worst was towards the end, when she was talking about how nobody would think a thing about it. At the same time, I could see what she meant, and maybe agree with her that people would get used to it. A dirty joke or two we might not even get to hear.

She might be right. It might make sense.

At this I felt as if I had been thrown down into a cellar and a flat door slammed on my head.

I wouldn't for anything let her know about that.

I said it was an interesting idea, but one thing made it impossible.

What was that?

I had neglected to tell her. With all the sickness and fuss and everything. But I had put this house on the market. This house was sold.

Oh. Oh. Why had I not told her this?

I had no inkling, I said then, truthfully. I had no inkling that she had such a plan in her head.

"So it just didn't come to me soon enough," she said. "Like a lot of things in my life. Something must be the matter with me. I don't get around to thinking about things. I always think there's plenty of time."

I had rescued myself, but not without a cost. I had to put the house—this house—up for sale and sell it as quickly as I could. Almost the same as she had done with hers.

And I sold it almost that quickly, though I was not forced to accept such a ridiculous offer as she had. And then I had to face the job of dealing with all that had been accumulating since my parents moved in on their honeymoon, not having the money for any kind of a trip.

The neighbours were amazed. They weren't longtime neighbours, they hadn't known my mother, but they said they had got so used to my coming and going, my regularity.

They wanted to know what my plans were now, and I realized that I didn't have any. Beyond doing the work I'd always done, and I had already been cutting down on that, looking forward to a careful old age.

———

I began scouting around town for a place to live, and it turned out that of all the places that came near to suiting me, only one was vacant. And that one was an apartment in the building on the site of Oneida's old house. Not on the top floor, with the view, where she was, but on the bottom. I had never been much for views, anyway, and I took it. Not knowing what else I could do.

Of course I meant to tell her. But the word got out before I could bring myself round to it. She had her own plans, anyway. It was summer by this time, our programs were off the air. It was a time when we did not regularly see each other. And I didn't think, when it came right down to it, that I should have to apologize or ask her permission. When I went up to look at the place and sign the lease she hadn't been anywhere in sight.

One thing I came to understand on that visit, or when I thought about it afterwards. A man I didn't quite recognize spoke to me, and after a minute I realized he was somebody I'd known for years and greeted on the street for half my life. If I'd seen him there I might have known him, in spite of certain ravages of age. But here I hadn't, and we laughed about that, and he wanted to know if I was moving into the boneyard.

I said I hadn't realized they called it that, but yes, I guessed I was.

Then he wanted to know whether I played euchre, and I said I did, up to a point.

"That'll be good," he said.

And I thought then, *Just living long enough wipes out the*

problems. Puts you in a select club. No matter what your disabilities may have been, just living till now wipes them out, to a good measure. Everybody's face will have suffered, never just yours.

That made me think of Oneida, and how she looked while she was talking to me about moving in. She was not slender anymore but gaunt, tired, no doubt, from the nights of getting up with me, but her age was telling, beyond that. Her beauty had been delicate all along. A blond woman's easily flushing kind of looks, with that strange mixture of apology and high-class confidence about it was what she'd had, and lost. When she set out to make her proposal to me, she looked strained and her expression was somewhat peculiar.

Of course if I had ever had the right to choose, I would naturally, according to my height, have picked a smaller girl. Like the university girl, dainty and dark-haired, who was related to the Krebses and worked there for a summer.

One day that girl had said to me in a friendly way that I could get a better job done on my face, nowadays. I'd be amazed, she said. And it wouldn't cost, with OHIP.

She was right. But how could I explain that it was just beyond me to walk into some doctor's office and admit that I was wishing for something I hadn't got?

Oneida was looking better than formerly when she showed up in the midst of my packing and discarding. She'd had her hair done, and the colour changed somewhat, maybe browner.

"You mustn't throw everything out in one fell swoop," she said. "All you'd collected for that town history."

I said I was being selective, though that was not entirely true. It seemed to me that both of us were pretending to care about what happened, more than we really did. When I thought about the town history now, it seemed as if one town must after all be much like another.

We did not mention my going into the apartment building. As if that had all been discussed and taken for granted long ago.

She said that she was going off on one of her trips, and this time she named the place. Savary Island, as if that was enough.

I asked politely where that was and she said, "Oh, it's off the coast."

As if that answered the question.

"Where an old friend of mine lives," she said.

Of course that might be true.

"She's on e-mail. She says that's what I should do. I'm not keen on it somehow. But I might as well try it."

"I suppose you never know till you try."

I felt as if I should say something more. Ask about the weather there, or something, out where she was going. But before I could think of what to say she gave a most unusual little shriek or cry, and then put her hand to her mouth and moved with large cautious steps to my window.

"Careful, careful," she said. "Look. Look."

She was laughing almost soundlessly, a laugh that might even indicate that she was in pain. She moved one hand behind her back to hush me as I got to my feet.

In the backyard of my house there was a birdbath. I had put it in years ago so that my mother could watch the birds. She was very fond of birds and could recognize them by their song as well as their appearance. I had neglected it for a good while and had just filled it up that morning.

Now what?

It was full of birds. Black-and-white, dashing up a storm.

Not birds. Something larger than robins, smaller than crows.

She said, "Skunks. Little skunks. More white in them than black."

But how beautiful. Flashing and dancing and never getting in each other's way, so you could not tell how many there were, where each body started or stopped.

While we watched, they lifted themselves up one by one and left the water and proceeded to walk across the yard, swiftly but in a straight diagonal line. As if they were proud of themselves but discreet. Five of them.

"My Lord," said Oneida. "In town."

Her face looked dazzled.

"Have you ever seen such a sight?"

I said no. Never.

I thought she might say another thing, and spoil it, but no, neither of us did.

We were as glad as we could be.

CORRIE

"I T isn't a good thing to have the money concentrated all in the one family, the way you do in a place like this," Mr. Carlton said. "I mean, for a girl like my daughter Corrie here. For example, I mean, like her. It isn't good. Nobody on the same level."

Corrie was right across the table, looking their guest in the eye. She seemed to think this was funny.

"Who's she going to marry?" her father continued. "She's twenty-five."

Corrie raised her eyebrows, made a face.

"You missed a year," she said. "Twenty-six."

"Go ahead," her father said. "Laugh all you like."

She laughed out loud, and, indeed, what else could she do? the guest thought. His name was Howard Ritchie, and he was only a few years older than she was, but already equipped with a wife and a young family, as her father had immediately found out.

Her expressions changed very quickly. She had bright-white teeth and short, curly, nearly black hair. High cheekbones that caught the light. Not a soft woman. Not much meat on the bone, which was the sort of thing her father might find to say next. Howard Ritchie thought of her as the type of girl who spent a lot of time playing golf and tennis. In spite of her quick tongue, he expected her to have a conventional mind.

He was an architect, just getting started on a career. Mr. Carlton insisted on referring to him as a church architect, because he was at present restoring the tower of the town's Anglican Church. A tower that had been on the verge of toppling until Mr. Carlton came to its rescue. Mr. Carlton was not an Anglican—he had pointed that out several times. His church was the Methodist, and he was Methodist to the core, which was why he kept no liquor in the house. But a fine church like the Anglican ought not be let go to rack and ruin. No hope looking to the Anglicans to do anything—they were a poor class of Irish Protestants who would have taken the tower down and put up something that was a blemish on the town. They didn't have the shekels, of course, and they wouldn't understand the need for an architect, rather than a carpenter. A church architect.

The dining room was hideous, at least in Howard's opinion. This was the mid-fifties, but everything looked as if it had been in place before the turn of the century. The food was barely all right. The man at the head of the table never stopped talking. You'd think the girl would be exhausted by it, but she seemed mostly to be on the verge of laughing. Before she was done with her dessert, she lit a cigarette. She offered Howard one, saying, quite audibly, "Don't mind Daddy." He accepted, but didn't think the better of her.

Spoiled rich miss. Unmannerly.

Out of the blue, she asked him what he thought of the Saskatchewan premier, Tommy Douglas.

He said that his wife supported him. Actually, his wife didn't think Douglas was far left enough, but he wasn't going to get into that.

"Daddy loves him. Daddy's a Communist."

This brought a snort from Mr. Carlton that didn't squelch her.

"Well, you laugh at his jokes," she told her father.

Shortly after that, she took Howard out to look at the grounds. The house was directly across the street from the factory which made men's boots and work shoes. Behind the house, however, were wide lawns and the river that curled halfway around the town. There was a worn path down to its bank. She led the way, and he was able to see what he hadn't been sure of before. She was lame in one leg.

"Isn't it a steep climb back up?" he asked.

"I'm not an invalid."

"I see you've got a rowboat," he said, meaning that as a partway apology.

"I'd take you out in it but not right now. Now we've got to watch the sunset." She pointed out an old kitchen chair that she said was for watching the sunset, and demanded that he sit there. She herself sat on the grass. He was about to ask if she would be able to get up all right, but thought better of it.

"I had polio," she said. "That's all it is. My mother had it too, and she died."

"That's too bad."

"I suppose so. I can't remember her. I'm going to Egypt next week. I was very keen on going, but now I don't seem to care so much. Do you think it'd be fun?"

"I have to earn a living."

He was amazed at what he'd said, and of course it set her off giggling.

"I was speaking in general terms," she said grandly, when the giggling finished.

"Me too."

Some creepy fortune hunter was bound to snap her up, some Egyptian or whatever. She seemed both bold and childish. At first, a man might be intrigued by her, but then her forwardness, her self-satisfaction, if that was what it was, would become tiresome. Of course, there was money, and to some men that never became tiresome.

"You mustn't ever mention my leg in front of Daddy or he will go apoplectic," she said. "Once he fired not just a kid who teased me but his entire family. I mean, even cousins."

From Egypt there arrived peculiar postcards, sent to his firm, not his house. Well, of course, how could she have known his home address?

Not a single pyramid on them. No Sphinx.

Instead, one showed the Rock of Gibraltar with a note that called it a pyramid in collapse. Another showed some flat dark-brown fields, God knows where, and said, "Sea of Melancholia." There was another message in fine print:

"Magnifying glass obtainable send money." Fortunately, nobody in the office got hold of these.

He did not intend to reply, but he did: "Magnifying glass faulty please refund money."

He drove to her town for an unnecessary inspection of the church steeple, knowing that she had to be back from the Pyramids but not knowing whether she would be at home or off on some other jaunt.

She was home, and would be for some time. Her father had suffered a stroke.

There was not really much for her to do. A nurse came in every other day. And a girl named Lillian Wolfe was in charge of the fires, which were always lit when Howard arrived. Of course, she did other chores as well. Corrie herself couldn't quite manage to get a good fire going or put a meal together; she couldn't type, couldn't drive a car, not even with a built-up shoe to help her. Howard took over when he came. He looked after the fires and saw to various things around the house and was even taken to visit Corrie's father, if the old man was able.

He hadn't been sure how he would react to the foot, in bed. But in some way it seemed more appealing, more unique, than the rest of her.

She had told him that she was not a virgin. But that turned out to be a complicated half-truth, owing to the interference of a piano teacher, when she was fifteen. She had gone along with what the piano teacher wanted because she felt sorry for people who wanted things so badly.

"Don't take that as an insult," she said, explaining that she had not continued to feel sorry for people in that way.

"I should hope not," he said.

Then he had things to tell her about himself. The fact that he had produced a condom did not mean that he was a regular seducer. In fact, she was only the second person he had gone to bed with, the first being his wife. He had been brought up in a fiercely religious household and still believed in God, to some extent. He kept that a secret from his wife, who would have made a joke of it, being very left-wing.

Corrie said she was glad that what they were doing—what they had just done—appeared not to bother him, in spite of his belief. She said that she herself had never had any time for God, because her father was enough to cope with.

It wasn't difficult for them. Howard's job often required him to travel for a daytime inspection or to see a client. The drive from Kitchener didn't take long. And Corrie was alone in the house now. Her father had died, and the girl who used to work for her had gone off to find a city job. Corrie had approved of this, even giving her money for typing lessons, so that she could better herself.

"You're too smart to mess around doing housework," she had said. "Let me know how you get along."

Whether Lillian Wolfe spent the money on typing lessons or on something else was not known, but she did continue to do housework. This was discovered on an occasion when Howard and his wife were invited to dinner, with others, at the home of some newly important people in Kitchener. There was Lillian waiting on table, coming face-to-face with the man she had seen in Corrie's house. The man she had seen with his arm around Corrie when she came in to take the plates away or fix the fire. Conversation made plain that this dinner-table wife had been his wife then as she was now.

Howard said that he had not told Corrie about the dinner party right away, because he hoped it would become unimportant.

The host and hostess of the evening were nothing like close friends of his, or of his wife. Certainly not of his wife, who made fun of them on political grounds afterwards. It had been a social business event. And the household wasn't likely the sort in which the maids gossiped with the mistress.

Indeed, it wasn't. Lillian said that she had not gossiped about it at all. She said this in a letter. It was not her mistress whom she had a notion of speaking to, if she had to. It was his own wife. Would his wife be interested in getting this information? was the way she put it. The letter was sent to his office address, which she had been clever enough to find out. But she was also acquainted with his home address. She had been spying. She mentioned that and also referred to his wife's coat with the silver-fox collar. This coat bothered his wife, and she often felt obliged to tell people that she had inherited, not bought, it. That was the truth. Still, she liked to wear it on certain occasions, like that dinner party, to hold her own, it seemed, even with people whom she had no use for.

"I would hate to have to break the heart of such a nice lady with a big silver-fox collar on her coat," Lillian had written.

"How would Lillian know a silver-fox collar from a hole in the ground?" Corrie said, when he felt that he had to relay the news to her. "Are you sure that's what she said?"

"I'm sure."

He had burned the letter at once, had felt contaminated by it.

"She's learned things, then," Corrie said. "I always thought she was sly. I guess killing her is not an option?"

He didn't even smile, so she said very soberly, "I'm just kidding."

It was April, but still cold enough that you would like to have a fire lit. She had planned to ask him to do it, all through supper, but his strange, sombre attitude had prevented her.

He told her that his wife hadn't wanted to go to that dinner. "It's all just pure rotten luck."

"You should have taken her advice," she said.

"It's the worst," he said. "It's the worst that could happen."

They were both staring into the black grate. He had touched her only once, to say hello.

"Well, no," Corrie said. "Not the worst. No."

"No?"

"No," she said. "We could give her the money. It's not a lot, really."

"I don't have—"

"Not you. I could."

"Oh, no."

"Yes."

She made herself speak lightly, but she had gone deathly cold. For what if he said no? No, I can't let you. No, it's a sign. It's a sign that we have to stop. She was sure that there'd been something like that in his voice, and in his face. All that old sin stuff. Evil.

"It's nothing to me," she said. "And, even if you could get hold of it easily, you couldn't do it. You'd feel you were taking it away from your family—how could you?"

Family. She should never have said that. Never have said that word.

But his face actually cleared. He said, No, no, but there was doubt in his voice. And then she knew that it would be all right. After a while, he was able to speak practically and he remembered another thing from the letter. It had to be in bills, he said. She had no use for cheques.

He spoke without looking up, as if about a business deal. Bills were best for Corrie too. They would not implicate her.

"Fine," she said. "It's not an outrageous sum, anyway."

"But she is not to know that we see it that way," he warned.

A postal box was to be taken, in Lillian's name. The bills in an envelope addressed to her, left there twice a year. The dates to be set by her. Never a day late. Or, as she had said, she might start to worry.

He still did not touch Corrie, except for a grateful, almost formal good-bye. This subject must be altogether separate from what is between us, was what he seemed to be saying. We'll start fresh. We will be able again to feel that we're not hurting anybody. Not doing any wrong. That was how he would put it in his unspoken language. In her own language she made one half-joke that did not go over.

"Already we've contributed to Lillian's education—she wasn't this smart before."

"We don't want her getting any smarter. Asking for more."

"We'll cross that bridge when we come to it. Anyway, we could threaten to go to the police. Even now."

"But that would be the end of you and me," he said. He had already said good-bye and turned his head away. They were on the windy porch.

He said, "I could not stand for there to be an end of you and me."

"I'm glad to hear that," Corrie said.

The time came quickly when they did not even speak of it. She handed over the bills already in their envelope. At first he made a small grunt of disgust, but later that turned into a sigh of acquiescence, as if he had been reminded of a chore.

"How the time goes around."

"Doesn't it just?"

"Lillian's ill-gotten gains," Corrie might say, and though he didn't care for the expression at first, he got used to saying it himself. In the beginning, she would ask if he'd ever seen Lillian again, if there had been any further dinner parties.

"They weren't that kind of friends," he reminded her. He hardly ever saw them, didn't know if Lillian was still working for them or not.

Corrie hadn't seen her, either. Her people lived out in the country, and if Lillian came to see them they weren't likely to shop in this town, which had rapidly gone downhill. There was nothing now on the main street but a convenience store, where people went to buy Lotto tickets and whatever groceries they had run out of, and a furniture store, where the same tables and sofas sat forever in the windows, and the doors seemed never to be open—and maybe wouldn't be, until the owner died in Florida.

After Corrie's father died, the shoe factory had been taken over by a large firm that had promised—so she believed—to keep it running. Within a year, however, the building was empty, such equipment as was wanted moved to another town, nothing left, except a few outmoded tools that had once had to do with making boots and shoes. Corrie got it into her head to establish a quaint little museum to display these things. She herself would set it up and give tours describing how things used to be done. It was surprising how knowledgeable she became, helped by some photographs that her father had had taken to illustrate a talk that perhaps he himself had given—it was badly typed—to the Women's Institute when they were studying local industries. Already by the end of the summer Corrie had shown a few visitors around. She was sure that things would pick up the next year, after she had put a sign up on the highway and written a piece for a tourist brochure.

In the early spring, she looked out of her window one morning and saw some strangers starting to tear the building down. It turned out that the contract she'd thought she had to use the building so long as a certain amount of the rent was paid did not allow her to display or appropriate any objects found within the building, no matter how long they had been considered worthless. There was no question of these ancient bits of hardware belonging to her, and, in fact, she was fortunate not to be hauled up in court now that the company—which had once seemed so obliging—had found out what she was up to.

If Howard had not taken his family to Europe the previous summer, when she embarked on this project, he could have looked at the agreement for her and she would have been saved a lot of trouble.

Never mind, she said when she had calmed down, and soon she found a new interest.

It began with her deciding that she was sick of her big and empty house—she wanted to get out, and she set her sights on the public library down the street.

It was a handsome, manageable redbrick building and,

being a Carnegie Library, was not easy to get rid of, even though few people used it anymore—not nearly enough to justify a librarian's wages.

Corrie went down there twice a week and unlocked the doors and sat behind the librarian's desk. She dusted the shelves if she felt like it, and phoned up the people who were shown by the records to have had books out for years. Sometimes the people she reached claimed that they had never heard of the book—it had been checked out by some aunt or grandmother who used to read and was now dead. She spoke then of library property, and sometimes the book actually showed up in the returns bin.

The only thing not agreeable about sitting in the library was the noise. It was made by Jimmy Cousins, who cut the grass around the library building, starting again practically as soon as he'd finished because he had nothing else to do. So she hired him to do the lawns at her house—something she'd been doing herself for the exercise, but her figure didn't really need it and it took forever with her lameness.

Howard was somewhat dismayed by the change in her life. He came more seldom now, but was able to stay longer. He was living in Toronto, though working for the same firm. His children were teenagers or else in university. The girls were doing very well, the boys not quite so well as he might have wished, but that was the way of boys. His wife was working full-time and sometimes more than full-time in the office of a provincial politician. Her pay was next to nothing, but she was happy. Happier than he'd ever known her.

The past spring he had taken her to Spain, as a birthday surprise. Corrie hadn't heard from him for some time then. It would have been lacking in taste for him to write to her from the birthday-present holiday. He would never do a thing like that, and she would not have liked him to do it, either.

"You'd think my place were a shrine, the way you carry on," Corrie said after he got back, and he said, "Exactly right." He loved everything about the big rooms now, with their ornate ceilings and dark, gloomy panelling. There was a grand absurdity to them. But he was able to see that it was different for her, that she needed to get out once in a while. They began to take little trips, then somewhat longer trips, staying overnight in motels—though never more than one night—and eating at moderately fancy restaurants.

They never ran into anyone they knew. Once upon a time they would have done so—they were sure of it. Now things were different, though they didn't know why. Was it because they weren't in such danger, even if it did happen? The fact being that the people they might have met, and never did, would not have suspected them of being the sinful pair they still were. He could have introduced her as a cousin without making any impression—a lame relation he had thought to drop in on. He did have relatives whom his wife never wanted to bother with. And who would have gone after a middle-aged mistress with a dragging foot? Nobody would have stored that information up to spill at a dangerous moment.

We met Howard up at Bruce Beach with his sister, was it? He was looking good. His cousin, maybe. A limp?

It wouldn't have seemed worth the trouble.

They still made love, of course. Sometimes with caution, avoiding a sore shoulder, a touchy knee. They had always been conventional in that way, and remained so, congratulating themselves on not needing any fancy stimulation. That was for married people.

Sometimes Corrie would fill up with tears, hiding her face against him.

"It's just that we're so lucky," she said.

She never asked him whether he was happy, but he indicated in a roundabout way that he was. He said that he had developed more conservative, or maybe just less hopeful, ideas in his work. (She kept to herself the thought that he had always been rather conservative.) He was taking piano lessons, to the surprise of his wife and family. It was good to have that kind of interest of your own, in a marriage.

"I'm sure," Corrie said.

"I didn't mean—"

"I know."

One day—it was in September—Jimmy Cousins came into the library to tell her that he wouldn't be able to cut her grass that day. He had to go to the cemetery and dig a grave. It was for someone who used to live around here, he said.

Corrie, with her finger in *The Great Gatsby,* asked for the person's name. She said that it was interesting how many people showed up here—or their bodies did—with this last request and bother for their relatives. They might have lived their entire lives in cities nearby or distant, and seemed quite satisfied in those places, but had no wish to stay there when they were dead. Old people got such ideas.

Jimmy said that it wasn't such an old person. The name was Wolfe. The first name slipped his mind.

"Not Lillian? Not Lillian Wolfe?"

He believed it was.

And her name proved to be right there, in the library edition of the local paper, which Corrie never read. Lillian had died in Kitchener, at the age of forty-six. She was to be buried from the Church of the Lord's Anointed, the ceremony at two o'clock.

Well.

This was one of the two days a week that the library was supposed to be open. Corrie couldn't go.

The Church of the Lord's Anointed was a new one in town. Nothing flourished here anymore but what her father had called "freak religions." She could see the building from one of the library windows.

She was at the window before two o'clock, watching a respectably sized group of people go in.

Hats didn't seem to be required nowadays, on women or men.

How would she tell him? A letter to the office, it would have to be. She could phone there, but then his response would have to be so guarded, so matter-of-fact, that half the wonder of their release would be lost.

She went back to *Gatsby,* but she was just reading words, she was too restless. She locked the library and walked around town.

People were always saying that this town was like a funeral, but in fact when there was a real funeral it put on its best show of liveliness. She was reminded of that when she saw, from a block away, the funeral-goers coming out of the church doors, stopping to chat and ease themselves out of solemnity. And then, to her surprise, many of them went around the church to a side door, where they reentered.

Of course. She had forgotten. After the ceremony, after the closed coffin had been put in its place in the hearse, everybody except those close enough to follow the dead and see her put into the ground would head for the after-the-service refreshments. These would be waiting in another part of the church, where there was a Sunday School room and a hospitable kitchen.

She didn't see any reason that she shouldn't join them.

But at the last moment she would have walked past.

Too late. A woman called to her in a challenging—or, at least, confidently unfuneral—voice from the door where the other people had gone in.

This woman said to her, close up, "We missed you at the service."

Corrie had no notion who the woman was. She said that she was sorry not to have attended but she'd had to keep the library open.

"Well, of course," the woman said, but had already turned to consult with somebody carrying a pie.

"Is there room in the fridge for this?"

"I don't know, honey, you'll just have to look and see."

Corrie had thought from the greeting person's flowered dress that the women inside would all be wearing something similar. Sunday best if not mourning best. But maybe her ideas of Sunday best were out of date. Some of the women here were just wearing pants, as she herself was.

Another woman brought her a slice of spice cake on a plastic plate.

"You must be hungry," she said. "Everybody else is."

A woman who used to be Corrie's hairdresser said, "I told everybody you would probably drop in. I told them you couldn't till you'd closed up the library. I said it was too bad you had to miss the service. I said so."

"It was a lovely service," another woman said. "You'll want tea once you're done with that cake."

And so on. She couldn't think of anybody's name. The United Church and the Presbyterian Church were just hanging on; the Anglican Church had closed ages ago. Was this where everybody had gone?

There was only one other woman at the reception who was getting as much attention as Corrie, and who was dressed as Corrie would have expected a funeral-going woman to be. A lovely lilac-grey dress and a subdued grey summer hat.

The woman was being brought over to meet her. A string of modest genuine pearls around her neck.

"Oh, yes." She spoke in a soft voice, as pleased as the occasion would allow. "You must be Corrie. The Corrie I've heard so much about. Though we never met, I felt I knew you. But you must be wondering who I am." She said a name that meant nothing to Corrie. Then shook her head and gave a small, regretful laugh.

"Lillian worked for us ever since she came to Kitchener," she said. "The children adored her. Then the grandchildren. They truly adored her. My goodness. On her day off I was just the most unsatisfactory substitute for Lillian. We all adored her, actually."

She said this in a way that was bemused, yet delighted. The way women like that could be, showing such charming self-disparagement. She would have spotted Corrie as the only person in the room who could speak her language and not take her words at face value.

Corrie said, "I didn't know she was sick."

"She went that fast," the woman with the teapot said, offering more to the lady with the pearls and being refused.

"It takes them her age faster than it does the real old ones," the tea lady said. "How long was she in the hospital?" she asked in a slightly menacing way of the pearls.

"I'm trying to think. Ten days?"

"Shorter time than that, what I heard. And shorter still when they got around to letting her people know at home."

"She kept it all very much to herself." This from the employer, who spoke quietly but held her ground. "She was absolutely not a person to make a fuss."

"No, she wasn't," Corrie said.

At that moment, a stout, smiling young woman came up and introduced herself as the minister.

"We're speaking of Lillian?" she asked. She shook her head in wonder. "Lillian was blessed. Lillian was a rare person."

All agreed. Corrie included.

"I suspect Milady the Minister," Corrie wrote to Howard, in the long letter she was composing in her head on the way home.

Later in the evening she sat down and started that letter, though she would not be able to send it yet—Howard was spending a couple of weeks at the Muskoka cottage with his family. Everybody slightly disgruntled, as he had described it in advance—his wife without her politics, he without his piano—but unwilling to forgo the ritual.

"Of course, it's absurd to think that Lillian's ill-gotten gains would build a church," she wrote. "But I'd bet she built the steeple. It's a silly-looking steeple, anyway. I never thought before what a giveaway those upside-down ice-cream-cone steeples are. The loss of faith is right there, isn't it? They don't know it, but they're declaring it."

She crumpled the letter up and started again, in a more jubilant manner.

"The days of the Blackmail are over. The sound of the cuckoo is heard in the land."

She had never realized how much it weighed on her, she wrote, but now she could see it. Not the money—as he well knew, she didn't care about the money, and, anyway, it had become a smaller amount in real terms as the years passed, though Lillian had never seemed to realize that. It was the queasy feeling, the never-quite-safeness of it, the burden on their long love, that had made her unhappy. She had that feeling every time she passed a postbox.

She wondered if by any chance he would hear the news before her letter could get it to him. Not possible. He hadn't reached the stage of checking obituaries yet.

It was in February and again in August of every year that she put the special bills in the envelope and he slipped the envelope into his pocket. Later, he would probably check the bills and type Lillian's name on the envelope before delivering it to her box.

The question was, had he looked in the box to see if this summer's money had been picked up? Lillian had been alive when Corrie made the transfer but surely not able to get to the mailbox. Surely not able.

It was shortly before Howard left for the cottage that Corrie had last seen him and that the transfer of the envelope had taken place. She tried to figure out exactly when it was, whether he would have had time to check the box again after delivering the money or whether he would have gone straight to the cottage. Sometimes while at the cottage in the past he'd found time to write Corrie a letter. But not this time.

She goes to bed with the letter to him still unfinished.

And wakes up early, when the sky is brightening, though the sun is not yet up.

There's always one morning when you realize that the birds have all gone.

She knows something. She has found it in her sleep.

There is no news to give him. No news, because there never was any.

No news about Lillian, because Lillian doesn't matter and she never did. No post office box, because the money goes straight into an account or maybe just into a wallet. General expenses. Or a modest nest egg. A trip to Spain. Who cares? People with families, summer cottages, children to educate, bills to pay—they don't have to think about how to spend such an amount of money. It can't even be called a windfall. No need to explain it.

She gets up and quickly dresses and walks through every room in the house, introducing the walls and the furniture to this new idea. A cavity everywhere, most notably in her chest. She makes coffee and doesn't drink it. She ends up in her bedroom once more, and finds that the introduction to the current reality has to be done all over again.

The briefest note, the letter tossed.

"Lillian is dead, buried yesterday."

She sends it to his office, it does not matter. Special delivery, who cares?

She turns off the phone, so as not to suffer waiting. The silence. She may simply never hear again.

But soon a letter, hardly more to it than there was to hers.

"All well now, be glad. Soon."

So that's the way they're going to leave it. Too late to do another thing. When there could have been worse, much worse.

TRAIN

THIS is a slow train anyway, and it has slowed some more for the curve. Jackson is the only passenger left, the next stop, Clover, being about twenty miles ahead. And after that Ripley, and Kincardine and the lake. He is in luck and it's not to be wasted. Already he has taken his ticket stub out of its overhead notch.

He heaves his bag, and sees it land just nicely, in between the rails. No choice now—the train's not going to get any slower.

He takes his chance. A young man in good shape, agile as he'll ever be. But the leap, the landing, disappoints him. He's stiffer than he'd thought, the stillness pitches him forward, his palms come down hard on the gravel between the ties, he's scraped the skin. Nerves.

The train is out of sight, he hears it putting on a bit of speed, clear of the curve. He spits on his hurting hands, getting the gravel out. Then picks up his bag and starts walking back in the direction he has just covered on the train. If he followed the train he would show up at Clover station well after dark. He'd still be able to complain that he'd fallen asleep and wakened all mixed up, thinking he'd slept through his stop when he hadn't. Jumped off all confused, then had to walk.

He would have been believed. Coming home from so far away, home from the war, he could have got mixed up in his head. It's not too late, he would be where he was supposed to be before midnight.

But all the time he's thinking this, he's walking in the opposite direction.

He doesn't know many names of trees. Maples, that everybody knows. Pines. Not much else. He'd thought that where he jumped was in some woods, but it wasn't. The trees are just along the track, thick on the embankment, but he can see the flash of fields behind them. Fields green or rusty or yellow. Pasture, crops, stubble. He knows just that much. It's still August.

And once the noise of the train has been swallowed up he realizes there isn't the perfect quiet around that he would have expected. Plenty of disturbance here and there, a shaking of the dry August leaves that wasn't wind, the racket of some unseen birds chastising him.

Jumping off the train was supposed to be a cancellation. You roused your body, readied your knees, to enter a different block of air. You looked forward to emptiness. And instead, what did you get? An immediate flock of new surroundings, asking for your attention in a way they never did when you were sitting on the train and just looking out the window. What are you doing here? Where are you going? A sense of being watched by things you didn't know about. Of being a disturbance. Life around coming to some conclusions about you from vantage points you couldn't see.

People he'd met in the last few years seemed to think that if you weren't from a city, you were from the country. And that was not true. There were distinctions you could miss unless you lived there, between country and town. Jackson himself was the son of a plumber. He had never been in a stable in his life or herded cows or stooked grain. Or found himself as now stumping along a railway track that seemed to have reverted from its normal purpose of carrying people and freight to become a province of wild apple trees and thorny berry bushes and trailing grape-vines and crows—he knew that bird at least—scolding from perches you could not see. And right now a garter snake slithering between the rails, perfectly confident he won't be quick enough to tramp on and murder it. He does know enough to figure that it's harmless, but the confidence riles him.

The little Jersey, whose name was Margaret Rose, could usually be counted on to show up at the stable door for milking twice a day, morning and evening. Belle didn't often have to call her. But this morning she was too inter-ested in something down by the dip of the pasture field, or in the trees that hid the railway tracks on the other side of the fence. She heard Belle's whistle and then her call, and started out reluctantly. But then decided to go back for another look.

Belle set the pail and stool down and started tramping through the morning-wet grass.

"So-boss. So-boss."

She was half coaxing, half scolding.

Something moved in the trees. A man's voice called out that it was all right.

Well of course it was all right. Did he think she was afraid of him? Better for him to be afraid of the cow with the horns still on.

Climbing over the rail fence, he waved in what he might have considered a reassuring way.

That was too much for Margaret Rose, she had to put on a display. Jump one way, then the other. Toss of the wicked little horns. Nothing much, but Jerseys can always surprise you in an unpleasant way, with their speed and spurts of temper. Belle called out, to scold her and to reassure him.

"She won't hurt you. Just don't move. It's her nerves."

Now she noticed the bag he had hold of. That was what had caused the trouble. She had thought he was just out walking the tracks, but he was going somewhere.

"She's upset with your bag. If you could just lay it down for a moment. I have to get her back towards the barn to milk her."

He did as she asked, and then stood watching, not wanting to move an inch.

She got Margaret Rose headed back to where the pail was, and the stool, on this side of the barn.

"You can pick it up now," she called. And spoke companionably as he got nearer. "As long as you don't wave it around at her. You're a soldier, aren't you? If you wait till I get her milked I can get you some breakfast. That's a stupid name when you have to holler at her. Margaret Rose."

She was a short sturdy woman with straight hair, grey mixed in with what was fair, and childish bangs.

"I'm the one responsible for it," she said, as she got herself settled. "I'm a royalist. Or I used to be. I have porridge made, on the back of the stove. It won't take me long to milk. If you wouldn't mind going round the barn and waiting where she can't see you. It's too bad I can't offer you an egg. We used to keep hens but the foxes kept getting them and we just got fed up."

We. We used to keep hens. That meant she had a man around somewhere.

"Porridge is good. I'll be glad to pay you."

"No need. Just get out of the way for a bit. She's got herself too interested to let her milk down."

He took himself off, around the barn. It was in bad shape. He peered between the boards to see what kind of a car she had, but all he could make out in there was an old buggy and some other wrecks of machinery.

The place showed some sort of tidiness, but not exactly industry. On the house, white paint all peeling and going grey. A window with boards nailed across it, where there must have been broken glass. The dilapidated henhouse where she had mentioned the foxes getting the hens. Shingles in a pile.

If there was a man on the place he must have been an invalid, or else paralyzed with laziness.

There was a road running by. A small fenced field in front of the house, a dirt road. And in the field a dappled peaceable-looking horse. A cow he could see reasons for keeping, but a horse? Even before the war people on farms were getting rid of them, tractors were the coming thing. And she hadn't looked like the sort to trot round on horse-back just for the fun of it.

Then it struck him. The buggy in the barn. It was no relic, it was all she had.

For a while now he'd been hearing a peculiar sound. The road rose up a hill, and from over that hill came a clip-clop, clip-clop. Along with the clip-clop some little tinkle or whistling.

Now then. Over the hill came a box on wheels, being pulled by two quite small horses. Smaller than the one in the field but no end livelier. And in the box sat a half dozen or so little men. All dressed in black, with proper black hats on their heads.

The sound was coming from them. It was singing. Discreet high-pitched little voices, as sweet as could be. They never looked at him as they went by.

That chilled him. The buggy in the barn and the horse in the field were nothing in comparison.

He was still standing there looking one way and another when he heard her call, "All finished." She was standing by the house.

"This is where to go in and out," she said of the back door. "The front is stuck since last winter, it just refuses to open, you'd think it was still frozen."

They walked on planks laid over an uneven dirt floor, in a darkness provided by the boarded-up window. It was as chilly there as it had been in the hollow where he'd slept. He had wakened again and again, trying to scrunch himself into a position where he could stay warm. The woman didn't shiver here—she gave off a smell of healthy exertion and what was likely the cow's hide.

She poured the fresh milk into a basin and covered it with a piece of cheesecloth she kept by, then led him into the main part of the house. The windows there had no curtains, so the light was coming in. Also the woodstove had been in use. There was a sink with a hand pump, a table with oilcloth on it worn in some places to shreds, and a couch covered with a patchy old quilt.

Also a pillow that had shed some feathers.

So far, not so bad, though old and shabby. There was a use for everything that you could see. But raise your eyes and up there on shelves was pile on pile of newspapers or magazines or just some kind of papers, up to the ceiling.

He had to ask her, Was she not afraid of fire? A woodstove for instance.

"Oh, I'm always here. I mean, I sleep here. There isn't any-place else I can keep the drafts out. I'm watchful. I haven't had a chimney fire even. A couple of times it got too hot and I just threw some baking powder on it. Nothing to it.

"My mother had to be here anyway," she said. "There was no place else for her to be comfortable. I had her cot in here. I kept an eye on everything. I did think of moving all the papers into the front room but it's really too damp in there, they would all be ruined."

Then she said she should have explained. "My mother's dead. She died in May. Just when the weather got decent. She lived to hear about the end of the war on the radio. She understood perfectly. She lost her speech a long time ago but she could understand. I got so used to her not speaking that sometimes I think she's here but of course she's not."

Jackson felt it was up to him to say he was sorry.

"Oh well. It was coming. Just lucky it wasn't in the winter."

She served him oatmeal porridge and poured tea.

"Not too strong? The tea?"

Mouth full, he shook his head.

"I never economize on tea. If it comes to that, why not drink hot water? We did run out when the weather got so bad last winter. The hydro gave out and the radio gave out and the tea gave out. I had a rope round the back door to hang on to when I went out to milk. I was going to let Margaret Rose into the back kitchen but I figured she'd get too upset with the storm and I couldn't hold her. Anyway, she survived. We all survived."

Finding a space in the conversation, he asked, were there any dwarfs in the neighbourhood?

"Not that I've noticed."

"In a cart?"

"Oh. Were they singing? It must have been the little Mennonite boys. They drive their cart to church and they sing all the way. The girls have to go in the buggy with the parents but they let the boys ride in the cart."

"They looked like they never saw me."

"They wouldn't. I used to say to Mother that we lived on the right road because we were just like the Mennonites. The horse and buggy and we drink our milk unpasteurized. The only thing is, neither one of us can sing.

"When Mother died they brought so much food I was eating it for weeks. They must have thought there'd be a wake or something. I'm lucky to have them. But then I say to myself they are lucky too. Because they are supposed to practise charity and here I am practically on their doorstep and an occasion for charity if you ever saw one."

He offered to pay her when he'd finished but she batted her hand at his money.

But there was one thing, she said. If before he went he could manage to fix the horse trough.

What this involved was actually making a new horse trough, and in order to do that he had to hunt around for any materials and tools he could find. It took him all day, and she served him pancakes and Mennonite maple syrup for supper. She said that if he'd only come a week later she might have fed him fresh jam. She picked the wild berries growing along the railway track.

They sat on kitchen chairs outside the back door until after the sun went down. She was telling him something about how she came to be here, and he was listening but not paying full attention because he was looking around and thinking how this place was on its last legs but not absolutely hopeless, if somebody wanted to settle down and fix things up. A certain investment of money was needed, but a greater investment of time and energy. It could be a challenge. He could almost bring himself to regret that he was moving on.

Another reason that he didn't pay full attention to what Belle—her name was Belle—kept telling him was that she was talking about her life which he couldn't very well imagine.

Her father—she called him her daddy—had bought this place just for the summers, she said, and then he decided that they might as well live here all the year round. He could work anywhere, because he made his living with a column for the *Toronto Evening Telegram*. The mailman took what was written and it was sent off on the train. He wrote about all sorts of things that happened. He even put Belle in, referring to her as Pussycat. And mentioning Belle's mother occasionally but calling her Princess Casamassima, out of a book whose name, she said, meant nothing anymore. Her mother might have been the reason they stayed year-round. She had caught the terrible flu of 1918 in which so many people died, and when she came out of it she was strange. Not really mute, because she could make words, but had lost many of them. Or they had lost her. She had to learn all over again to feed herself and go to the bathroom. Besides the words she had to learn to keep her clothes on in the hot weather. So you wouldn't want her just wandering around and being a laughingstock on some city street.

Belle was away at a school in the winters. The name of the school was Bishop Strachan and she was surprised that he had never heard of it. She spelled it out. It was in Toronto and it was full of rich girls but also had girls like herself who got special money from relations or wills to go there. It taught her to be rather snooty, she said. And it didn't give her any idea of what she would do for a living.

But that was all settled for her by the accident. Walking along the railway track, as he often liked to do on a summer evening, her father was hit by a train. She and her mother had both gone to bed before it happened and Belle thought it must be a farm animal loose on the tracks, but her mother was moaning dreadfully and seemed to know first thing.

Sometimes a girl she had been friends with at school would write to ask her what on earth she could find to do up there, but little did they know. There was milking and cooking and taking care of her mother and she had the hens at that time as well. She learned how to cut up potatoes so each part has an eye, and plant them and dig them up the next summer. She had not learned to drive and when the war came she sold her daddy's car. The Mennonites let her have a horse that was not good for farm work anymore, and one of them taught her how to harness and drive it.

One of the old friends, called Robin, came up to visit her and thought the way she was living was a hoot. She wanted her to go back to Toronto, but what about her mother? Her mother was a lot quieter now and kept her clothes on, also enjoyed listening to the radio, the opera on Saturday afternoons. Of course she could do that in Toronto, but Belle didn't like to uproot her. Robin said it was herself she was talking about, scared of uproot. She—Robin—went away and joined whatever they called the women's army.

The first thing he had to do was to make some rooms other than the kitchen fit to sleep in, come the cold weather. He had some mice to get rid of and even some rats, now coming in from the cooling weather. He asked her why she'd never invested in a cat and heard a piece of her peculiar logic. She said it would always be killing things and dragging them for her to look at, which she didn't want to do. He kept a sharp ear open for the snap of the traps, and got rid of them before she knew what had happened. Then he lectured about the papers filling up the kitchen, the firetrap problem, and she agreed to move them if the front room could be got free of damp. That became his main job. He invested in a heater and repaired the walls, and convinced her to spend the better part of a month climbing up and getting the papers, rereading and reorganizing them and fitting them onto the shelves he had made.

She told him then that the papers contained her father's book. Sometimes she called it a novel. He did not think to ask anything about it, but one day she told him it was about two people named Matilda and Stephen. A historical novel.

"You remember your history?"

He had finished five years of high school with respectable marks and a very good showing in trigonometry and geography but did not remember much history. In his final year, anyway, all you could think about was that you were going to the war.

He said, "Not altogether."

"You'd remember altogether if you went to Bishop Strachan. You'd have had it rammed down your throat. English history, anyway."

She said that Stephen had been a hero. A man of honour, far too good for his times. He was that rare person who wasn't all out for himself or looking to break his word the moment it was convenient to do so. Consequently and finally he was not a success.

And then Matilda. She was a straight descendant of William the Conqueror and as cruel and haughty as you might expect. Though there might be people stupid enough to defend her because she was a woman.

"If he could have finished it would have been a very fine novel."

Jackson of course knew that books existed because people sat down and wrote them. They didn't just appear out of the blue. But why, was the question. There were books already in existence, plenty of them. Two of which he had to read at school. *A Tale of Two Cities* and *Huckleberry Finn*, each of them with language that wore you down though in different ways. And that was understandable. They were written in the past.

What puzzled him, though he didn't intend to let on, was why anybody would want to sit down and do another one, in the present. Now.

A tragedy, said Belle briskly, and Jackson didn't know if it was her father she was talking about or the people in the book that had not got finished.

Anyway, now that this room was livable his mind was on the roof. No use to fix up a room and have the state of the roof render it unlivable again in a year or two. He had managed to patch it so that it would do her a couple of more winters, but he could not guarantee more than that. And he still planned to be on his way by Christmas.

The Mennonite families on the next farm ran to older girls, and the younger boys he had seen were not strong enough yet to take on heavier chores. Jackson had been able to hire himself out to them, during the fall harvest. He had been brought in to eat with the others and to his surprise found that the girls behaved giddily as they served him, they were not at all mute as he had expected. The mothers kept an eye on them, he noticed, and the fathers kept an eye on him. He was pleased to know that he could satisfy both sets of parents. They could see that nothing was stirring with him. All safe.

And of course with Belle not a thing had to be spoken of.

She was—he had found this out—sixteen years older than he was. To mention it, even to joke about it, would spoil everything. She was a certain kind of woman, he a certain kind of man.

The town where they shopped, when they needed to, was called Oriole. It was in the opposite direction from the town where he had grown up. He tied up the horse in the United Church shed there, since there were of course no hitching posts left on the main street. At first he was leery of the hardware store and the barbershop. But soon he understood something about small towns which he should have realized just from growing up in one. They did not have much to do with each other, unless it was for games run off in the ballpark or the hockey arena, where all was a fervent made-up sort of hostility. When they needed to shop for something their own stores could not supply they went to a city. The same when they wanted to consult a doctor other than the ones their own town could offer. He didn't run into anybody familiar, and nobody showed a curiosity about him, though they might look twice at the horse. In the winter months, not even that, because the back roads were not plowed and people taking their milk to the creamery or eggs to the grocery had to make do with horses, just as he and Belle did.

Belle always stopped to see what movie was on though she had no intention of going to see any of them. Her knowledge of movies and movie stars was intensive but came from some years back, something like Matilda and Stephen. For instance she could tell you who Clark Gable was married to in real life before he became Rhett Butler.

Soon Jackson was going to get his hair cut when he needed to and buying his tobacco when he had run out. He smoked now like a farmer, rolling his own and never lighting up indoors.

Secondhand cars didn't become available for a while, but when they did, with the new models finally on the scene, and farmers who'd made money in the war ready to turn in the old ones, he had a talk with Belle. The horse Freckles was God knows how old and stubborn on any sort of hill.

He found that the car dealer had been taking notice of him, though not counting on a visit.

"I always thought you and your sister was Mennonites but ones that wore a different kind of outfit," the dealer said.

That shook Jackson up a little but at least it was better than husband and wife. It made him realize how he must have aged and changed over the years, and how the person who had jumped off the train, that skinny nerve-racked soldier, would not be so recognizable in the man he was now. Whereas Belle, so far as he could see, was stopped at some point in life where she remained a grown-up child. And her talk reinforced this impression, jumping back and forth, into the past and out again, so that it seemed she made no difference between their last trip to town and the last movie she had seen with her mother and father, or the comical occasion when Margaret Rose—now dead—had tipped her horns at a worried Jackson.

It was the second car that they had owned, a used one of course, that took them to Toronto in the summer of 1962. This was a trip they had not anticipated and it came at an awkward time for Jackson. For one thing, he was building a new horse barn for the Mennonites, who were busy with the crops, and for another, he had his own harvest of vegetables coming on that he had sold to the grocery store in Oriole. But Belle had a lump that she had finally been persuaded to pay attention to, and she was booked now for an operation in Toronto.

What a change, Belle kept saying. Are you so sure we are still in Canada?

This was before they got past Kitchener. Once they got on the new highway she was truly alarmed, imploring him to find a side road or else turn around and go home. He found himself speaking sharply at that—the traffic was surprising him too. She stayed quiet all the way after that, and he had no way of knowing whether she had her eyes closed because she had given up or because she was praying. He had never known her to pray.

Even this morning she had tried to get him to change his mind about going. She said the lump was getting smaller, not larger. Since the health insurance for everybody had come in, she said, nobody did anything but run to the doctor, and make their lives into one long drama of hospitals and operations, which did nothing but prolong the period of being a nuisance at the end of life.

She calmed down and cheered up once they got to their turnoff and were actually in the city. They found themselves on Avenue Road, and in spite of exclamations about how everything had changed, she seemed to be able on every block to recognize something she knew. There was the apartment building where one of the teachers from Bishop Strachan had lived. In its basement there was a shop where you could buy milk and cigarettes and the newspaper. Wouldn't it be strange, she said, if you could go in there and still find the *Telegram*, where there would be not only her father's name but his smudgy picture, taken when he still had all his hair?

Then a little cry, and down a side street she had seen the very church—she could swear it was the very church—in which her parents had been married. They had taken her there to show her, though it wasn't a church they had gone to. They did not go to any church, far from it. It was sort of a joke. Her father said they had been married in the basement but her mother said the vestry.

Her mother could talk readily then, she was like anybody else.

Perhaps there was a law at the time, to make you get married in a church or it wasn't legal.

At Eglinton she saw the subway sign.

"Just think, I have never been on a subway train."

She said this with some sort of mixed pain and pride.

"Imagine remaining so ignorant."

At the hospital they were ready for her. She continued to be lively, telling them about her horrors in the traffic and about the changes, wondering if there was still such a show put on at Christmas by Eaton's store. And did anybody still read the *Telegram*?

"You should have driven in through Chinatown," one of the nurses said. "Now that's something."

"I'll look forward to seeing it on my way home." She laughed, and said, "If I get to go home."

"Now don't be silly."

Another nurse was talking to Jackson about where he'd parked the car, and telling him where to move it so he wouldn't get a ticket. Also making sure that he knew about the accommodations for out-of-town relations, much cheaper than you'd have to pay at a hotel.

Belle would be put to bed now, they said. A doctor would come to have a look at her, and Jackson could come back later to say good night. He might find her a little dopey by that time.

She overheard, and said that she was dopey all the time so he wouldn't be surprised, and there was a little merriment all round.

The nurse took him to sign something before he left. He hesitated where it asked what relation. Then he wrote "Friend."

When he came back in the evening he did see a change, though he would not have described Belle then as dopey. They had put her into some kind of green cloth sack that left her neck and most of her arms quite bare. He had seldom seen her so bare, or noticed the raw-looking cords that stretched between her collarbone and chin.

She was angry that her mouth was dry.

"They won't let me have anything but the meanest little sip of water."

She wanted him to go and get her a Coke, something that she never had drunk in her life as far as he knew.

"There's a machine down the hall—there must be. I see people going by with a bottle in their hands and it makes me so thirsty."

He said he couldn't go against orders.

Tears came into her eyes and she turned pettishly away.

"I want to go home."

"Soon you will."

"You could help me find my clothes."

"No I couldn't."

"If you won't I'll do it myself. I'll get to the train station myself."

"There isn't any passenger train that goes up our way anymore."

Abruptly then, she seemed to give up on her plans for escape. In a few moments she started to recall the house and all the improvements that they—or mostly he—had made on it. The white paint shining on the outside, and even the back kitchen whitewashed and furnished with a plank floor. The roof reshingled and the windows restored to their plain old style, and most of all glories, the plumbing that was such a joy in the wintertime.

"If you hadn't shown up I'd have soon been living in absolute squalor."

He didn't voice his opinion that she already had been.

"When I come out of this I am going to make a will," she said. "All yours. You won't have wasted your labours."

He had of course thought about this, and you would have expected that the prospects of ownership would have brought a sober satisfaction to him, though he would have expressed a truthful and companionable hope that nothing would happen too soon. But not now. It seemed to have little to do with him, to be quite far away.

She returned to her fret.

"Oh, I wish I was there and not here."

"You'll feel a lot better when you wake up after the operation."

Though from everything that he had heard that was a whopping lie.

Suddenly he felt so tired.

He had spoken closer to the truth than he could have guessed. Two days after the lump's removal Belle was sitting up in a different room, eager to greet him and not at all disturbed by the moans coming from a woman behind the curtain in the next bed. That was more or less what she—Belle—had sounded like yesterday, when he never got her to open her eyes or notice him at all.

"Don't pay any attention to her," said Belle. "She's completely out of it. Probably doesn't feel a thing. She'll come round tomorrow bright as a dollar. Or else she won't."

A somewhat satisfied, institutional authority was showing, a veteran's callousness. She was sitting up in bed and swallowing some kind of bright orange drink through a conveniently bent straw. She looked a lot younger than the woman he had brought to the hospital such a short time before.

She wanted to know if he was getting enough sleep, if he'd found someplace where he liked to eat, if the weather had been not too warm for walking, if he had found time to visit the Royal Ontario Museum, as she thought she had advised.

But she could not concentrate on his replies. She seemed to be in a state of amazement. Controlled amazement.

"Oh, I do have to tell you," she said, breaking right into his explanation of why he had not got to the museum. "Oh, don't look so alarmed. You'll make me laugh with that face on, it'll hurt my stitches. Why on earth should I be thinking of laughing anyway? It's a dreadfully sad thing really, it's a tragedy. You know about my father, what I've told you about my father—"

The thing he noticed was that she said father instead of Daddy.

"My father and my mother—"

She seemed to have to search around and get started again.

"The house was in better shape than when you first got to see it. Well, it would be. We used that room at the top of the stairs for our bathroom. Of course we had to carry the water up and down. Only later, when you came, I was using the downstairs. With the shelves in it, you know, that had been a pantry?"

How could she not remember that he was the one who had taken out the shelves and put in the bathroom?

"Oh well, what does it matter?" she said, as if she followed his thoughts. "So I had heated the water and I carried it upstairs to have my sponge bath. And I took off my clothes. Well, I would. There was a big mirror over the sink, you see it had a sink like a real bathroom, only you had to pull out the plug and let the water back into the pail when you were finished. The toilet was elsewhere. You get the picture. So I proceeded to wash myself and I was bare naked, naturally. It must have been around nine o'clock at night so there was plenty of light. It was summer, did I say? That little room facing the west?

"Then I heard steps and of course it was Daddy. My father. He must have been finished putting Mother to bed. I heard the steps coming up the stairs and I did notice they sounded heavy. Somewhat not like usual. Very deliberate. Or maybe that was just my impression afterwards. You are apt to dramatize things afterwards. The steps stopped right outside the bathroom door and if I thought anything I thought, Oh, he must be tired. I didn't have any bolt across the door because of course there wasn't one. You just assumed somebody was in there if the door was closed.

"So he was standing outside the door and I didn't think anything of it and then he opened the door and he just stood and looked at me. And I have to say what I mean. Looking at all of me, not just my face. My face looking into the mirror and him looking at me in the mirror and also what was behind me and I couldn't see. It wasn't in any sense a normal look.

"I'll tell you what I thought. I thought, He's walking in his sleep. I didn't know what to do, because you are not supposed to startle anybody that is sleepwalking.

"But then he said, 'Excuse me,' and I knew he was not asleep. But he spoke in a funny kind of voice, I mean it was a strange voice, very much as if he was disgusted with me. Or mad at me, I didn't know. Then he left the door open and just went away down the hall. I dried myself and got into my nightgown and went to bed and went to sleep right away. When I got up in the morning there was the water I hadn't drained, and I didn't want to go near it, but I did.

"But everything seemed normal and he was up already typing away. He just yelled good morning and then he asked me how to spell some word. The way he often did, because I was a better speller. So I gave it to him and then I said he should learn how to spell if he was going to be a writer, he was hopeless. But sometime later in the day when I was washing some dishes he came up right behind me and I froze. He just said, 'Belle, I'm sorry.' And I thought, Oh, I wish he had not said that. It scared me. I knew it was true he was sorry but he was putting it out in the open in a way I could not ignore. I just said, 'That's okay,' but I couldn't make myself say it in an easy voice or as if it really was okay.

"I couldn't. I had to let him know he had changed us. I went to throw out the dishwater and then I went back to whatever else I was doing and not another word. Later I got Mother up from her nap and I had supper ready and I called him but he didn't come. I said to Mother that he must have gone for a walk. He often did when he got stuck in his writing. I helped Mother cut up her food, but I couldn't help thinking about disgusting things. Primarily about noises I heard sometimes coming from their room, and I muffled myself so I wouldn't hear. Now I wondered about Mother sitting there eating her supper, and I wondered what she thought of it or understood of it at all.

"I didn't know where he could have gone. I got Mother ready for bed though that was his job. Then I heard the train coming and all at once the commotion and the screeching which was the train brakes and I must have known what had happened though I don't know exactly when I knew.

"I told you before. I told you he got run over by the train.

"But I'm telling you this. And I am not telling you just to be harrowing. At first I couldn't stand it and for the longest time I was actually making myself think that he was walking along the tracks with his mind on his work and never heard the train. That was the story all right. I was not going to think it was about me or even what it primarily was about.

"Sex.

"Now I see. Now I have got a real understanding of it and it was nobody's fault. It was the fault of human sex in a tragic situation. Me growing up there and Mother the way she was and Daddy, naturally, the way he would be. Not my fault nor his fault.

"There should be acknowledgement, that's all I mean, places where people can go if they are in a situation. And not be all ashamed and guilty about it. If you think I mean brothels, you are right. If you think prostitutes, right again. Do you understand?"

Jackson, looking over her head, said yes.

"I feel so released. It's not that I don't feel the tragedy, but I have got outside the tragedy, is what I mean. It is just the mistakes of humanity. You mustn't think because I'm smiling that I don't have compassion. I have serious compassion. But I have to say I am relieved. I have to say I somehow feel happy. You are not embarrassed by listening to all this?"

"No."

"You realize I am in an abnormal state. I know I am. Everything so clear. I am so grateful for it."

The woman on the next bed had not let up on her rhythmical groaning, all through this. Jackson felt as if that refrain had entered into his head.

He heard the nurse's squishy shoes in the hall and hoped that they would enter this room. They did.

The nurse said that she had come to give a sleepy-time pill. He was afraid that he would be required to kiss Belle good night. He had noticed that a lot of kissing went on in the hospital. He was glad that when he stood up there was no mention of it.

"See you tomorrow."

He woke up early, and decided to take a walk before breakfast. He had slept all right but told himself he ought to take
a break from the hospital air. It wasn't that he was worried
so much by the change in Belle. He thought that it was possible or even probable that she would get back to normal,
either today or in a couple of more days. She might not even
remember the story she had told him. Which would be a
blessing.

The sun was well up, as you could expect at this time of
year, and the buses and streetcars were already pretty full.
He walked south for a bit, then turned west onto Dundas
Street, and after a while found himself in the Chinatown
he had heard about. Loads of recognizable and many not so
recognizable vegetables were being trundled into shops, and
small skinned apparently edible animals were already hanging up for sale. The streets were full of illegally parked trucks
and noisy, desperate-sounding snatches of the Chinese language. Chinese. All the high-pitched clamour sounded like
they had a war going on, but probably to them it was just
everyday. Nevertheless he felt like getting out of the way, and
he went into a restaurant run by Chinese but advertising an
ordinary breakfast of eggs and bacon. When he came out of
there he intended to turn around and retrace his steps.

But instead he found himself heading south again. He had
got onto a residential street lined with tall and fairly narrow brick houses. They must have been built before people
in the area felt any need for driveways or possibly before
they even had cars. Before there were such things as cars.
He walked until he saw a sign for Queen Street, which he
had heard of. He turned west again and after a few blocks he

came to an obstacle. In front of a doughnut shop he ran into a small crowd of people.

They were stopped by an ambulance, backed right up on the sidewalk so you could not get by. Some of them were complaining about the delay and asking loudly if it was even legal to park an ambulance on the sidewalk and others were looking peaceful enough while they chatted about what the trouble might be. Death was mentioned, some of the onlookers speaking of various candidates and others saying that was the only legal excuse for the vehicle being where it was.

The man who was finally carried out, bound to the stretcher, was surely not dead or they'd have had his face covered. He was unconscious however and his skin the grey of cement. He was not being carried out through the dough-nut shop, as some had jokingly predicted—that was some sort of dig at the quality of the doughnuts—but through the main door of the building. It was a decent enough brick apartment building five storeys high, a Laundromat as well as the doughnut shop on its main floor. The name carved over its main door suggested pride as well as some foolish-ness in its past.

Bonnie Dundee.

A man not in ambulance uniform came out last. He stood there looking with exasperation at the crowd that was now thinking of breaking up. The only thing to wait for now was the grand wail of the ambulance as it found its way onto the street and tore away.

Jackson was one of those who didn't bother to walk away. He wouldn't have said he was curious about any of this, more that he was just waiting for the inevitable turn he had been expecting, to take him back to where he'd come from. The man who had come out of the building walked over and asked if he was in a hurry.

No. Not specially.

This man was the owner of the building. The man taken away in the ambulance was the caretaker and superintendent.

"I've got to get to the hospital and see what's the trouble with him. Right as rain yesterday. Never complained. Nobody close that I can call on, so far as I know. The worst, I can't find the keys. Not on him and not where he usually keeps them. So I got to go home and get my spares and I just wondered, could you keep a watch on things meanwhile? I got to go home and I got to go to the hospital too. I could ask some of the tenants but I'd just rather not, if you know what I mean. I don't want them bugging me what's the matter when I don't know any better than they do."

He asked again if Jackson was sure he would not mind, and Jackson said no, fine.

"Just keep an eye for anybody going in, out, ask to see their keys. Tell them it's an emergency, won't be long."

He was leaving, then turned around.

"You might as well sit down."

There was a chair Jackson had not noticed. Folded and pushed out of the way so the ambulance could park. It was just one of those canvas chairs but comfortable enough and sturdy. Jackson set it down with thanks in a spot where it would not interfere with passersby or apartment dwellers. No notice was taken of him. He had been about to mention the hospital and the fact that he himself had to get back there before too long. But the man had been in a hurry, and he already had enough on his mind, and he had made the point that he would be as quick as he could.

Jackson realized, once he got sitting down, just how long he'd been on his feet walking here or there.

The man had told him to get a coffee or something to eat from the doughnut shop if he felt the need.

"Just tell them my name."

But that name Jackson did not even know.

When the owner came back he apologized for being late. The fact was that the man who had been taken away in the ambulance had died. Arrangements had to be made. A new set of keys had become necessary. Here they were. There'd be some sort of funeral involving those in the building who had been around a long time. Notice in the paper might bring in a few more. A troublesome spell, till this was sorted out.

It would solve the problem. If Jackson could. Temporarily. It only had to be temporarily.

Jackson heard himself say, Yes, all right with him.

If he wanted to take a little time, that could be managed. He heard this man—his new boss—say so. Right after the funeral and some disposal of goods. A few days he could have then, to get his affairs together and do the proper moving-in.

That would not be necessary, Jackson said. His affairs were together and his possessions were on his back.

Naturally this roused a little suspicion. Jackson was not surprised a couple of days later to hear that his new employer had made a visit to the police. But all was well, apparently. He had emerged as just one of those loners who may have got themselves in too deep some way or another but have not been guilty of breaking any law.

It looked as if there was nobody looking for him anyway.

As a rule, Jackson liked to have older people in the building. And as a rule, single people. Not what you would call zombies. People with interests. You might sometimes say talent. The sort of talent that had been noticed once, made some kind of a living once, though not enough to hang on to all through a life. An announcer whose voice had been familiar on the radio years ago during the war but whose vocal cords were shot to pieces now. Most people probably believed he was dead. But here he was in his bachelor suite, keeping up with the news and subscribing to the *Globe and Mail* which he passed on to Jackson in case there was anything of interest to him in it.

Once, there was.

Marjorie Isabella Treece, daughter of Willard Treece, longtime columnist for the *Toronto Evening Telegram,* and his wife, Helena (née Abbott) Treece, lifelong friend of Robin (née Shillingham) Ford, has passed away after a courageous battle with cancer. Oriole paper please copy. July 18, 1965.

No mention of where she had been living. Probably in Toronto, with Robin so much in the picture. She had lasted maybe longer than you might have expected and might even have been in reasonable comfort and spirits, till of course near the end. She had shown a certain gift for adapting to circumstances. More, perhaps, than he possessed himself.

Not that he spent his time picturing the rooms he'd shared with her or the work he'd done on her place. He didn't have to—such things were often recalled in dreams, and his feeling then was more of exasperation than of longing, as if he had to get to work right away on something that had not been finished.

In the Bonnie Dundee, the tenants were generally uneasy about anything that might be called improvements, thinking that these might cause a raise in their rent. He talked them around, with respectful manners and good fiscal sense. The place improved and became one with a waiting list. The owner complained that it was getting to be a haven for loonies. But Jackson said they were generally tidier than average and old enough not to misbehave. There was a woman who had once played in the Toronto Symphony and an inventor who had missed out so far with his inventions but was hopeful, and a Hungarian refugee actor whose accent was against him but who still had a commercial running somewhere in the world. They were all well behaved and somehow scared up the money to go to the Epicure Restaurant and tell their stories through the afternoon. Also they had a few friends who were truly famous and might show up in a blue moon for a visit. And not to be sneezed at was the fact that the Bonnie Dundee had an in-house preacher on shaky terms with his church, whatever it was, but always able to officiate when called upon.

People did get in the habit of staying until his final offices were necessary, but it was better than skipping and running.

An exception was the young couple named Candace and Quincy, who never settled their rent and skipped out in the middle of the night. The owner happened to have been in charge when they came looking for a room, and he excused himself for his bad choice by saying that a fresh face was needed around the place. Candace's face, not the boyfriend's. The boyfriend was a jerk.

On a hot summer day Jackson had the double back doors, the delivery doors, open, to let in what air he could while he worked at varnishing a table. It was a pretty table he'd got for nothing because its polish was all worn away. He thought it would look nice in the entryway, to put the mail on.

He was able to be out of the office because the owner was in there checking some rents.

There was a light touch on the front doorbell. Jackson was ready to haul himself up, cleaning his brush, because he thought the owner in the midst of figures might not care to be disturbed. But it was all right, he heard the door being opened, a woman's voice. A voice on the edge of exhaustion, yet able to maintain something of its charm, its absolute assurance that whatever it said would win over anybody who came within listening range.

She would probably have got that from her father the preacher. Jackson was thinking this before the whole impact hit him.

This was the last address she had, she said, for her daughter. She was looking for her daughter. Candace, her daughter. Who might have been travelling with a friend. She, the mother, had come here from British Columbia. From Kelowna, where she and the girl's father lived.

Ileane. Jackson knew her voice without a doubt. That woman was Ileane.

He heard her ask if it was possible for her to sit down. Then the owner pulling out his—Jackson's—chair.

Toronto so much hotter than she had expected, though she knew Ontario, had grown up there.

She wondered if she could possibly ask for a glass of water.

She must have put her head down in her hands as her voice grew muffled. The owner came out into the hall and dropped some change into the machine to get a 7UP. He might have thought that more ladylike than a Coke.

Around the corner he saw Jackson listening, and he made a gesture that he—Jackson—should take over, being perhaps more used to distraught tenants. But Jackson shook his head violently.

No.

She did not stay distraught long.

She begged the owner's pardon and he said the heat could play those tricks today.

Now about Candace. They had left within the month, it could be three weeks ago. No forwarding address.

"In such cases there usually isn't."

She got the hint.

"Oh of course I can settle—"

There was some muttering and rustling while this was done.

Then, "I don't suppose you could let me see where they were living—"

"The tenant isn't in now. But even if he was I don't think he'd agree to it."

"Of course. That's silly."

"Was there anything you were particularly interested in?"

"Oh no. No. You've been kind. I've taken your time."

She had got up now, and they were moving. Out of the office, down the couple of steps to the front door. Then the door was opened and street noises swallowed up her further farewells if there were any.

However she had been disappointed, she would get herself through it with a good grace.

Jackson came out of hiding as the owner returned to the office.

"Surprise," was all the owner said. "We got our money."

He was a man who was basically incurious, at least about personal matters. A thing which Jackson valued in him.

Of course Jackson would like to have seen her. Now that she was gone he almost regretted his chance. He would never stoop so low as to ask the owner was her hair still dark, black almost, her body tall and slim and with very little bosom to it. He hadn't got much of an impression of the daughter. Her hair was blond but very likely dyed. No more than twenty years old though it was sometimes hard to tell nowadays. Very much under the thumb of the boyfriend. Run away from home, run away from your bills, break your parents' hearts, all for a sulky piece of business like the boyfriend.

Where was Kelowna? In the west somewhere. Alberta, British Columbia. A long way to come looking. Of course that mother was a persistent woman. An optimist. Probably that was true of her still. She had married. Unless the girl was born out of wedlock and that struck him as very unlikely. She'd be sure, sure of herself the next time, she wouldn't be one for tragedy. The girl wouldn't be, either. She'd come home when she'd had enough. She might bring along a baby but that was all the style nowadays.

Shortly before Christmas in the year 1940 there had been an uproar in the high school. It had even reached the third floor where the clamour of typewriters and adding machines usually kept all the downstairs noises at bay. The oldest girls in the school were up there—girls who last year had been learning Latin and biology and European history and were now learning to type.

One of these was Ileane Bishop, who oddly enough was a minister's daughter, although there were no bishops in her father's United Church. Ileane had arrived with her family when she was in grade nine and for five years, due to the custom of alphabetical seating, she had sat behind Jackson Adams. By that time Jackson's phenomenal shyness and silence had been accepted by everybody else in the class, but it was new to her, and during the next five years, by not acknowledging it she had produced a thaw. She borrowed erasers and pen nibs and geometry tools from him, not so much to break the ice as because she was naturally scatterbrained. They exchanged answers to problems and marked each other's tests. When they met on the street they said hello, and to her his hello was actually more than a mumble—it had two syllables and an emphasis to it. Nothing much was presumed beyond that, except that they had certain jokes. Ileane was not a shy girl but she was clever and aloof and not particularly popular, and that might have suited him.

From her position on the stairs, when everybody came out to watch the ruckus, Ileane was surprised to see that one of the two boys causing it was Jackson. The other was Billy Watts. Boys who only a year ago had sat hunched over books and shuffled dutifully between one classroom and another were now transformed. In army uniforms they looked twice the size they had been, and their boots made a powerful racket as they galloped around. They were shouting out that school was cancelled for the day, because everybody had to join the war. They were distributing cigarettes everywhere, tossing them on the floor where they could be picked up by boys who didn't even shave.

Careless warriors, whooping invaders. Drunk up to their eyeballs.

"I'm no piker," was what they were yelling.

The principal was trying to order them out. But because this was still early in the war and there was as yet some awe and special respect concerning the boys who had signed up, he was not able to show the ruthlessness he would have called upon a year later.

"Now now," he said.

"I'm no piker," Billy Watts told him.

Jackson had his mouth open probably to say the same, but at that moment his eyes met the eyes of Ileane Bishop and a certain piece of knowledge passed between them.

Ileane Bishop understood that Jackson was truly drunk but that the effect of this was to enable him to play drunk, therefore the drunkenness displayed could be managed. (Billy Watts was just drunk, through and through.) With this understanding Ileane walked down the stairs, smiling, and accepted a cigarette which she held unlit between her fingers. She linked arms with both heroes and marched them out of the school.

Once outside they lit up their cigarettes.

There was a conflict of opinion about this later, in Ileane's father's congregation. Some said Ileane had not actually smoked hers, just pretended, to pacify the boys, while others said she certainly had. Smoked. Their minister's daughter. Smoked.

Billy did put his arms around Ileane and tried to kiss her, but he stumbled and sat down on the school steps and crowed like a rooster.

Within two years he would be dead.

Meanwhile he had to be got home, and Jackson pulled him so that they could get his arms over their shoulders and drag him along. Fortunately his house was not far from the school. They left him there, passed out on the steps. Then they entered into a conversation.

Jackson did not want to go home. Why not? Because his stepmother was there, he said. He hated his stepmother. Why? No reason.

Ileane knew that his mother had died in a car accident when he was very small—this was sometimes mentioned to account for his shyness. She thought that the drink was probably making him exaggerate, but she didn't try to make him talk about it any further.

"Okay," she said. "You can stay at my place."

It just happened that Ileane's mother was away, looking after Ileane's sick grandmother. Ileane was at the time keeping house in a haphazard style for her father and her two younger brothers. This was unfortunate in some opinions. Not that her mother would have made a fuss, but she would have wanted to know the ins and outs, and who was this boy? At the very least she would have made Ileane go to school as usual.

A soldier and a girl, suddenly so close. Where there had been nothing all this time but logarithms and declensions.

Ileane's father didn't pay attention to them. He was more interested in the war than some of his parishioners thought a minister should be, and this made him proud to have a soldier in the house. Also he was unhappy not to be able to send his daughter to university. He had to save up to send her brothers there some day, they would have to earn a living. That made him go easy on Ileane whatever she did.

Jackson and Ileane didn't go to the movies. They didn't go to the dance hall. They went for walks, in any weather and often after dark. Sometimes they went into the restaurant and drank coffee, but did not try to be friendly to anybody. What was the matter with them, were they falling in love? When they were walking they might brush hands, and he made himself get used to that. Then when she changed the accidental to the deliberate, he found that he could get used to that also, overcoming a slight dismay.

He grew calmer, and was even prepared for kissing.

Ileane went by herself to Jackson's house to collect his bag. His stepmother showed her bright false teeth and tried to look as if she was ready for some fun.

She asked what they were up to.

"You better watch that stuff," she said.

She had a reputation for being a loudmouth. A dirty mouth, actually.

"Ask him if he remembers I used to wash his bottom," she said.

Ileane, reporting this, said that she herself had been especially courteous, even snooty, because she could not stand the woman.

But Jackson went red, cornered and desperate, the way he used to when asked a question in school.

"I shouldn't even have mentioned her," Ileane said. "You

get in the habit of caricaturing people, living in a parson-age."

He said it was okay.

That time turned out to be Jackson's last leave. They wrote to each other. Ileane wrote about finishing her typing and shorthand and getting a job in the office of the Town Clerk. She was determinedly satirical about everything, more than she had been in school. Maybe she thought that someone at war needed joking. And she insisted on being in the know. When hurry-up marriages had to be arranged through the clerk's office, she would refer to the Virgin Bride.

And when she mentioned some minister visiting the par-sonage and sleeping in the spare room, she said she won-dered if the mattress would induce Peculiar Dreams.

He wrote about the crowds on the *Île de France* and the ducking around to avoid U-boats. When he got to England he bought a bicycle and he told her about places he had biked around to see, if they were not out of bounds.

These letters though more prosaic than hers were always signed "With Love." When D-day did come there was what she called an agonizing silence but she understood the rea-son for it, and when he wrote again all was well, though details were not permitted.

In this letter he spoke as she had been doing, about marriage.

And at last VE-day and the voyage home. There were showers of summer stars, he said, all overhead.

Ileane had learned to sew. She was making a new summer dress in honour of his homecoming, a dress of lime-green rayon silk with a full skirt and cap sleeves, worn with a narrow belt of gold imitation leather. She meant to wind a ribbon of the same green material around the crown of her summer hat.

"All this is being described to you so you will notice me and know it's me and not go running off with some other beautiful woman who happens to be at the train station."

He mailed his letter to her from Halifax, telling her that he would be on the evening train on Saturday. He said that he remembered her very well and there was no danger of getting her mixed up with another woman even if the train station happened to be swarming with them that evening.

On their last evening before he left, they had sat up late in the parsonage kitchen where there was the picture of King George VI you saw everywhere that year. And the words beneath it.

> And I said to the man who stood at the gate of the year,
> "Give me a light that I may tread safely into the unknown."
> And he replied, "Go out into the darkness and put your hand into the hand of God. That shall be to you better than light and safer than a known way."

Then they went upstairs very quietly and he went to bed in the spare room. Her coming to him must have been by mutual agreement but perhaps he had not quite understood what for.

It was a disaster. But by the way she behaved, she might not even have known that. The more disaster, the more frantically she carried on. There was no way he could stop her trying, or explain. Was it possible a girl could know so little? They parted finally as if all had gone well. And the next morning said good-bye in the presence of her father and brothers. In a short while the letters began.

He got drunk and tried once more, in Southampton. But the woman said, "That's enough, sonny boy, you're down and out."

A thing he didn't like was women or girls dressing up. Gloves, hats, swishy skirts, all some demand and bother about it. But how could she know that? Lime green. He wasn't sure he knew the colour. It sounded like acid.

Then it came to him quite easily, that a person could just not be there.

Would she tell herself or tell anybody else, that she must have mistaken the date? He could make himself believe that she would find some lie, surely. She was resourceful, after all.

Now that she is gone out onto the street, Jackson does feel a wish to see her. He could never ask the owner what she looked like, whether her hair was dark or grey, and she herself still skinny or gone stout. Her voice even in distress had been marvellously unchanged. Drawing all importance to itself, to its musical levels, and at the same time setting up its so-sorries.

She had come a long way, but she was a persistent woman. You could say so.

And the daughter would come back. Too spoiled to stay away. Any daughter of Ileane's would be spoiled, arranging the world and the truth to suit herself, as if nothing could foil her for long.

If she had seen him, would she have known him? He thought so. No matter what the changes. And she'd have forgiven him, yes, right on the spot. To keep up her notion of herself, always.

The next day whatever ease he had felt about Ileane passing from his life was gone. She knew this place, she might come back. She might settle herself in for a while, walking up and down these streets, trying to find where the trail was warm. Humbly but not really humbly making inquiries of people, in that pleading but spoiled voice. It was possible he would run into her right outside this door. Surprised only for a moment, as if she had always expected him. Holding out the possibilities of life, the way she thought she could.

Things could be locked up, it only took some determination. When he was as young as six or seven he had locked up his stepmother's fooling, what she called her fooling or her teasing. He had run out into the street after dark and she got him in but she saw there'd be some real running away if she didn't stop so she stopped. And said that he was no fun because she could never say that anybody hated her.

He spent three more nights in the building called Bonnie Dundee. He wrote an account for the owner of every apartment and when upkeep was due and what it would consist of. He said that he had been called away, without indicating why or where to. He emptied his bank account and packed the few things belonging to him. In the evening, late in the evening, he got on the train.

He slept off and on during the night and in one of those snatches he saw the little Mennonite boys go by in their cart. He heard their small voices singing.

In the morning he got off in Kapuskasing. He could smell the mills, and was encouraged by the cooler air. Work there, sure to be work in a lumbering town.

IN SIGHT OF THE LAKE

A WOMAN goes to her doctor to have a prescription renewed. But the doctor is not there. It's her day off. In fact the woman has got the day wrong, she has mixed up Monday with Tuesday.

This is the very thing she wanted to talk to the doctor about, as well as renewing the prescription. She has wondered if her mind is slipping a bit.

"What a laugh," she has expected the doctor to say. "Your mind. You of all people."

(It isn't that the doctor knows her all that well, but they do have friends in common.)

Instead, the doctor's assistant phones a day later to say that the prescription is ready and that an appointment has been made for the woman—her name is Nancy—to be examined by a specialist about this mind problem.

It isn't mind. It's just memory.

Whatever. The specialist deals with elderly patients.

Indeed. Elderly patients who are off their nut.

The girl laughs. Finally, somebody laughs.

She says that the specialist's office is located in a village called Hymen, twenty or so miles away from where Nancy lives.

"Oh dear, a marriage specialist," says Nancy.

The girl doesn't get it, begs her pardon.

"Never mind, I'll be there."

What has happened in the last few years is that specialists are located all over the place. Your CAT scan is in one town and your cancer person in another, pulmonary problems in a third, and so on. This is so you won't have to travel to the city hospital, but it can take about as long, since not all these towns have hospitals and you have to ferret out where the doctor is once you get there.

It is for this reason that Nancy decides to drive to the village of the Elderly Specialist—as she decides to call him—on the evening before the day of her appointment. That should give her lots of time to find out where he is, so there will be no danger of her arriving all flustered or even a little late, creating a bad impression right off the bat.

Her husband could go with her, but she knows that he wants to watch a soccer game on television. He is an economist who watches sports half the night and works on his book the other half, though he tells her to say he is retired.

She says she wants to find the place herself. The girl in the doctor's office has given her directions to the town.

The evening is beautiful. But when she turns off the highway, driving west, she finds that the sun is just low enough to shine into her face. If she sits up quite straight, however, and lifts her chin, she can get her eyes into shadow. Also, she has good sunglasses. She can read the sign, which tells her that she has eight miles to go to the village of Highman.

Highman. So that's what is was, no joke. Population 1,553. Why do they bother to put the 3 on?

Every soul counts.

She has a habit of checking out small places just for fun, to see if she could live there. This one seems to fill the bill. A decent-sized market, where you could get fairly fresh vegetables, though they would probably not be from the fields round about, okay coffee. Then a Laundromat, and a pharmacy, which could fill your prescriptions even if they didn't stock the better class of magazines.

There are signs of course that the place has seen better days. A clock that no longer tells the time presides over a window which promises Fine Jewellery but now appears to be full of any old china, crocks and pails and wreaths twisted out of wires.

She gets to look at some of this trash because she has chosen to park in front of the shop where it is displayed. She thinks that she may as well search out this doctor's office on foot. And almost too soon to give her satisfaction she does see a dark brick one-storey building in the utilitarian style of the last century and she is ready to bet that is it. Doctors in small towns used to have their working quarters as part of their houses, but then they had to have space where cars could park, and they put up something like this. Reddish-brown bricks, and sure enough the sign, Medical/Dental. A parking lot behind the building.

In her pocket she has the doctor's name and she gets out

the scrap of paper to check it. The names on the frosted glass door are Dr. H. W. Forsyth, Dentist, and Dr. Donald McMillen, Physician.

These names are not on Nancy's piece of paper. And no wonder, because nothing is written there but a number. It is the shoe size of her husband's sister, who is dead. The number is O 7½. It takes her a while to figure that out, the O standing for Olivia but scribbled in a hasty way. She can only recall faintly something about buying slippers when Olivia was in the hospital.

That's no use to her anyway.

One solution may be that the doctor she will see has newly moved into this building and the name on the door has not been changed yet. She should ask somebody. First she should ring the bell on the off chance that somebody is in there, working late. She does this, and it is a good thing in a way that nobody comes, because the doctor's name that she is after has for a moment slipped below the surface of her mind.

Another idea. Isn't it quite possible that this person—the crazy-doctor, as she has chosen to call him in her head—isn't it quite possible that he (or she—like most people of her age she does not automatically allow for that possibility) that he or she does operate out of a house? It would make sense and be cheaper. You don't need a lot of apparatus for the crazy doctoring.

So she continues her walk away from the main street. The doctor's name that she is after has come back to her, as such things are apt to do when there is no longer a crisis. The houses she walks by were mostly built in the nineteenth century. Some of wood, some of brick. The brick

ones often two full storeys high, the wooden ones somewhat more modest, a storey and a half with slanting ceilings
in the upstairs rooms. Some front doors open just a few feet
from the sidewalk. Others onto wide verandas, occasionally glassed in. A century ago, on an evening like this one,
people would have been sitting on their verandas or perhaps
on the front steps. Housewives who had finished washing
the dishes and sweeping up the kitchen for the last time that
day, men who had coiled up the hose after giving the grass
a soaking. No garden furniture such as now sat here empty,
showing off. Just the wooden steps or dragged-out kitchen
chairs. Conversation about the weather or a runaway horse
or some person who has taken to bed and was not expected
to recover. Speculation about herself, once she was out of
earshot.

But wouldn't she have put their minds at ease by this time,
stopping and asking them, Please, can you tell me, where is
the doctor's house?

New item of conversation. What does she want the doctor for?

(This once she has put herself out of earshot.)

Now every single person is inside with their fans on or their
air-conditioning. Numbers on the houses appear, just as in a
city. No sign of a doctor.

Where the sidewalk ends there is a large brick building
with gables and a clock tower. Perhaps a school, before the
children were bused to some larger and drearier centre of
learning. The hands stopped at twelve, for noon or midnight, which certainly is not the right time. Profusion of

summer flowers that seem professionally arranged—some spilling out of a wheelbarrow and more out of a milk pail on its side. A sign she cannot read because the sun is shining straight onto it. She climbs up on the lawn to see it at another angle.

Funeral Home. Now she sees the built-on garage that probably holds the hearse.

Never mind. She had better get on with things.

She turns onto a side street where there are very well kept places indeed, proving that even a town this size can have its suburb. The houses all slightly different yet somehow looking all the same. Gently coloured stone or pale brick, peaked or rounded windows, a rejection of the utilitarian look, the ranch style of past decades.

Here there are people. They haven't all managed to shut themselves up with the air-conditioning. A boy is riding a bicycle, taking diagonal routes across the pavement. Something about his riding is odd, and she cannot figure it out at first.

He is riding backward. That's what it is. A jacket flung in such a way that you could not see—or she cannot see—what is wrong.

A woman who might be too old to be his mother—but who is very trim and lively looking all the same—is standing out in the street watching him. She is holding on to a skipping rope and talking to a man who could not be her husband—both of them are being too cordial.

The street is a curved dead end. No going farther.

Interrupting the adults, Nancy excuses herself. She says that she is looking for a doctor.

"No, no," she says. "Don't be alarmed. Just his address. I thought you might know."

Then comes the problem of realizing that she is still not sure of the name. They are too polite to show any surprise at this but they cannot help her.

The boy on one of his perverse sallies comes swinging around, barely missing all three.

Laughter. No reprimand. A perfect young savage and they seem to positively admire him. They all remark on the beauty of the evening, and Nancy turns to go back the way that she has come.

Except that she does not go all the way, not as far as the funeral home. There is a side street she ignored before, perhaps because it was unpaved and she had not thought of a doctor living in such circumstances.

There is no sidewalk, and the houses are surrounded with trash. A couple of men are busy under the hood of a truck, and she has an idea it would not do to interrupt them. Besides, she has glimpsed something interesting ahead.

There is a hedge that comes right out to the street. It is high enough that she does not expect to be able to see over it, but thinks she might be able to peek through.

That is not necessary. When she gets past the hedge she finds that the lot—about the size of four town lots—is quite open to the road she is walking on. It appears to be some sort of park, with flagstone paths diagonally crossing the mown and flourishing grass. In between the paths, and bursting from the grass, there are flowers. She knows some of them— the dark gold and light yellow daisies for instance, pink and rosy and red-hearted white phlox—but she is no great gardener herself and here there are clumped or trailing displays of all colours that she could not name. Some of them climb trellises, some spread free. Everything artful but nothing stiff, not even the fountain that shoots up seven feet or so before falling down into its rock-lined pool. She has walked in off the street to get a little of its cool spray, and there she finds a wrought-iron bench, where she can sit down.

A man has come along one of the paths, carrying a pair of shears. Gardeners are evidently expected to work late here. Though to tell the truth, he does not look like a hired workman. He is tall and very thin and dressed in a black shirt and pants that tightly fit his body.

It has not occurred to her that this could be anything but a town park.

"This is really beautiful," she calls to him in her most assured and approving voice. "You keep it up so well."

"Thank you," he says. "You're welcome to rest there."

Informing her by some dryness of voice that this is not a park but private property, and that he himself is not a village employee but the owner.

"I should have asked your permission."

"That's okay."

Preoccupied, bending and snipping at a plant that is encroaching on the path.

"It's yours, is it? All of it?"

After a moment's busyness, "All of it."

"I should have known. It's too imaginative to be public. Too unusual."

No answer. She is going to ask him whether he likes to sit here himself, in the evenings. But she better not bother. He doesn't seem an easy person to be around. One of those who pride themselves, probably, on that very fact. After a moment she will thank him and get up.

But instead, after a moment he comes and sits down beside her. He speaks just as if a question has been put to him.

"Actually, I only feel comfortable when I'm doing something that needs attending to," he says. "If I sit down I have to keep my eyes off everything, or I'll just see some more work."

She should have known right away that he was a man who doesn't like banter. But still she is curious.

What was here before?

Before he made the garden?

"A knitting factory. All these little places had something like that, you could get away with the starvation wages then. But in time that went under and there was a contractor who thought he was going to turn it into a nursing home. There was some trouble then, the town wouldn't give him a licence, they had some idea there'd be a lot of old people around and make it depressing. So he set fire to it or he knocked it down, I don't know."

He's not from around here. Even she knows that if he was he'd never talk so openly.

"I'm not from around here," he says. "I had a friend who was, though, and when he died I came up just to get rid of the place and go."

"Then I got hold of this land cheap because the contractor had left it just a hole in the ground and it was an eyesore."

"I'm sorry if I seem inquisitive."

"That's all right. If I don't feel like explaining something I don't do it."

"I haven't been here before," she says. "Of course I haven't, or I'd have seen this spot. I was walking around looking for something. I thought I could find it better if I parked my car and walked. I was looking for a doctor's office, actually."

She explains about not being sick, just having an appointment tomorrow, and not wanting to be running around in the morning looking for the place. Then she tells him about parking her car and being surprised that the name of the doctor she wanted was not listed anywhere.

"I couldn't look in the phone book either because you know how the phone books and the phone booths have all disappeared now. Or else you find their insides ripped out. I'm beginning to sound quite silly."

She tells him the name of the doctor, but he says it doesn't ring a bell.

"But I don't go to doctors."

"You're probably just as smart not to."

"Oh, I wouldn't say that."

"At any rate, I'd better get back to my car."

Standing up when she does, he says he will walk with her.

"So I won't get lost?"

"Not altogether. I always try to stretch my legs this time of the evening. Garden work can leave you cramped."

"I'm sure there's some sensible explanation about this doctor. Do you ever think that there used to be more sensible explanations about things than there are now?"

He does not answer. Thinking perhaps of the friend who died. The garden perhaps a memorial to the friend who died.

Instead of being embarrassed now when she has spoken and he has not answered, she feels a freshness, a peace in the conversation.

They walk along without meeting a soul.

Soon they reach the main street, with the medical building just a block away. The sight of it makes her feel somewhat less easy, and she does not know why, but after a moment she does. She has an absurd but alarming notion that the sight of the medical building has provoked. What if the right name, the name she said she could not find, has been waiting there all along. She moves more quickly, she finds that she is shaky, and then, having quite good eyesight she reads the two useless names just as before.

She pretends to have been hurrying to look at the assortment in the window, the china-headed dolls and ancient skates and chamber pots and quilts already in tatters.

"Sad," she says.

He is not paying attention. He says that he has just thought of something.

"This doctor," he says.

"Yes?"

"I wonder if he might be connected with the home?"

They are walking again, passing a couple of young men sitting on the sidewalk, one with his legs stretched out so they have to move around him. The man with her takes no notice of them, but his voice has dropped.

"Home?" she says.

"You wouldn't have noticed if you came in from the highway. But if you keep going out of town towards the lake you pass it. Not more than half a mile out. You go past the gravel pile on the south side of the road and it's just a little farther on, on the other side. I don't know if they have a live-in doctor there or not, but it stands to reason they might have."

"They might have," she says. "It stands to reason."

Then she hopes he doesn't think she is copying him on purpose, making a silly joke. It is true that she wants to go on talking to him longer, silly jokes or whatever.

But now comes another of her problems—she has to think about the whereabouts of her keys, as she often does before getting into the car. She is regularly worried about whether she's locked the keys inside or dropped them somewhere. She can feel the approach of familiar, tiresome panic. But then she finds them, in her pocket.

"It's worth a try," he says, and she agrees.

"There's plenty of room to turn off the road and take a look. If there's a doctor out there regularly, there's no need for him to have his name up in town. Or her name, as the case might be."

As if he too is not entirely anxious for them to part.

"I have you to thank."

"Just a hunch."

He holds the door while she gets in, and closes it, waits there until she is turned to go in the right direction, then waves good-bye.

When she is on her way out of the town she catches sight of him again in the rearview mirror. He is bending over, speaking to the couple of boys or young men who were sitting on the pavement with their backs against the wall of the store. He had ignored them in such a way that she is surprised to see him talking to them now.

Maybe a remark to be made, some joke about her vagueness or silliness. Or just her age. A mark against her, with the nicest man.

She had thought that she would come back through the village to thank him again and tell him if it was the right doctor. She could just slow down and laugh and call out the window.

But now she thinks that she will just take the lakeshore route and stay out of his way.

Forget him. She sees the gravel pile coming up, she has to pay attention to where she is going.

Just as he has said. A sign. A notice of the Lakeview Rest Home. And there really is, from here, a view of the lake, a thread of pale blue along the horizon.

A spacious parking lot. One long wing with what looks like separate compartments, or good-sized rooms at least, with their own little gardens or places to sit. A latticed fence quite high in front of every one of them for privacy, or safety. Though nobody is sitting out there now that she can see.

Of course not. Bedtime comes early in these establishments.

She likes how the lattice provides a touch of fantasy. Public buildings have been changing in the past few years, just as private houses have. The relentless, charmless look—the only one permitted in her youth—has disappeared. Here she parks in front of a bright dome that has a look of welcome, of cheerful excess. Some people would find it fakey, she supposes, but isn't it the very thing you would want? All that glass must cheer the spirits of the old people, or even, perhaps, of some people not so old but just off kilter.

She looks for a button to push, a bell to ring, as she walks up to the door. But that is not necessary—the door opens on its own. And once she gets inside there is an even greater expression of space, of loftiness, a blue tinge to the glass. The floor is all silvery tiles, the sort that children love to slide on, and for a moment she thinks of the patients sliding and slipping for pleasure and the idea makes her lighthearted. Of course it cannot be as slippery as it looks, you wouldn't want people breaking their necks.

"I didn't dare try it myself," she says in a charming voice to somebody in her head, perhaps her husband. "It wouldn't have done, would it? I could have found myself in front of the doctor, the very one who was getting ready to test my mental stability. And then what would he have to say?"

At the moment there is no doctor to be seen.

Well, there wouldn't be, would there? Doctors don't sit behind desks here waiting for patients to show up.

And she isn't even here for a consultation. She will have to explain again that she is making sure of the time and place of an appointment for tomorrow. All this has made her feel rather tired.

There is a rounded desk, waist high, whose panels of dark wood look like mahogany, though they probably are not. Nobody behind it at the moment. It is after hours of course. She looks for a bell but does not see one. Then she looks to see if there is a list of doctors' names or the name of the doctor in charge. She doesn't see that either. You would think there would be a way of getting hold of somebody, no matter what the hour. Somebody on call in a place like this.

No important clutter behind the desk either. No computer or telephone or papers or coloured buttons to press. Of course she has not been able to get right behind the desk, there may well be some lock, or some compartments she can't see. Buttons a receptionist could reach and she can't.

She gives up on the desk for the moment, and takes a closer look at the space she has found herself in. It's a hexagon, with doors at intervals. Four doors—one is the large door that lets in the light and any visitors, another is an official and private-looking door behind the desk, not that easy of access, and the other two doors, exactly alike and facing each other, would obviously take you into the long wings, to the corridors and rooms where the inmates are housed. Each of these has an upper window, and the window glass looks clear enough for anybody to manage to see through.

She goes up to one of these possibly accessible doors and knocks, then tries the knob and cannot budge it. Locked. She cannot see through the window properly, either. Close up the glass is all wavy and distorted.

In the door directly opposite there is the same problem with the glass and the same problem with the knob.

The click of her shoes on the floor, the trick of the glass, the uselessness of the polished knobs have made her feel more discouraged than she would care to admit.

She does not give up, however. She tries the doors again in the same order, and this time she shakes both knobs as well as she can and also calls out, "Hello?" in a voice that sounds at first trivial and silly, then aggrieved, but not more hopeful.

She squeezes herself in behind the desk and bangs that door, with practically no hope. It doesn't even have a knob, just a keyhole.

There is nothing to do but get out of this place and go home.

All very cheerful and elegant, she thinks, but there is no pretense here of serving the public. Of course they shove the residents or patients or whatever they call them into bed early, it is the same old story everywhere, however glamorous the surroundings.

Still thinking about this, she gives the entry door a push. It is too heavy. She pushes again.

Again. It does not budge.

She can see the pots of flowers outside in the open air. A car going by on the road. The mild evening light.

She has to stop and think.

There are no artificial lights on in here. The place will get dark. Already in spite of the lingering light outside, it seems to be getting dark. No one will come, they have all completed their duties, or at least the duties that brought them through this part of the building. Wherever they have settled down now is where they will stay.

She opens her mouth to yell but it seems that no yell is forthcoming. She is shaking all over and no matter how she tries she cannot get her breath down into her lungs. It is as if she has a blotter in her throat. Suffocation. She knows that she has to behave differently, and more than that, she has to believe differently. Calm. Calm. Breathe. Breathe.

She doesn't know if the panic has taken a long time or a short time. Her heart is pounding but she is nearly safe.

There is a woman here whose name is Sandy. It says so on the brooch she wears, and Nancy knows her anyway.

"What are we going to do with you?" says Sandy. "All we want is to get you into your nightie. And you go and carry on like a chicken that's scared of being et for dinner.

"You must have had a dream," she says. "What did you dream about now?"

"Nothing," says Nancy. "It was back when my husband was alive and when I was still driving the car."

"You have a nice car?"

"Volvo."

"See? You're sharp as a tack."

DOLLY

THAT fall there had been some discussion of death. Our deaths. Franklin being eighty-three years old and myself seventy-one at the time, we had naturally made plans for our funerals (none) and for the burials (immediate) in a plot already purchased. We had decided against cremation, which was popular with our friends. It was just the actual dying that had been left out or up to chance.

One day we were driving around in the country not too far from where we live, and we found a road we hadn't known about. The trees, maples and oaks and others, were second growth, though of an impressive size, indicating that there had been cleared land. Farms at one time, pastures and houses and barns. But not a sign of this was left. The road was unpaved but not untravelled. It looked as if it might see several vehicles a day. Maybe there were trucks that used it as a shortcut.

This was important, Franklin said. No way did we want to be there for a day or two, or possibly a week, with no discovery. Nor did we want to leave the car empty, with the police having to tramp through the trees in search of remains that the coyotes might already have got into.

Also, the day must not be too melancholy. No rain or early snow. The leaves turned but not many fallen. Plastered with gold, as they were on that day. But perhaps the sun would not be shining, else the gold, the glamour of the day, might make us feel like spoilers.

We had a difference about the note. That is, about whether we should leave a note or not. I thought that we owed people an explanation. They should be told that there was no question of a fatal illness, no onset of pain that blocked out the prospect of a decent life. They should be assured that this was a clearheaded, you might almost say a lighthearted decision.

Gone while the going is good.

No. I retracted that. Flippancy. An insult.

Franklin's idea was that any explanation at all was an insult. Not to others but to ourselves. To ourselves. We belonged to ourselves and to each other and any explanation at all struck him as snivelling.

I saw what he meant but I was still inclined to disagree.

And that very fact—our disagreement—seemed to put the possibility out of his head.

He said that it was rubbish. All right for him but I was too young. We could talk again when I was seventy-five.

I said that the only thing that bothered me, a little, was

the way there was an assumption that nothing more was going to happen in our lives. Nothing of importance to us, nothing to be managed anymore.

He said that we had just had an argument, what more did I want?

It was too polite, I said.

I have never felt that I am younger than Franklin, except maybe when the war comes up in conversation—I mean the Second World War—and that seldom happens nowadays. For one thing, he does more strenuous exercise than I do. At one time he was the overseer of a stable—I mean the sort of stable where people board riding horses, not racehorses. He still goes there two or three times a week, and rides his own horse, and talks to the man in charge who occasionally wants his advice. Though mostly he says he tries to keep out of the way.

He is in fact a poet. He is really a poet and really a horse trainer. He has held one-term jobs at various colleges, but never so far away that he can't keep in touch with the stables. He admits to giving readings, but only as he says once in a blue moon. He doesn't stress the poetic employment. Sometimes I am annoyed with this attitude—I call it his aw-shucks persona—but I can see the point. When you're busy with horses people can see that you are busy, but when you're busy at making up a poem you look as if you're in a state of idleness and you feel a little strange or embarrassed having to explain what's going on.

Another problem might be that though he is a reticent sort of man, the poem that he is best known for is what people around here—that is, where he grew up—are apt to call raw. Pretty raw, I have heard him say himself, not apologizing but just maybe warning somebody off. He has a feeling for the sensibilities of those people he knows who can be upset by certain things, though he is a great defender of freedom of speech in general.

Not that there haven't been changes around here, concerning what you can say out loud and read in print. Prizes help, and being mentioned in the papers.

All the years that I taught in a high school I didn't teach literature, as you might expect, but mathematics. Then staying home I grew restless and undertook something else— writing tidy and I hope entertaining biographies of Canadian novelists who have been undeservedly forgotten or have never received proper attention. I don't think I would have got the job if it wasn't for Franklin, and the literary reputation that we don't talk about—I was born in Scotland and really didn't know any Canadian writers.

I never would have counted Franklin or any poet as deserving of the sympathy I gave the novelists, I mean for their faded or even vanished condition. I don't know exactly why. Perhaps I think poetry is more of an end in itself.

I liked the work, I thought it worthwhile, and after years in classrooms I was glad of the control and the quiet. But there might come a time, say around four in the afternoon, when I just wanted to relax and have some company.

And it was around that time on a dreary closed-in day when a woman came to my door with a load of cosmetics. At any other time I wouldn't have been glad to see her, but I was then. Her name was Gwen, and she said she hadn't called on me before because they had told her I wasn't the type.

"Whatever that is," she said. "But anyway I had the idea, just let her speak for herself, all she has to do is say no."

I asked her if she would like a cup of the coffee I had just made and she said sure.

She said she was just getting ready anyway to pack it in. She set her burdens down with a groan.

"You don't wear makeup. I wouldn't wear none neither if I wasn't in the business."

If she had not told me that, I would have thought her face was as bare as mine. Bare, sallow, and with an amazing nest of wrinkles round the mouth. Glasses that magnified her eyes, which were the lightest blue. The only blatant thing about her was brassy thin hair cut straight across her forehead in bangs.

Maybe it had made her uneasy, to be asked in. She kept taking jumpy little looks around.

"It's bad cold today," she said.

And then in a rush, "I don't see any kind of an ashtray around here, do I?"

I found one in a cupboard. She got out her cigarettes and sank back in relief.

"You don't smoke?"

"I used to."

"Didn't everybody."

I poured her coffee.

"Black," she said. "Oh, isn't this the great stuff? I hope

I didn't interrupt whatever you were doing. You writing letters?"

And I found myself telling her about the neglected writers, even naming the one I was working on at the moment. Martha Ostenso, who wrote a book called *Wild Geese* and a horde of others all now forgotten.

"You mean like all this stuff will get printed? Like in the paper?"

In a book, I said. She exhaled somewhat dubiously, and I realized that I wanted to tell her something more interesting.

"Her husband is supposed to have written parts of the novel, but the odd thing is his name isn't anywhere on it."

"Maybe he didn't want the guys to kid him," she said. "Like, you know, what are they going to think about the kind of guy writes books."

"I hadn't thought of that."

"But he wouldn't mind taking the money," she said. "You know men."

Then she began to smile and shake her head and said, "You must be one smart person. Wait till I get to tell them at home that I saw a book that was just getting written."

To take her off the subject, which had begun to embarrass me, I asked who were those at home.

Various people whom I didn't get straight, or maybe didn't bother to. I'm not sure about the order in which they were mentioned except that her husband was the final one and he was dead.

"Last year. Except he wasn't my husband officially. You know."

"Mine wasn't either," I said. "Isn't, I mean."

"Is that right? There's so many doing that now, isn't there?

It used to be, oh my, isn't it awful, and now it's just, what the hell? And then there's the ones that live together year after year and finally it's, oh, we're getting married. You think then, whatever for? For the presents, is it, or just the thought of getting dolled up in the white dress. Makes you laugh, I could die."

She said she had a daughter who went through the whole fancy-dancy that way and much good it did her because she was now in jail for trafficking. Stupid. It was the man she went and married that got her into it. So now it was necessary to sell cosmetics as well as look after the daughter's two young children, who had nobody else.

All the time she was telling me this she seemed in high good humour. It was when she got onto the subject of another quite successful daughter, a registered nurse who was retired and living in Vancouver, that she became dubious and a little fretful.

This daughter wanted her mother to ditch the whole lot of them and come and live with her.

"But I don't like Vancouver. Everybody else does, I know. Just don't like it."

No. The trouble was, really, if she went to live with that daughter, she would have to quit smoking. It wasn't Vancouver, it was the giving up smoking.

I paid for some lotion that would restore my youth and she promised to drop it off next time she came around.

I told Franklin all about her. Gwen, her name was.

"It's another world. I rather enjoyed it," I said. Then I didn't quite like myself for saying that.

He said that maybe I needed to get out more, and should put my name in for some supply teaching.

When she came by soon with the lotion, I was surprised. After all I had already paid. She didn't even try to sell me anything more, which seemed almost a relief to her, not a tactic. I made coffee again, and we talked easily, even in a rush, as before. I gave her the copy of *Wild Geese* that I had been using to write about Martha Ostenso. I said she could keep it, because I would be getting another one when the series came out.

She said she would read it. No matter what. She didn't know when she had ever read a book through because of being so busy, but this time she promised.

She said she had never met a person like me, that was so educated and so easy. I felt a little flattered, yet cautious at the same time, as you feel when you realize that some student has a crush on you. Then there was embarrassment, as if I had no right to be so superior.

It was dark when she went out to start her car, and she couldn't get it going. She tried again and again and the engine made a willing noise, then stopped. When Franklin came into the yard and couldn't get past it I hurried to tell him the trouble. She got out of the driver's seat when she saw him coming, and began to explain, saying it had been acting up on her like the devil lately.

He tried to get it going, while we stood by his truck, out of the way. He couldn't manage it either. He went inside to call the garage in the village. She didn't want to go in again, though it was cold out. The presence of the man of the house seemed to have made her reticent. I waited with her. He came to the door to call to us that the garage was closed.

There was nothing to do then but ask her to stay for supper, and overnight. She was immensely apologetic, then more comfortable, once she got sitting down with a new cigarette. I started taking things out for the meal. Franklin was off changing his clothes. I asked her if she wanted to phone whoever was at her house.

She said, yes, she better.

I was thinking that she might have somebody there who could come take her home. I wasn't looking forward to talking all evening with Franklin sitting listening. Of course he could go to his own room—he wouldn't call it his study—but I would feel that this banishment was my fault. Also we would want to watch the news, and she would want to talk through it. Even my brightest women friends did that, and he hated it.

Or she might sit quiet and strangely bewildered. Just as bad.

There seemed to be nobody answering. So she called the people next door—that was where the children were—and there was a great deal of apologetic laughing, then a talk with the children to urge them to be good, then more assurances and heartfelt thanks to the people who would be keeping them. Though it turned out that those friends had somewhere to go tomorrow so that the children would have to go with them, and it was really not so handy after all.

Franklin was coming back into the kitchen just as she hung up the phone. She turned to me and said that they might have made up stuff about going out, that was what they were like. Never mind all the favours she had done for them when they needed it.

Both she and Franklin then were struck at the same time.

"Oh my Lord," said Gwen.

"No it isn't," said Franklin. "It's just me."

And they stood halted in their tracks. How could they have missed it, they said. Realizing, I supposed, that it would not do to spread their arms and fall upon each other. Instead, they made some strange disconnected movements, as if they had to look all around them in order to be sure this was reality. Also repeating each other's names in tones of some mockery and dismay. Not the names I would have expected them to say either.

"Frank."

"Dolly."

After a moment I realized that Gwen, Gwendolyn, could indeed be teased into Dolly.

And any young man would rather be called Frank than Franklin.

They did not forget about me, or Franklin didn't, except for that one moment.

"You've heard me mention Dolly?"

His voice insisted on our going back to normal, while Dolly's or Gwen's voice insisted on the enormous or even supernatural joke of their finding each other.

"I can't tell you the last time when I ever heard myself called that. Not anybody else in the world that knows me by that name. Dolly."

The odd thing now was that I began to participate in the general merriment. For wonder would have to be changed into merriment before my eyes, and that was happening.

The whole discovery had to take that quick turn. And so eager was I apparently to do my share that I produced a bottle of wine.

Franklin does not drink anymore. He never drank much, then quietly gave it up altogether. So it was up to Gwen and myself to chatter and explain, in our newly discovered high spirits, and to keep remarking on the coincidence of things.

She told me that she had been a nursemaid when she knew Franklin. She had been working in Toronto, looking after two little English children whose parents had sent them out to Canada so that they could miss the war. There was other help in the house so she got most of her evenings off and she would go out to have a good time, as what young girl wouldn't? She met Franklin when he was on his last leave before going overseas and they had as crazy a time as you could imagine. He might have written her a letter or two, but she was just too busy for letters. Then when the war was over she got on a boat as soon as possible to transport the English children home and she met a man on that boat whom she married.

But it didn't last, England was so dreary after the war that she thought she would die, so she came on home.

That was a part of her life I didn't already know about. But I did know about her two weeks with Franklin, and so, as I have said, did many others. At least if they read poetry. They knew how lavish she was with her love, but they didn't know as I did how she believed that she couldn't get pregnant because she had been a twin and wore her dead sis's hair in a locket around her neck. She had all kinds of notions like that and gave Franklin a magic tooth—he didn't know whose—to keep him safe when he left to go overseas. He managed to lose it right away, but his life was spared.

She had a rule also that if she stepped off a curb on the wrong foot the whole day would go bad for her, and so they would have to go back and do it again. Her rules enthralled him.

To tell the truth I was privately un-enthralled when told this. I had thought how men are charmed by stubborn quirks if the girl is good-looking enough. Of course that has gone out of fashion. At least I hope it has. All that delight in the infantile female brain. (When I first went teaching they told me there was a time, not long ago, when women never taught mathematics. Weakness of intellect prevented it.)

Of course that girl, that charmer I had badgered him into telling me about, might be generally made up. She might be anybody's creation. But I did not think so. She was her own sassy choice. She'd loved herself so thoroughly.

Naturally I kept my mouth shut about what he'd told me and what had gone into the poem. And Franklin remained quiet about that most of the time too, except to say something about what Toronto was like in those teeming war days, about the stupid liquor laws or the farce of the Church Parade. If I had thought at this point that he might make her a gift of any of his writing, it seemed I was mistaken.

He got tired and went to bed. Gwen or Dolly and I made up her bed on the couch. She sat on the side of it with her last cigarette, telling me not to worry, she was not going to burn the house down, she never lay down till it was finished.

Our room was cold, the windows opened much wider than usual. Franklin was asleep. He was really asleep, I could always tell if he was shamming.

I hate going to sleep knowing there are dirty dishes on the table, but I had felt suddenly too tired to do them with Gwen helping as I knew she would. I meant to get up early in the morning to clear things away.

But I woke to full daylight and a clatter in the kitchen and the smell of breakfast as well as the smell of cigarettes. Conversation too, and it was Franklin talking when I would have expected Gwen. I heard her laughing at whatever he said. I got up at once and hurried into my clothes and fixed my hair, a thing I never usually bother with so early.

All the safety and merriment of the evening was gone from me. I made a good deal of noise coming down the stairs.

Gwen was at the sink with a row of sparkling clean glass jars on the draining board.

"Done the dishes all by hand because I was scared I wouldn't get the hang of your dishwasher," she said. "Then I got hold of these jars up there and I thought I might as well do them while I was at it."

"They haven't been washed in a century," I said.

"Yeah, I didn't think so."

Franklin said he'd gone out and tried the car again, but no go. He had got hold of the garage though, and they'd said that somebody could come up and look at it this afternoon. But he thought instead of waiting around he'd tow the car down there and they could get at it this morning.

"Gives Gwen a chance to get at the rest of the kitchen," I said, but neither one was interested in my joke. He said no, Gwen had better go with him, they'd want to talk to her since it was her car.

I noticed that he had a little trouble saying the name Gwen, having to push aside Dolly.

I said I had been joking.

He asked if he could make me any breakfast and I said no.

"How she keeps her figure," Gwen said. And somehow even this compliment turned into a thing they could laugh at together.

Neither gave any sign of knowing how I felt, though it seemed to me I was behaving oddly, with every remark I made coming out like some brittle kind of mockery. They are so full of themselves, I thought. It was an expression that came from I don't know where. When Franklin went out to prepare the car to be towed she followed, as if she didn't want to lose sight of him for a moment.

As she left she called back that she could never thank me enough.

Franklin tooted the horn to wish me good-bye, a thing he never did normally.

I wanted to run after them, pound them to pieces. I walked up and down as this grievous excitement got more and more of a hold on me. There was no doubt at all about what I should do.

In a fairly short time I went out and got into my car, having dropped my house key through the slot in the front door. I had a suitcase beside me, though I had already more or less forgotten what I'd put in it. I had written a terse note saying that I had to check some facts about Martha Ostenso and then I started to write a longer note which I intended to address to Franklin but did not want Gwen to see when she came back with him as she surely would. It said that he must be free to do as he wished and that the only thing that was unbearable to me was the deception or perhaps it was self-deception. There was nothing for it but for him to admit what he wanted. It was ridiculous and cruel to make me watch it and so I would just get out of the way.

I went on to say that no lies, after all, were as strong as the lies we tell ourselves and then unfortunately have to keep telling to make the whole puke stay down in our stomachs, eating us alive, as he would find out soon enough. And so on, a berating that became in even so short a space somewhat repetitive and rambling and more and more without dignity or grace. I understood now that it would have to be rewritten before I could let it go to Franklin so I had to take it with me and send it through the mail.

At the end of our driveway I turned in the other direction from the village and the garage, and in no time, as it seemed, I was driving east on a major highway. Where was I going? If I didn't make up my mind soon I was going to find myself in Toronto, and it seemed to me that far from getting into a hiding place there I was bound to run into places and people all tied up with my former happiness, and Franklin.

To keep this from happening I turned and headed for Cobourg. A town that we had never been in together.

It wasn't even noon yet. I got a room in a downtown motel. I passed the maids who were cleaning up the rooms that had been occupied last night. My room, having been unoccupied, was very cold. I turned the heat on and decided to go for a walk. Then when I opened the door I couldn't do it. I was shivering and shaking. I locked the door and got into bed with all my clothes on and I still shook so I pulled the covers up to my ears.

When I woke up it was well into a bright afternoon and my clothes were plastered to me with sweat. I turned the heat off and found a few clothes in the suitcase, which I changed into, and I went out. I walked very fast. I was hungry but felt that I could never slow down, or sit down, to eat.

What had happened to me was not uncommon, I thought. Not in books or in life. There should be, there must be, some well-worn way of dealing with it. Walking like this, of course. But you had to stop, even in a town this size you have to stop for cars and red lights. Also there were people going round in such clumsy ways, stopping and starting, and hordes of schoolchildren like the ones I used to keep in order. Why so many of them and so idiotic with their yelps and yells and the redundancy, the sheer un-necessity of their existence. Everywhere an insult in your face.

As the shops and their signs were an insult, and the noise of the cars with their stops and starts. Everywhere the proclaiming, this is life. As if we needed it, more of life.

Where the shops finally did peter out there were some cabins. Empty, boards nailed across their windows, waiting to be demolished. Where people used to stay on humbler holidays, before the motels. And then I remembered that I too had stayed there. Yes, in one of those places when they were reduced—maybe it was the off-season—reduced to taking in afternoon sinners and I had been one of them. I was still a student teacher and I would not even have remembered that it was in this town if it wasn't for something about those now boarded-up cabins. The man a teacher, older. A wife at home, undoubtedly children. Lives to be tampered with. She mustn't know, it would break her heart. I didn't care in the least. Let it break.

I could remember more if I tried, but it wasn't worth it. Except that it slowed me down to a more normal pace and turned me back towards the motel. And there on the dresser was the letter I'd written. Sealed but without a stamp. I went out again, found the post office, bought a stamp, dropped the envelope where it should go. Hardly any thought and no misgiving. I could have left it on the table, what did it matter? All is over.

On the walk I had noticed a restaurant, down some steps. I found it again, and looked at the posted menu.

Franklin did not like eating out. I did. I walked some more, at a normal pace this time, waiting for the place to open. I saw a scarf I liked in a window, and I thought that I should go in and buy it, that it would be good for me. But when I picked it up I had to drop it. Its silky feel made me sick.

In the restaurant I drank wine and waited a long time for my food. There was hardly anybody there—they were just setting up the band for the evening. I went into the washroom and was surprised how much like myself I looked. I wondered if it was possible that some man—some old man—would ever think of picking me up. The idea was grotesque—not because of his possible age but because there could be no thought in my head of any man but Franklin, ever.

I could eat hardly any food when it did come. It was not the food's fault. Just the oddity of sitting alone, eating alone, the gaping solitude, the unreality.

I had thought to bring sleeping pills, though I hardly ever used them. In fact I'd had them for so long that I wondered if they would work. But they did—I fell asleep and did not waken once, not until nearly six o'clock in the morning.

Some big trucks were already pulling out of their berths at the motel.

I knew where I was, I knew what I had done. And I knew that I had made a terrible mistake. I got dressed and, as soon as I could, got out of the motel. I could barely tolerate the friendly chat of the woman behind the desk. She said that there was snow coming later on. Take care, she told me.

The traffic was already getting heavy on the highway. And then there was an accident which slowed things down further.

I thought of Franklin maybe out looking for me. An accident could happen to him too. We might never see each other again.

I did not think of Gwen except as a person who had got in the way and created absurd problems. Her little stout legs, her foolish hair, her nest of wrinkles. A caricature you might say, somebody you could not blame and should never have taken seriously either.

Then I was home. Our house had not changed. I turned up the drive, and I saw his car. Thank God he was there.

I did notice that the car was not parked in its usual place.

The reason being that another car, Gwen's car, was in that spot.

I couldn't take it in. All this way I had thought of her, when I thought of her at all, as a person who would already be set aside, who after the first disturbance could not maintain herself as a character in our lives. I was still full of the relief of being home and his being home, safe. Assurance had spread all over me so that my body was ready, still, to spring out of the car and run to the house. I had even been feeling for my house key, having forgotten what I had done with it.

I wouldn't have needed it, anyway. Franklin was open-

ing the door of our house. He did not call out in surprise
or relief, not even when I had left the car and was out and
going towards him. He just came down the house steps in a
measured way, and his words held me off as I reached him.
He said, "Wait."

Wait. Of course. She was there.

"Get back in the car," he said. "We can't talk out here, it's
too cold."

When we were in the car he said, "Life is totally
unpredictable."

His voice was unusually gentle and sad. He didn't look at
me but stared straight ahead at the windshield, at our house.

"No use saying I'm sorry," he told me.

"You know," he went on, "it's not even the person. It's
like a sort of aura. It's a spell. Well of course it is really the
person but it surrounds them and embodies them. Or they
embody—I don't know. Do you understand? It just strikes
like an eclipse or something."

He shook his bent head. All dismay.

He was longing to talk about her, you could see that. But
this spiel was surely something that would have made him
sick, normally. That was what made me lose hope.

I felt myself getting bitterly cold. I was going to ask him if
he had alerted the other party to this transformation. Then
I thought that of course he had and she was with us, in the
kitchen with the things she polished.

His enchantment was so dreary. It was like anybody
else's. Dreary.

"Don't talk any more," I said. "Just don't talk."

He turned and looked at me for the first time and spoke
without any of that special wondering hush in his voice.

"Christ, I'm kidding," he said. "I thought you'd catch on. All right. All right. Oh for God's sake, shut up. Listen."

For I was howling now with anger and relief.

"All right, I was a little mad at you. I felt like giving you a hard time. What was I supposed to think when I came home and you were just gone? All right, I'm an asshole. Stop. Stop."

I didn't want to stop. I knew it was all right now, but it was such a comfort to howl. And I found a fresh grievance.

"What is her car doing here, then?"

"They can't do anything with it, it's junk."

"But why is it here?"

He said it was here because the non-junk parts of it, and that wasn't much, now belonged to him. Us.

Because he had bought her a car.

"A car? New?"

New enough to run better than what she had.

"The thing is she wants to go to North Bay. She has relatives or something there and that's where she wants to go when she can get a car fit to take her."

"She has relatives here. Wherever she lives here. She has three-year-old kids to look after."

"Well apparently the ones in North Bay would suit her better. I don't know about any three-year-olds. Maybe she'll take them along."

"Did she ask you to buy her a car?"

"She wouldn't ask for anything."

"So now," I said. "Now she's in our life."

"She's in North Bay. Let's go in the house. I haven't even got a jacket on."

On our way I asked if he had told her about his poem. Or maybe read it to her.

He said, "Oh God no, why would I do that?"

The first thing I saw in the kitchen was the sparkle of glass jars. I yanked a chair out and climbed up on it and began putting them away on top of the cupboard.

"Can you help me?" I said, and he handed them up to me.

I wondered—could he have been lying about the poem? Could she have heard it read to her? Or been left to read it by herself?

If so, her response had not been satisfactory. Whose ever could be?

Suppose she said that it was lovely? He would have hated that.

Or she might have wondered out loud how he could get away with what he had got away with. The smut, she might have said. That would have been better, but not as much better as you might think.

Who can ever say the perfect thing to the poet about his poetry? And not too much or not too little, just enough.

He put his arms around me, lifted me down from the chair.

"We can't afford rows," he said.

No indeed. I had forgotten how old we were, forgotten everything. Thinking there was all the time in the world to suffer and complain.

I could see the key now, the one I had put through the slot. It was in a crack between the hairy brown mat and the doorsill.

I would have to be on the lookout for that letter I had written as well.

Supposing I should die before it came? You can think yourself in reasonable shape and then die, just like that. Ought I to leave a note for Franklin to find, just in case?

If a letter comes addressed to you from me, tear it up.

The thing was, he would do what I asked. I wouldn't, in his place. I would rip it open, no matter what promises had been made.

He'd obey.

What a mix of rage and admiration I could feel, at his being willing to do that. It went back through our whole life together.

FINALE

The final four works in this book are not quite stories. They form a separate unit, one that is autobiographical in feeling, though not, sometimes, entirely so in fact. I believe they are the first and last—and the closest— things I have to say about my own life.

THE EYE

WHEN I was five years old my parents all of a sudden produced a baby boy, which my mother said was what I had always wanted. Where she got this idea I did not know. She did quite a bit of elaborating on it, all fictitious but hard to counter.

Then a year later a baby girl appeared, and there was another fuss but more subdued than with the first one.

Up until the time of the first baby I had not been aware of ever feeling different from the way my mother said I felt. And up until that time the whole house was full of my mother, of her footsteps her voice her powdery yet ominous smell that inhabited all the rooms even when she wasn't in them.

Why do I say ominous? I didn't feel frightened. It wasn't

that my mother actually told me what I was to feel about things. She was an authority on that without having to question a thing. Not just in the case of a baby brother but in the matter of Red River Cereal which was good for me and so I must be fond of it. And in my interpretation of the picture that hung at the foot of my bed, showing Jesus suffering the little children to come unto him. Suffering meant something different in those days, but that was not what we concentrated on. My mother pointed out the little girl half hiding round a corner because she wanted to come to Jesus but was too shy. That was me, my mother said, and I supposed it was though I wouldn't have figured it out without her telling me and I rather wished it wasn't so.

The thing I really felt miserable about was Alice in Wonderland huge and trapped in the rabbit hole, but I laughed because my mother seemed delighted.

It was with my brother's coming, though, and the endless carryings-on about how he was some sort of present for me, that I began to accept how largely my mother's notions about me might differ from my own.

I suppose all this was making me ready for Sadie when she came to work for us. My mother had shrunk to whatever territory she had with the babies. With her not around so much, I could think about what was true and what wasn't. I knew enough not to speak about this to anybody.

The most unusual thing about Sadie—though it was not a thing stressed in our house—was that she was a celebrity. Our town had a radio station where she played her guitar and sang the opening welcome song which was her own composition.

"Hello, hello, hello, everybody—"

And half an hour later it was, "Good-bye, good-bye, good-bye, everybody." In between she sang songs that were requested, as well as some she picked out herself. The more sophisticated people in town tended to joke about her songs and about the whole station which was said to be the smallest one in Canada. Those people listened to a Toronto station that broadcast popular songs of the day—three little fishes and a momma fishy too—and Jim Hunter hollering out the desperate war news. But people on the farms liked the local station and the kind of songs Sadie sang. Her voice was strong and sad and she sang about loneliness and grief.

> Leanin' on the old top rail,
> In a big corral.
> Lookin' down the twilight trail
> For my long lost pal—

Most of the farms in our part of the country had been cleared and settled around a hundred and fifty years ago, and you could look out from almost any farmhouse and see another farmhouse only a few fields away. Yet the songs the farmers wanted were all about lone cowhands, the lure and disappointment of far-off places, the bitter crimes that led to criminals dying with their mothers' names on their lips, or God's.

This was what Sadie sang with such sorrow in a full-throated alto, but in her job with us she was full of energy and confidence, happy to talk and mostly to talk about herself. There was usually nobody to talk to but me. Her jobs and my mother's kept them divided most of the time and somehow I don't think they would have enjoyed talking together anyway. My mother was a serious person as I have indicated, one who used to teach school before she taught me. She maybe would have liked Sadie to be somebody she could help, teaching her not to say "youse." But Sadie did not give much indication that she wanted the help anybody could offer, or to speak in any way that was different from how she had always spoken.

After dinner, which was the noon meal, Sadie and I were alone in the kitchen. My mother took time off for a nap and if she was lucky the babies napped too. When she got up she put on a different sort of dress as if she expected a leisurely afternoon, even though there would certainly be more diapers to change and also some of that unseemly business that I tried never to catch sight of, when the littlest one guzzled at a breast.

My father took a nap too—maybe fifteen minutes on the porch with the *Saturday Evening Post* over his face, before he went back to the barn.

Sadie heated water on the stove and washed the dishes with me helping and the blinds down to keep out the heat. When we were finished she mopped the floor and I dried it, by a method I had invented—skating around and around it on rags. Then we took down the coils of sticky yellow flypaper that had been put up after breakfast and were already heavy with dead or buzzing nearly dead black flies, and hung up the fresh coils which would be full of newly dead ones by suppertime. All this while Sadie was telling me about her life.

I didn't make easy judgments about ages then. People were either children or grown-ups and I thought her a grown-up. Maybe she was sixteen, maybe eighteen or twenty. Whatever her age, she announced more than once that she was not in any hurry to get married.

She went to dances every weekend but she went by herself. By herself and for herself, she said.

She told me about the dance halls. There was one in town, off the main street, where the curling rink was in the winter. You paid a dime for a dance, then went up and danced on a platform with people gawking all around, not that she cared. She always liked to pay her own dime, not to be beholden. But sometimes a fellow got to her first. He asked if she wanted to dance and the first thing she said was, Can you? Can you dance? she asked him bluntly. Then he would look at her funny and say yes, meaning why else would he be here? And it would turn out usually that what he meant by dance was shuffling around on two feet with his sweaty big meats of hands grabbing at her. Sometimes she just broke off and left him stranded, danced by herself—which was what she liked to do anyway. She finished up the dance that had been paid for, and if the money-taker objected and tried to make her pay for two when it was only one, she told him that was enough out of him. They could all laugh at her dancing by herself if they liked.

The other dance hall was just out of town on the highway. You paid at the door there and it wasn't for one dance but the whole night. The place was called the Royal-T. She paid her own way there too. There was generally a better class of dancer, but she did try to get an idea of how they managed before she let them take her out on the floor. They were usually town fellows while the ones at the other place were country. Better on their feet—the town ones—but it was not always the feet you had to look out for. It was where they wanted to get hold of you. Sometimes she had to read them the riot act and tell them what she would do to them if they didn't quit it. She let them know she'd come there to dance and paid her own way to do it. Furthermore she knew where to jab them. That would straighten them out. Sometimes they were good dancers and she got to enjoy herself. Then when they played the last dance she bolted for home.

She wasn't like some, she said. She didn't mean to get caught.

Caught. When she said that, I saw a big wire net coming down, some evil little creatures wrapping it around and around you and choking you so you could never get out. Sadie must have seen something like this on my face because she said not to be scared.

"There's nothing in this world to be scared of, just look out for yourself."

"You and Sadie talk together a lot," my mother said.

I knew something was coming that I should watch for but I didn't know what.

"You like her, don't you?"

I said yes.

"Well of course you do. I do too."

I hoped that was going to be all and for a moment I thought it was.

Then, "You and I don't get so much time now we have the babies. They don't give us much time, do they?

"But we do love them, don't we?"

Quickly I said yes.

She said, "Truly?"

She wasn't going to stop till I said truly, so I said it.

———

My mother wanted something very badly. Was it nice friends? Women who played bridge and had husbands who went to work in suits with vests? Not quite, and no hope of that anyway. Was it me as I used to be, with my sausage curls that I didn't mind standing still for, and my expert Sunday School recitations? No time for her to manage that anymore. And something in me was turning traitorous, though she didn't know why, and I didn't know why either. I hadn't made any town friends at Sunday School. Instead, I worshipped Sadie. I heard my mother say that to my father. "She worships Sadie."

My father said Sadie was a godsend. What did that mean? He sounded cheerful. Maybe it meant he wasn't going to take anybody's side.

"I wish we had proper sidewalks for her," my mother said. "Maybe if we had proper sidewalks she could learn to roller-skate and make friends."

I did wish for roller skates. But now without any idea why, I knew that I was never going to admit it.

Then my mother said something about it being better when school started. Something about me being better or something concerning Sadie that would be better. I didn't want to hear.

Sadie was teaching me some of her songs and I knew I wasn't very good at singing. I hoped that wasn't what had to get better or else stop. I truly did not want it to stop.

My father didn't have much to say. I was my mother's business, except for later on when I got really mouthy and had to be punished. He was waiting for my brother to get older and be his. A boy would not be so complicated.

And sure enough my brother wasn't. He would grow up to be just fine.

Now school has started. It started some weeks ago, before the leaves turned red and yellow. Now they were mostly gone. I am not wearing my school coat but my good coat, the one with the dark velvet cuffs and collar. My mother is wearing the coat she wears to church, and a turban covers most of her hair.

My mother is driving to whatever place it is that we are going to. She doesn't drive often, and her driving is always more stately and yet uncertain than my father's. She peeps her horn at any curve.

"Now," she says, but it takes a little while for her to get the car into place.

"Here we are then." Her voice seems meant to be encouraging. She touches my hand to give me a chance to hold hers, but I pretend not to notice and she takes her hand away.

The house has no driveway or even a sidewalk. It's decent but quite plain. My mother has raised her gloved hand to knock but it turns out we don't have to. The door is opened for us. My mother has just started to say something encouraging to me—something like, It will go more quickly than you think—but she doesn't get finished. The tone in which she spoke to me had been somewhat stern but slightly comforting. It changes when the door is opened into something more subdued, softened as if she was bowing her head.

The door has been opened to let some people go out, not just to let us go in. One of the women going out calls back over her shoulder in a voice that does not try to be soft at all.

"It's her that she worked for, and that little girl."

Then a woman who is rather dressed up comes and speaks to my mother and helps her off with her coat. That done, my mother takes my coat off and says to the woman that I was especially fond of Sadie. She hopes it was all right to bring me.

"Oh the dear little thing," the woman says and my mother touches me lightly to get me to say hello.

"Sadie loved children," the woman said. "She did indeed."

I notice that there are two other children there. Boys. I know them from school, one being in the first grade with me, and the other one older. They are peering out from what is likely the kitchen. The younger one is stuffing a whole cookie into his mouth in a comical way and the other, older, one is making a disgusted face. Not at the cookie stuffer, but at me. They hate me of course. Boys either ignored you if they met you somewhere that wasn't school (they ignored you there too) or they made these faces and called you horrid names. If I had to go near one I would stiffen and wonder what to do. Of course it was different if there were adults around. These boys stayed quiet but I was slightly miserable until somebody yanked the two of them into the kitchen. Then I became aware of my mother's especially gentle and sympathetic voice, more ladylike even than the voice of the spokeswoman she was talking to, and I thought maybe the face was meant for her. Sometimes people imitated her voice when she called for me at school.

The woman she was talking to and who seemed to be in charge was leading us to a part of the room where a man and a woman sat on a sofa, looking as if they did not quite understand why they were here. My mother bent over and spoke to them very respectfully and pointed me out to them.

"She did so love Sadie," she said. I knew that I was supposed to say something then but before I could the woman sitting there let out a howl. She did not look at any of us and the sound she made seemed like a sound you might make if some animal was biting or gnawing at you. She slapped away at her arms as if to get rid of whatever it was, but it did not go away. She looked at my mother as if my mother was the person who should do something about this.

The old man told her to hush.

"She's taking it very hard," said the woman who was guiding us. "She doesn't know what she's doing." She bent down lower and said, "Now, now. You'll scare the little girl."

"Scare the little girl," the old man said obediently.

By the time he finished saying that, the woman was not making the noise anymore and was patting her scratched arms as if she didn't know what had happened to them.

My mother said, "Poor woman."

"An only child too," said the conducting woman. To me she said, "Don't you worry."

I was worried but not about the yelling.

I knew Sadie was somewhere and I did not want to see her. My mother had not actually said that I would have to see her but she had not said that I wouldn't have to, either.

Sadie had been killed when walking home from the Royal-T dance hall. A car had hit her just on that little bit of gravel road between the parking space belonging to the dance hall and the beginning of the proper town sidewalk. She would have been hurrying along just the way she always did, and was no doubt thinking cars could see her, or that she had as much right as they did, and perhaps the car behind her swerved or perhaps she was not quite where she thought she was. She was hit from behind. The car that hit her was getting out of the way of the car that was behind it, and that second car was looking to make the first turn onto a town street. There had been some drinking at the dance hall, though you could not buy liquor there. And there was always some honking and yelling and whipping around too fast when the dancing was over. Sadie scurrying along without even a flashlight would behave as if it was everybody's business to get out of her way.

"A girl without a boyfriend going to dances on foot," said the woman who was still being friends with my mother. She spoke quite softly and my mother murmured something regretful.

It was asking for trouble, the friendly woman said still more softly.

I had heard talk at home that I did not understand. My mother wanted something done that might have had to do with Sadie and the car that hit her, but my father said to leave it alone. We've got no business in town, he said. I did not even try to figure this out because I was trying not to think about Sadie at all, let alone about her being dead. When I had realized that we were going into Sadie's house I longed not to go, but didn't see any way to get out of it except by behaving with enormous indignity.

Now after the old woman's outburst it seemed to me we might turn around and go home. I would never have to admit the truth, which was that I was in fact desperately scared of any dead body.

Just as I thought this might be possible, I heard my mother and the woman she seemed now to be conniving with speak of what was worse than anything.

Seeing Sadie.

Yes, my mother was saying. Of course, we must see Sadie. Dead Sadie.

I had kept my eyes pretty well cast down, seeing mostly just those boys who were hardly taller than I was, and the old people who were sitting down. But now my mother was taking me by the hand in another direction.

There had been a coffin in the room all the time but I had thought it was something else. Because of my lack of experience I didn't know exactly what such a thing looked like. A shelf to put flowers on, this object we were approaching might have been, or a closed piano.

Perhaps the people being around it had somehow disguised its real size and shape and purpose. But now these people were making way respectfully and my mother spoke in a new very quiet voice.

"Come now," she said to me. Her gentleness sounded hateful to me, triumphant.

She bent to look into my face, and this, I was sure, was to prevent me from doing what had just occurred to me—keeping my eyes squeezed shut. Then she took her gaze away from me but kept my hand tightly held in hers. I did manage to lower my lids as soon as she took her eyes off me, but I did not shut them quite lest I stumble or somebody push me right where I didn't want to be. I was able to see just a blur of the stiff flowers and the sheen of polished wood.

Then I heard my mother sniffling and felt her pulling away. There was a click of her purse being opened. She had to get her hand in there, so her hold on me weakened and I was able to get myself free of her. She was weeping. It was attention to her tears and sniffles that had set me loose.

I looked straight into the coffin and saw Sadie.

The accident had spared her neck and face but I didn't see all of that at once. I just got the general impression that there was nothing about her as bad as I had been afraid of. I shut my eyes quickly but found myself unable to keep from looking again. First at the little yellow cushion that was under her neck and that also managed to cover her throat and chin and the one cheek I could easily see. The trick was in seeing a bit of her quickly, then going back to the cushion, and the next time managing a little bit more that you were not afraid of. And then it was Sadie, all of her or at least all I could reasonably see on the side that was available.

Something moved. I saw it, her eyelid on my side moved. It was not opening or halfway opening or anything like that, but lifting just such a tiny bit as would make it possible, if you were her, if you were inside her, to be able to see out through the lashes. Just to distinguish maybe what was light outside and what was dark.

I was not surprised then and not in the least scared. Instantly, this sight fell into everything I knew about Sadie and somehow, as well, into whatever special experience was owing to myself. And I did not dream of calling anybody else's attention to what was there, because it was not meant for them, it was completely for me.

My mother had taken my hand again and said that we were ready to go. There were some more exchanges, but before any time had passed, as it seemed to me, we found ourselves outside.

My mother said, "Good for you." She squeezed my hand and said, "Now then. It's over." She had to stop and speak to somebody else who was on the way to the house, and then we got into the car and began to drive home. I had an idea that she would like me to say something, or maybe even tell her something, but I didn't do it.

There was never any other appearance of that sort and in fact Sadie faded rather quickly from my mind, what with the shock of school, where I learned somehow to manage with an odd mixture of being dead scared and showing off. As a matter of fact some of her importance had faded in that first week in September when she said she had to stay home now to look after her father and mother, so she wouldn't be working for us anymore.

And then my mother had found out she was working in the creamery.

Yet for a long time when I did think of her, I never questioned what I believed had been shown to me. Long, long afterwards, when I was not at all interested in any unnatural display, I still had it in my mind that such a thing had happened. I just believed it easily, the way you might believe and in fact remember that you once had another set of teeth, now vanished but real in spite of that. Until one day, one day when I may even have been in my teens, I knew with a dim sort of hole in my insides that now I didn't believe it anymore.

NIGHT

WHEN I was young, there seemed to be never a childbirth, or a burst appendix, or any other drastic physical event that did not occur simultaneously with a snowstorm. The roads would be closed, there was no question of digging out a car anyway, and some horses had to be hitched up to make their way into town to the hospital. It was just lucky that there were horses still around—in the normal course of events they would have been given up, but the war and gas rationing had changed all that, at least for the time being.

When the pain in my side struck, therefore, it had to do so at about eleven o'clock at night, and a blizzard had to be blowing, and since we were not stabling any horses at the moment, the neighbours' team had to be brought into action to take me to the hospital. A trip of no more than a mile and a half but an adventure all the same. The doctor was waiting, and to nobody's surprise he prepared to take out my appendix.

Did more appendixes have to be taken out then? I know it still happens, and it is necessary—I even know of somebody who died because it did not happen soon enough—but as I remember it was a kind of rite that quite a few people my age had to undergo, not in large numbers by any means but not all that unexpectedly, and perhaps not all that unhappily, because it meant a holiday from school and it gave you some kind of status—set you apart, briefly, as one touched by the wing of mortality, all at a time in your life when that could be gratifying.

So I lay, minus my appendix, for some days looking out a hospital window at the snow sifting in a sombre way through some evergreens. I don't suppose it ever crossed my head to wonder how my father was going to pay for this distinction. (I think he sold a woodlot that he had kept when he disposed of his father's farm. He would have hoped to use it for trapping or sugaring. Or perhaps he felt an unmentionable nostalgia.)

Then I went back to school, and enjoyed being excused from physical training for longer than necessary, and one Saturday morning when my mother and I were alone in the kitchen she told me that my appendix had been taken out in the hospital, just as I thought, but it was not the only thing removed. The doctor had seen fit to take it out while he was at it, but the main thing that concerned him was a growth. A growth, my mother said, the size of a turkey's egg.

But don't worry, she said, it's all over now.

The thought of cancer never entered my head and she never mentioned it. I don't think there could be such a revelation today without some kind of question, some probing about whether it was or it wasn't. Cancerous or benign—we would want to know at once. The only way I can explain our failure to speak of it was that there must have been a cloud around that word like the cloud around the mention of sex. Worse, even. Sex was disgusting but there must be some gratification there—indeed we knew there was, though our mothers were not aware of it—while even the word cancer made you think of some dark rotting ill-smelling creature that you would not look at even while you kicked it out of the way.

So I did not ask and wasn't told and can only suppose it was benign or was most skillfully got rid of, for here I am today. And so little do I think of it that all through my life when called upon to list my surgeries, I automatically say or write only "Appendix."

This conversation with my mother would probably have taken place in the Easter holidays, when all the snowstorms and snow mountains had vanished and the creeks were in flood, laying hold of anything they could get at, and the brazen summer was just looming ahead. Our climate had no dallying, no mercies.

In the heat of early June I got out of school, having made good enough marks to free me from the final examinations. I looked well, I did chores around the house, I read books as usual, nobody knew there was a thing the matter with me.

Now I have to describe the sleeping arrangements in the bedroom occupied by my sister and myself. It was a small room that could not accommodate two single beds side by side, so the solution was a pair of bunk beds, with a ladder in place to help whoever slept in the top bunk climb into bed. That was me. When I had been younger and prone to teasing, I would lift up the corner of my thin mattress and threaten to spit on my little sister lying helpless in the bunk below. Of course my sister—her name was Catherine—was not really helpless. She could hide under her covers, but my game was to watch until suffocation or curiosity drove her out, and at that moment to spit or successfully pretend to spit on her bared face, enraging her.

I was too old for such fooling, certainly too old by this time. My sister was nine when I was fourteen. The relationship between us was always unsettled. When I wasn't tormenting her, teasing her in some asinine way, I would take on the role of sophisticated counsellor or hair-raising storyteller. I would dress her up in some of the old clothes that had been put away in my mother's hope chest, being too fine to be cut up for quilts and too out of date for anybody to wear. I would put my mother's old caked rouge and powder on her face and tell her how pretty she looked. She was pretty, without a doubt, though the face I put on her gave her the look of a freakish foreign doll.

I don't mean to say that I was entirely in control of her, or even that our lives were constantly intertwined. She had her own friends, her own games. These tended towards domesticity rather than glamour. Dolls were taken for walks in their baby carriages, or sometimes kittens were dressed up and walked in the dolls' stead, always frantic to get out. Also there were play sessions when somebody got to be the teacher and could slap the others over the wrists and make them pretend to cry, for various infractions and stupidities.

In the month of June, as I have said, I was free of school and left on my own, as I don't remember being in quite the same way in any other time of my growing-up. I did some chores in the house, but my mother must have been well enough, as yet, to handle most of that work. Or perhaps we had just enough money at the time to hire what she—my mother—would call a maid, though everybody else said hired girl. I don't remember, at any rate, having to tackle any of the jobs that piled up for me in later summers, when I fought quite willingly to maintain the decency of our house. It seems that the mysterious turkey egg must have given me some invalid status, so that I could spend part of the time wandering about like a visitor.

Though not trailing any special clouds. Nobody in our family would have got away with that. It was all inward—this uselessness and strangeness I felt. And not continual uselessness either. I remember squatting down to thin the baby carrots as you had to do every spring, so the root would grow to a decent size to be eaten.

It must have been just that every moment of the day was not filled up with jobs, as it was in summers before and after.

So maybe that was the reason that I had begun to have trouble getting to sleep. At first, I think, that meant lying awake maybe till around midnight and wondering at how wide awake I was, with the rest of the household asleep. I would have read, and got tired in the usual way, and turned out my light and waited. Nobody would have called out to me earlier, telling me to put out my light and get to sleep. For the first time ever (and this too must have marked a special status) I was left to make up my own mind about such a thing.

It took a while for the house to change from the light of day and from the household lights turned on late into the evening. Leaving behind the general clatter of things to be done, hung up, finished with, it became a stranger place in which people and the work that dictated their lives fell away, their uses for everything around them fell away, all the furniture retreated into itself and no longer existed because of anybody's attention.

You might think this was a liberation. At first, perhaps it was. The freedom. The strangeness. But as my failure to fall asleep prolonged itself, and as it finally took hold altogether until dark changed into dawn, I became more and more disturbed by it. I started saying rhymes, then real poetry, first to make myself go under but then hardly of my own volition. The activity seemed to mock me. I was mocking myself, as the words turned into absurdity, into the silliest random speech.

I was not myself.

I had been hearing that said of people now and then, all my life, without thinking what it could mean.

So who do you think you are, then?

I'd been hearing that too, without attaching to it any real menace, just taking it as a sort of routine jeering.

Think again.

By this time it wasn't sleep I was after. I knew mere sleep wasn't likely. Maybe not even desirable. Something was taking hold of me and it was my business, my hope, to fight it off. I had the sense to do that, but only barely, as it seemed. Whatever it was was trying to tell me to do things, not exactly for any reason but just to see if such acts were possible. It was informing me that motives were not necessary.

It was only necessary to give in. How strange. Not out of revenge, or for any normal reason, but just because you had thought of something.

And I did think of it. The more I chased the thought away, the more it came back. No vengeance, no hatred—as I've said, no reason, except that something like an utterly cold deep thought that was hardly an urging, more of a contemplation, could take possession of me. I must not even think of it but I did think of it.

The thought was there and hanging in my mind.

The thought that I could strangle my little sister, who was asleep in the bunk below me and whom I loved more than anybody in the world.

I might do it not for any jealousy, viciousness, or anger, but because of madness, which could be lying right beside me there in the night. Not a savage madness either, but something that could be almost teasing. A lazy, teasing, half-sluggish suggestion that seemed to have been waiting a long time.

It might be saying why not. Why not try the worst?

The worst. Here in the most familiar place, the room where we had lain for all of our lives and thought ourselves most safe. I might do it for no reason I or anybody could understand, except that I could not help it.

The thing to do was to get up, to get myself out of that room and out of the house. I went down the rungs of the ladder and never cast a single look at my sister where she slept. Then quietly down the stairs, nobody stirring, into the kitchen where everything was so familiar to me that I could make my way without a light. The kitchen door was not really locked—I am not even sure that we possessed a key. A chair was pushed under the doorknob so that any-body trying to get in would make a great clatter. A slow careful removal of the chair could be managed without making any noise at all.

After the first night I was able to make my moves without a break, so that I could be outside, as it seemed, within a couple of smooth seconds.

Of course there were no streetlights—we were too far from town.

Everything was larger. The trees around the house were always called by their names—the beech tree, the elm tree, the oak tree, the maples always spoken of in the plural and not differentiated, because they clung together. Now they were all intensely black. So were the white lilac tree (no lon-ger with its blooms) and the purple lilac tree—always called lilac trees not bushes because they had grown too big.

The front and back and side lawns were easy to negotiate because I had mown them myself with the idea of giving us some townlike respectability.

The east side of our house and the west side looked on two different worlds, or so it seemed to me. The east side was the town side, even though you could not see any town. Not so much as two miles away, there were houses in rows, with streetlights and running water. And though I have said you could not see any of that, I am really not sure that you couldn't get a certain glow if you stared long enough.

To the west, the long curve of the river and the fields and the trees and the sunsets had nothing to interrupt them. Nothing to do with people, in my mind, or to do with ordi-nary life, ever.

Back and forth I walked, first close to the house and then

venturing here and there as I got to rely on my eyesight and could count on not bumping into the pump handle or the platform that supported the clothesline. The birds began to stir, and then to sing—as if each of them had thought of it separately, up there in the trees. They woke far earlier than I would have thought possible. But soon after those earliest starting songs, there got to be a little whitening in the sky. And suddenly I would be overwhelmed with sleepiness. I went back into the house, where there was suddenly darkness everywhere, and I very properly, carefully, silently, set the tilted chair under the doorknob, and went upstairs without a sound, managing doors and steps with the caution necessary, although I seemed already half asleep. I fell into my pillow, and I woke late—late in our house being around eight o'clock.

I would remember everything then, but it was so absurd—the bad part of it indeed was so absurd—that I could get rid of it fairly easily. My brother and sister had gone off to their classes in the public school, but their dishes were still on the table, a few bits of puffed rice floating in the excess milk.

Absurd.

When my sister got home from school we would swing in the hammock, one of us at either end.

It was in that hammock that I spent much of the days, which possibly accounted for my not getting to sleep at night. And since I did not speak of my night difficulties, nobody came up with the simple information that I'd be better off getting more action during the day.

My troubles returned with the night, of course. The demons got hold of me again. I knew enough soon to get up and out of my bunk without any pretending that things would get better and that I would in fact go to sleep if I just tried hard enough. I made my way as carefully out of the house as I had done before. I became able to find my way around more easily; even the inside of the rooms became more visible to me and yet more strange. I could make out the tongue-in-groove kitchen ceiling put in when the house was built maybe a hundred years ago, and the northern window frame partly chewed away by a dog that had been shut inside, one night long before I was born. I remembered what I had completely forgotten—that I used to have a sandbox there, placed where my mother could watch me out that north window. A great bunch of overgrown spirea was flowering in its place now and you could hardly see out at all.

The east wall of the kitchen had no windows in it but it had a door opening on a stoop where we stood to hang out the heavy wet washing, and haul it in when it was dry and smelling all fresh and congratulatory, from white sheets to dark heavy overalls.

At that stoop I sometimes halted in my night walks. I never sat down but it eased me to look towards town, maybe just to inhale the sanity of it. All the people getting up before long, having their shops to go to, their doors to unlock and milk bottles to take inside, their busyness.

One night—I can't say whether it could be the twentieth or the twelfth or only the eighth or the ninth that I had got up and walked—I got a sense, too late for me to change my pace, that there was somebody around the corner. There was somebody waiting there and I could do nothing but walk right on. I would be caught if I turned my back, and it would be worse that way than to be confronted.

Who was it? Nobody but my father. He too sitting on the stoop looking towards town and that improbable faint light. He was dressed in his day clothes—dark work pants, the next thing to overalls but not quite, and dark, rough shirt and boots. He was smoking a cigarette. One he rolled himself, of course. Maybe the cigarette smoke had alerted me to another presence, though it's possible that in those days the smell of tobacco smoke was everywhere, inside buildings and out, so there was no way to notice it.

He said good morning, in what might have seemed a natural way except that there was nothing natural about it. We weren't accustomed to giving such greetings in our family. There was nothing hostile about this—it was just thought unnecessary, I suppose, when we would see each other off and on all day.

I said good morning back. And it must have really been getting towards morning or my father would not have been dressed for a day's work in that way. The sky may have been whitening but hidden still between the heavy trees. The birds singing too. I had taken to staying away from my bunk till later and later, even though I didn't get comfort from doing so as I had at first. The possibilities that had once inhabited only the bedroom, the bunk beds, were taking up the corners everywhere.

Now that I come to think of it, why wasn't my father in his overalls? He was dressed as if he had to go into town for something, first thing in the morning.

I could not continue walking, the whole rhythm of it had been broken.

"Having trouble sleeping?" he said.

My impulse was to say no, but then I thought of the difficulties of explaining that I was just walking around, so I said yes.

He said that was often the case on summer nights.

"You go to bed tired out and then just as you think you're falling asleep you're wide awake. Isn't that the way?"

I said yes.

I knew now that he had not heard me getting up and walking around on just this one night. The person whose livestock was on the premises, whose earnings such as they were lay all close by, and who kept a handgun in his desk drawer, was certainly going to stir at the slightest creeping on the stairs and the easiest turning of a knob.

I am not sure what conversation he meant to follow then, as regards to my being awake. He seems to have declared wakefulness to be a nuisance, but was that to be all? I certainly did not intend to tell him more. If he had given the slightest intimation that he knew there was more, if he'd even hinted that he had come here intending to hear it, I don't think he'd have got anything out of me at all. I had to break the silence out of my own will, saying that I could not sleep. I had to get out of bed and walk.

Why was that?

I did not know.

Not bad dreams?

No.

"Stupid question," he said. "You wouldn't get chased out of your bed on account of good dreams."

He let me wait to go on, he didn't ask anything. I meant to back off but I kept talking. The truth was told with only the slightest modification.

When I spoke of my little sister I said that I was afraid I would hurt her. I believed that would be enough, that he would know enough of what I meant.

"Strangle her," I said then. I could not stop myself, after all.

Now I could not unsay it, I could not go back to the person I had been before.

My father had heard it. He had heard that I thought myself capable of, for no reason, strangling little Catherine in her sleep.

He said, "Well."

Then he said not to worry. He said, "People have those kinds of thoughts sometimes."

He said this quite seriously and without any sort of alarm or jumpy surprise. People have these kinds of thoughts or fears if you like, but there's no real worry about it, no more than a dream, you could say.

He did not say, specifically, that I was in no danger of doing any such thing. He seemed more to be taking it for granted that such a thing could not happen. An effect of the ether, he said. Ether they gave you in the hospital. No more sense than a dream. It could not happen, in the way that a meteor could not hit our house (of course it could, but the likelihood of its doing so put it in the category of couldn't).

He did not blame me, though, for thinking of it. Did not wonder at me, was what he said.

There were other things he could have said. He could have questioned me further about my attitude to my little sister or my dissatisfactions with my life in general. If this were happening today, he might have made an appointment for me to see a psychiatrist. (I think that is what I might have done for a child, a generation and an income further on.)

The fact is, what he did worked as well. It set me down, but without either mockery or alarm, in the world we were living in.

People have thoughts they'd sooner not have. It happens in life.

If you live long enough as a parent nowadays, you discover that you have made mistakes you didn't bother to know about along with the ones you do know about all too well. You are somewhat humbled at heart, sometimes disgusted with yourself. I don't think my father felt anything like this. I do know that if I had ever taxed him, with his use on me of the razor strap or his belt, he might have said something about liking or lumping it. Those strappings, then, would have stayed in his mind, if they stayed at all, as no more than the necessary and adequate curbing of a mouthy child's imagining that she could rule the roost.

"You thought you were too smart," was what he might have given as his reason for the punishments, and indeed you heard that often in those times, with the smartness figuring as an obnoxious imp that had to have the sass beaten out of him. Otherwise there was the risk of him growing up thinking he was smart. Or her, as the case might be.

However, on that breaking morning he gave me just what I needed to hear and what I was even to forget about soon enough.

I have thought that he was maybe in his better work clothes because he had a morning appointment to go to the bank, to learn, not to his surprise, that there was no extension to his loan. He had worked as hard as he could but the market was not going to turn around and he had to find a new way of supporting us and paying off what we owed at the same time. Or he may have found out that there was a name for my mother's shakiness and that it was not going to stop. Or that he was in love with an impossible woman.

Never mind. From then on I could sleep.

VOICES

WHEN my mother was growing up, she and her whole family would go to dances. These would be held in the schoolhouse, or sometimes in a farmhouse with a big enough front room. Young and old would be in attendance. Someone would play the piano—the household piano or the one in the school—and someone would have brought a violin. The square dancing had complicated patterns or steps, which a person known for a special facility would call out at the top of his voice (it was always a man) and in a strange desperate sort of haste which was of no use at all unless you knew the dance already. As everybody did, having learned them all by the time they were ten or twelve years old.

Married now, with three of us children, my mother was still of an age and temperament to enjoy such dances if she had lived in the true countryside where they were still going on. She would have enjoyed too the round dancing performed by couples, which was supplanting the old style to a certain extent. But she was in an odd situation. We were. Our family was out of town but not really in the country.

My father, who was much better liked than my mother, was a man who believed in taking whatever you were dealt. Not so my mother. She had risen from her farm girl's life to become a schoolteacher, but this was not enough, it had not given her the position she would have liked, or the friends she would have liked to have in town. She was living in the wrong place and had not enough money, but she was not equipped anyway. She could play euchre but not bridge. She was affronted by the sight of a woman smoking. I think people found her pushy and overly grammatical. She said things like "readily" and "indeed so." She sounded as if she had grown up in some strange family who always talked that way. And she hadn't. They didn't. Out on their farms, my aunts and uncles talked the way everybody else did. And they didn't like my mother very much, either.

I don't mean that she spent all her time wishing that things weren't as they were. Like any other woman with washtubs to haul into the kitchen and no running water and a need to spend most of the summer preparing food to be eaten in the winter, she was kept busy. She couldn't even devote as much time as she otherwise would have done in being disappointed with me, wondering why I was not bringing the right kind of friends, or any friends at all, home from the town school. Or why I was shying away from Sunday School recitations, something I used to make a grab at. And why I came home with the ringlets torn out of my hair—a desecration I had managed even before I got to school, because nobody else wore their hair the way she fixed mine. Or indeed why I had learned to blank out even the prodigious memory I once had for reciting poetry, refusing to use it ever again for showing off.

But I am not always full of sulks and disputes. Not yet. Here I am when about ten years old, all eager to dress up and accompany my mother to a dance.

The dance was being held in one of the altogether decent but not prosperous-looking houses on our road. A large wooden house inhabited by people I knew nothing about, except that the husband worked in the foundry, even though he was old enough to be my grandfather. You didn't quit the foundry then, you worked as long as you could and tried to save up money for when you couldn't. It was a disgrace, even in the middle of what I later learned to call the Great Depression, to find yourself having to go on the Old Age Pension. It was a disgrace for your grown children to allow it, no matter what straits they were in themselves.

Some questions come to mind now that didn't then.

Were the people who lived in the house giving this dance simply in order to create some festivity? Or were they charging money? They might have found themselves in difficulties, even if the man had a job. Doctor's bills. I knew how dreadfully that could fall upon a family. My little sister was delicate, as people said, and her tonsils had already been removed. My brother and I suffered spectacular bronchitis every winter, resulting in doctor's visits. Doctors cost money.

The other thing I might have wondered about was why I should have been chosen to accompany my mother, instead of my father doing that. But it really isn't such a puzzle. My father maybe didn't like to dance, and my mother did. Also, there were two small children to be looked after at home, and I wasn't old enough yet to do that. I can't remember my parents ever hiring a babysitter. I'm not sure the term was even familiar in those days. When I was in my teens I found employment that way, but times had changed by then.

We were dressed up. At the country dances my mother remembered, there was never any appearance in those sassy square dance outfits you would see later on television. Everybody wore their best, and not to do so—to appear in anything like those frills and neckerchieves that were the supposed attire of country folk—would have been an insult to the hosts and everybody else. I wore a dress my mother had made for me, of soft winter wool. The skirt was pink and the top yellow, with a heart of the pink wool sewn where my left breast would be one day. My hair was combed and moistened and shaped into those long fat sausage-like ringlets that I got rid of every day on the way to school. I had complained about wearing them to the dance on the grounds that nobody else wore them. My mother's retort was that nobody else was so lucky. I dropped the complaint because I wanted to go so much, or perhaps because I thought that nobody from school would be at the dance so it didn't matter. It was the ridicule of my school fellows that I feared always.

My mother's dress was not homemade. It was her best, too elegant for church and too festive for a funeral, and so hardly ever worn. It was made of black velvet, with sleeves to the elbows, and a high neckline. The wonderful thing about it was a proliferation of tiny beads, gold and silver and various colours, sewn all over the bodice and catching the light, changing whenever she moved or only breathed. She had braided her hair, which was still mostly black, then pinned it in a tight coronet on top of her head. If she had been anybody else but my mother I would have thought her thrillingly handsome. I think I did find her so, but as soon as we got into the strange house I had to notice that her best dress was nothing like any other woman's dress, though they must have put on their best too.

The other women I'm speaking of were in the kitchen. That was where we stopped and looked at things set out on a big table. All sorts of tarts and cookies and pies and cakes. And my mother too set down some fancy thing she had made and started to fuss around to make it look better. She commented on how mouthwatering everything looked.

Am I sure she said that—mouthwatering? Whatever she said, it did not sound quite right. I wished then for my father to be there, always sounding perfectly right for the occasion, even when he spoke grammatically. He would do that in our house but not so readily outside of it. He slipped into whatever exchange was going on—he understood that the thing to do was never to say anything special. My mother was just the opposite. With her everything was clear and ringing and served to call attention.

Now that was happening and I heard her laugh, delightedly, as if to make up for nobody's talking to her. She was inquiring where we might put our coats.

It turned out that we could put them anywhere, but if we wanted, somebody said, we could lay them down on the bed upstairs. You got upstairs by a staircase shut in by walls, and there was no light, except at the top. My mother told me to go ahead, she would be up in a minute, and so I did.

A question here might be whether there could really have been a payment for attending that dance. My mother could have stayed behind to arrange it. On the other hand, would people have been asked to pay and still have brought all those refreshments? And were the refreshments really as lavish as I remember? With everybody so poor? But maybe they were already feeling not so poor, with the war jobs and money that soldiers sent home. If I was really ten, and I think I was, then those changes would have been going on for two years.

The staircase came up from the kitchen and also from the front room, joining together into one set of steps that led up to the bedrooms. After I had got rid of my coat and boots in the tidied-up front bedroom, I could still hear my mother's voice ringing out in the kitchen. But I could also hear music coming from the front room, so I went down that way.

The room had been cleared of all furniture except the piano. Dark green cloth blinds, of the kind I thought particularly dreary, were pulled down over the windows. But there was no dreary sort of atmosphere in the room. Many people were dancing, decorously holding on to each other, shuffling or swaying in tight circles. A couple of girls still in school were dancing in a way that was just becoming popular, moving opposite each other and sometimes holding hands, sometimes not. They actually smiled a greeting when they saw me, and I melted with pleasure, as I was apt to do when any confident older girl paid any attention to me.

There was a woman in that room you couldn't help noticing, one whose dress would certainly put my mother's in the shade. She must have been quite a bit older than my mother—her hair was white, and worn in a smooth sophisticated arrangement of what were called marcelled waves, close to her scalp. She was a large person with noble shoulders and broad hips, and she was wearing a dress of golden-orange taffeta, cut with a rather low square neck and a skirt that just covered her knees. Her short sleeves held her arms tightly and the flesh on them was heavy and smooth and white, like lard.

This was a startling sight. I would not have thought it possible that somebody could look both old and polished, both heavy and graceful, bold as brass and yet mightily dignified. You could have called her brazen, and perhaps my mother later did—that was her sort of word. Someone better disposed might have said, stately. She didn't really show off, except in the whole style and colour of the dress. She and the man with her danced together in a respectful, rather absentminded style, like spouses.

I didn't know her name. I had never seen her before. I didn't know that she was notorious in our town, and maybe farther afield, for all I knew.

I think that if I was writing fiction instead of remembering something that happened, I would never have given her that dress. A kind of advertisement she didn't need.

Of course, if I had lived in the town, instead of just going in and out every day for school, I might have known that she was a notable prostitute. I would surely have seen her sometime, though not in that orange dress. And I would not have used the word prostitute. Bad woman, more likely. I would have known that there was something disgusting and dangerous and exciting and bold about her, without knowing exactly what it was. If somebody had tried to tell me, I don't think I would have believed them.

There were several people in town who looked unusual and maybe she would have seemed to me just another. There was the hunchbacked man who polished the doors of the town hall every day and as far as I know did nothing else. And the quite proper-looking woman who never stopped talking in a loud voice to herself, scolding people who were nowhere in sight.

I would have learned in time what her name was and eventually found out that she really did the things I could not believe she did. And that the man I saw dancing with her and whose name perhaps I never knew was the owner of the poolroom. One day when I was in high school a couple of girls dared me to go into the poolroom when we were walking past, and I did, and there he was, the same man. Though he was balder and heavier now, and wearing shabbier clothes. I don't recall that he said anything to me, but he did not have to. I bolted back to my friends, who were not quite friends after all, and told them nothing.

When I saw the owner of the poolroom, the whole scene of the dance came back to me, the thumping piano and the fiddle music and the orange dress, which I would by then have called ridiculous, and my mother's sudden appearance with her coat on that she had probably never taken off.

There she was, calling my name through the music in the tone I particularly disliked, the tone that seemed to specially remind me that it was thanks to her I was on this earth at all.

She said, "Where is your coat?" As if I had mislaid it somewhere.

"Upstairs."

"Well go and get it."

She would have seen it there if she herself had been upstairs at all. She must never have got past the kitchen, she must have been fussing around the food with her own coat unbuttoned but not removed, until she looked into the room where the dancing was taking place and knew who that orange dancer was.

"Don't delay," she said.

I didn't intend to. I opened the door to the stairway and ran up the first steps and found that where the stairs took their turn some people were sitting, blocking my way. They didn't see me coming—they were taken up, it seemed, with something serious. Not an argument, exactly, but an urgent sort of communication.

Two of these people were men. Young men in Air Force uniforms. One sitting on a step, one leaning forward on a lower step with a hand on his knee. There was a girl sitting on the step above them, and the man nearest to her was patting her leg in a comforting way. I thought she must have fallen on these narrow stairs and hurt herself, for she was crying.

Peggy. Her name was Peggy. "Peggy, Peggy," the young men were saying, in their urgent and even tender voices.

She said something I couldn't make out. She spoke in a childish voice. She was complaining, the way you complain about something that isn't fair. You say over and over that something isn't fair, but in a hopeless voice, as if you don't expect the thing that isn't fair to be righted. Mean is another word to be made use of in these circumstances. It's so mean. Somebody has been so mean.

By listening to my mother's talk to my father when we

got home I found out something of what had happened, but I was not able to get it straight. Mrs. Hutchison had shown up at the dance, driven by the poolroom man, who was not known to me then as the poolroom man. I don't know what name my mother called him by, but she was sadly dismayed by his behaviour. News had got out about the dance and some boys from Port Albert—that is, from the Air Force base—had decided to put in an appearance as well. Of course that would have been all right. The Air Force boys were all right. It was Mrs. Hutchison who was the disgrace. And the girl.

She had brought one of her girls with her.

"Maybe just felt like an outing," my father said. "Maybe just likes to dance."

My mother seemed not even to have heard this. She said that it was a shame. You expected to have a nice time, a nice decent dance within a neighbourhood, and then it was all ruined.

I was in the habit of assessing the looks of older girls. I had not thought Peggy was particularly pretty. Maybe her makeup had rubbed off with her crying. Her rolled-up mousey-coloured hair had got loose from some of its bobby pins. Her fingernails were polished but they still looked as if she chewed them. She didn't seem much more grown up than one of those whiny, sneaky, perpetually complaining older girls I knew. Nevertheless the young men treated her as if she was someone who deserved never to have encountered one rough moment, someone who rightfully should be petted and pleasured and have heads bowed before her.

One of them offered her a ready-made cigarette. This in itself I saw as a treat, since my father rolled his own and so did every other man I knew. But Peggy shook her head and complained in that hurt voice that she did not smoke. Then the other man offered a stick of gum, and she accepted it.

What was going on? I had no way of knowing. The boy who had offered the gum noticed me, while rummaging in his pocket, and he said, "Peggy? Peggy, here's a little girl I think wants to go upstairs."

She dropped her head so I couldn't look into her face. I smelled perfume as I went by. I smelled their cigarettes too and their manly woollen uniforms, their polished boots.

When I came downstairs with my coat on they were still there, but this time they had been expecting me, so they all kept quiet while I passed. Except that Peggy gave one loud sniffle, and the young man nearest to her kept stroking her upper leg. Her skirt was pulled up and I saw the fastener holding her stocking.

For a long time I remembered the voices. I pondered over the voices. Not Peggy's. The men's. I know now that some of the Air Force men stationed at Port Albert early in the war had come out from England, and were training there to fight the Germans. So I wonder if it was the accent of some part of Britain that I was finding so mild and entrancing. It was certainly true that I had never in my life heard a man speak in that way, treating a woman as if she was so fine and valued a creature that whatever it was, whatever unkindness had come near her, was somehow a breach of a law, a sin.

What did I think had happened to make Peggy cry? The question did not much interest me at the time. I was not a brave person myself. I cried when chased and beaten with shingles on the way home from my first school. I cried when the teacher in the town school singled me out, in front of the class, to expose the shocking untidiness of my desk. And when she phoned my mother about the same problem and my mother hanging up the phone herself wept, enduring misery because I was not a credit to her. It seemed as though some people were naturally brave and others weren't. Somebody must have said something to Peggy, and there she was snuffling, because like me she was not thick-skinned.

It must have been that orange-dressed woman who had been mean, I thought, for no particular reason. It had to have been a woman. Because if it had been a man, one of her Air Force comforters would have punished him. Told him to watch his mouth, maybe dragged him outside and beaten him up.

So it wasn't Peggy I was interested in, not her tears, her crumpled looks. She reminded me too much of myself. It was her comforters I marvelled at. How they seemed to bow down and declare themselves in front of her.

What had they been saying? Nothing in particular. All right, they said. It's all right, Peggy, they said. Now, Peggy. All right. All right.

Such kindness. That anybody could be so kind.

It is true that these young men, brought to our country to train for bombing missions on which so many of them would be killed, might have been speaking in the normal accents of Cornwall or Kent or Hull or Scotland. But to me they seemed to be unable to open their mouths without uttering some kind of blessing, a blessing on the moment. It didn't occur to me that their futures were all bound up with disaster, or that their ordinary lives had flown out the window and been smashed on the ground. I just thought of the blessing, how wonderful to get on the receiving end of it, how strangely lucky and undeserving was that Peggy.

And, for I don't know how long, I thought of them. In the cold dark of my bedroom they rocked me to sleep. I could turn them on, summon up their faces and their voices—but oh, far more, their voices were now directed to myself and not to any unnecessary third party. Their hands blessed my own skinny thighs and their voices assured me that I, too, was worthy of love.

And while they still inhabited my not yet quite erotic fantasies they were gone. Some, many, gone for good.

DEAR LIFE

I LIVED when I was young at the end of a long road, or a road that seemed long to me. Back behind me, as I walked home from primary school, and then from high school, was the real town with its activity and its sidewalks and its streetlights for after dark. Marking the end of town were two bridges over the Maitland River: one narrow iron bridge, where cars sometimes got into trouble over which one should pull off and wait for the other, and a wooden walkway which occasionally had a plank missing, so that you could look right down into the bright, hurrying water. I liked that, but somebody always came and replaced the plank eventually.

Then there was a slight hollow, a couple of rickety houses that got flooded every spring, but that people—different people—always came and lived in anyway. And then another bridge, over the mill race, which was narrow but deep enough to drown you. After that, the road divided, one part of it going south up a hill and over the river again to become a genuine highway, and the other jogging around the old fairgrounds to turn west.

That westward road was mine.

There was also a road heading north, which had a brief but real sidewalk and several houses close together, as if they were in town. One of them had a sign in the window that said "Salada Tea," evidence that groceries had once been for sale there. Then there was a school, which I had attended for two years of my life and wished never to see again. After those years, my mother had made my father buy an old shed in town so that he would be paying town taxes and I could go to the town school. As it turned out, she hadn't needed to do that, because in the year, in the very month, that I started school in town, war was declared with Germany and, as if by magic, the old school, the school where bullies had taken away my lunch and threatened to beat me up and where nobody seemed to learn anything in the midst of the uproar, had quieted down. Soon it had only one room and one teacher, who probably did not even lock the doors at recess. It appeared that the same boys who'd always asked me rhetorically and alarmingly if I wanted to fuck were just as eager to get jobs as their older brothers were to go into the Army.

I don't know if the school toilets had improved by then or not, but they had been the worst thing. It was not as if we didn't resort to an outhouse at home, but it was clean and even had a linoleum floor. At that school, for reasons of contempt or whatever, nobody seemed to bother to aim for the hole. In many ways it wasn't easy for me in town, either, because everybody else had been together since grade one, and there were many things that I hadn't learned yet, but it was a comfort to see my new school's unsoiled seats and to hear the noble urban sound of its flush toilets.

During my time at the first school, I did make one friend. A girl whom I'll call Diane arrived partway through my second year. She was about my age, and she lived in one of those houses with a sidewalk. She asked me one day if I could do the Highland fling, and when I said no she offered to teach me. With this in mind, we went to her place after school. Her mother had died and she had come to live with her grandparents. To dance the Highland fling, she told me, you needed clicking shoes, which she had and, of course, I didn't, but our feet were nearly the same size, so we could trade while she tried to teach me. Eventually we got thirsty and her grandmother gave us a drink of water, but it was horrid water from a dug well, just like at school. I explained about the superior water we got from a drilled well at home, and the grandmother said, without taking any sort of offence, that she wished they had that too.

But then, too soon, my mother was outside, having gone to the school and discovered my whereabouts. She honked the car horn to summon me and didn't even respond to the grandmother's friendly wave. My mother did not drive often, and when she did there was a nervous solemnity to the occasion. On the way home, I was told that I was never to enter that house again. (This proved not to be a difficulty, because Diane stopped appearing at school a few days later—she had been sent away somewhere.) I told my mother that Diane's mother was dead and she said yes, she knew. I told her about the Highland fling, and she said that I might learn it properly sometime, but not in that house.

I did not find out then—and I don't know when I did find out—that Diane's mother had been a prostitute and had died of some ailment it seemed that prostitutes caught. She'd wanted to be buried at home, and the minister of our own church had done the service. There had been controversy over the text he had used. Some people thought he should have left it out, but my mother believed that he had done the right thing.

The wages of sin is death.

My mother told me this a long time later, or what seemed a long time later, when I was at the stage of hating a good many things she said, and particularly when she used that voice of shuddering, even thrilled, conviction.

I kept running into the grandmother now and again. She always had a little smile for me. She said it was wonderful how I kept going to school, and she reported on Diane, who also continued at school for a notable time, wherever she was—though not for as long as I did. According to her grandmother, she then got a job in a restaurant in Toronto, where she wore an outfit with sequins on it. I was old enough at that point, and mean enough, to assume that it was probably a place where you also took the sequin outfit off.

Diane's grandmother wasn't the only one who thought I was taking a long time at school. Along my road, there were a number of houses set farther apart than they would have been in town but that still didn't have much in the way of property around them. One of them, on a small hill, belonged to Waitey Streets, a one-armed veteran of the First World War. He kept some sheep and had a wife I saw only once in all those years, when she was filling the drinking pail at the pump. Waitey liked to joke about the long time I had been at school and how it was a pity that I could never pass my exams and be done with it. And I joked back, pretending that was true. I was not sure what he really believed. This was the way you knew people on the road, and they knew you. You'd say hello, and they'd say hello and something about the weather, and if they had a car and you were walking, they would give you a ride. It wasn't like the real country, where people usually knew the insides of one another's houses and everybody had more or less the same way of making a living.

I wasn't taking longer to finish high school than any-body else who went through the full five grades would do. But few students did that. Nobody expected in those days that the same number of people who entered high school in grade nine would come out, all stuffed with knowledge and proper grammar, at the end of grade thirteen. People got part-time jobs and gradually those turned into full-time jobs. Girls got married and had babies, in that order or the other. In grade thirteen, with only about a quarter of the original class left, there was a sense of scholarship, of serious achievement, or perhaps just a special kind of serene imprac-ticality that hung on, no matter what happened to you later.

I felt as if I were a lifetime away from most of the people I had known in grade nine, let alone in that first school.

In a corner of our dining room was something that always surprised me a little when I got out the Electrolux to clean the floor. I knew what it was—a very new-looking golf bag, with the golf clubs and balls inside. I just wondered what it was doing in our house. I knew hardly anything about the game, but I had my ideas about the type of people who played it. They were not people who wore overalls, as my father did, though he put on better work pants when he went downtown. I could, to some extent, imagine my mother getting into the sporty kind of clothes you would have to wear, tying a scarf around her fine, blowing hair. But not actually trying to hit a ball into a hole. The frivolity of such an act was surely beyond her.

She must have thought differently at one time. She must have thought that she and my father were going to transform themselves into a different sort of people, people who enjoyed a degree of leisure. Golf. Dinner parties. Perhaps she had convinced herself that certain boundaries were not there. She had managed to get herself off a farm on the bare Canadian Shield—a farm much more hopeless than the one my father came from—and she had become a schoolteacher, who spoke in such a way that her own relatives were not easy around her. She might have got the idea that after such striving she would be welcomed anywhere.

My father had other ideas. It wasn't that he thought that town people or any people were actually better than he was. But he believed perhaps that was what they were thinking. And he preferred never to give them a chance to show it.

It seemed that, in the matter of golf, it was my father who had won.

It wasn't as if he'd been content to live the way his parents had expected him to live, taking over their decent farm. When he and my mother left their communities behind and bought this plot of land at the end of a road near a town they didn't know, their idea was almost certainly to become prosperous by raising silver foxes and, later on, mink. As a boy, my father had found himself happier following a trap-line than helping on the farm or going to high school—and richer, too, than he had ever been before—and this idea had come upon him and he had taken it up, as he thought, for a lifetime. He put what money he had collected into it, and my mother contributed her teacher's savings. He built all the pens and shelters in which the animals would live, and put up the wire walls that would contain their captive lives. The plot of land, twelve acres large, was the right size, with a hayfield and enough pasture for our own cow and what-ever old horses were waiting to be fed to the foxes. The pasture ran right down to the river and had twelve elm trees shading it.

There was quite a lot of killing going on, now that I think of it. The old horses had to be turned into meat and the fur-bearing animals culled every fall to leave just the breeders. But I was used to this and could easily ignore it all, constructing for myself a scene that was purified to resemble something out of the books I liked, such as *Anne of Green Gables* or *Pat of Silver Bush*. I had the help of the elm trees, which hung over the pasture, and the shining river, and the surprise of a spring that came out of the bank above the pasture, providing water for the doomed horses and the cow and also for me, out of a tin mug I brought there. Fresh manure was always around, but I ignored it, as Anne must have done at Green Gables.

In those days, I had to help my father sometimes, because my brother wasn't old enough yet. I pumped fresh water, and I walked up and down the rows of pens, cleaning out the animals' drinking tins and refilling them. I enjoyed this. The importance of the work, the frequent solitude were just what I liked. Later on, I had to stay in the house to help my mother, and I was full of resentment and quarrelsome remarks. "Talking back" it was called. I hurt her feelings, she said, and the outcome was that she would go to the barn to tell on me, to my father. Then he'd have to interrupt his work to give me a beating with his belt. (This was not an uncommon punishment at the time.) Afterwards, I'd lie weeping in bed and make plans to run away. But that phase also passed, and in my teens I became manageable, even jolly, noted for my funny recountings of things that I had heard about in town or that had happened at school.

Our house was of a decent size. We didn't know exactly when it had been built but it had to be less than a century old, because 1858 was the year the first settler had stopped at a place called Bodmin—which had now disappeared—built himself a raft, and come down the river to clear trees from the land that later became a whole village. That early village soon had a sawmill and a hotel and three churches and a school, the same school that was my first, and so dreaded by me. Then a bridge was built across the river, and it began to dawn on people how much more convenient it would be to live over on the other side, on higher ground, and the original settlement dwindled away to the disreputable, and then just peculiar, half-village that I have spoken of.

Our house would not have been one of the very first houses in that early settlement, because it was covered with brick, and they were all just wood, but it had probably gone up not long afterwards. It turned its back on the village; it faced west across slightly downsloping fields to the hidden curve where the river made what was called the Big Bend. Beyond the river was a patch of dark evergreen trees, probably cedar but too far away to tell. And even farther away, on another hillside, was another house, quite small at that distance, facing ours, that we would never visit or know and that was to me like a dwarf's house in a story. But we knew the name of the man who lived there, or had lived there at one time, for he might have died by now. Roly Grain, his name was, and he does not have any further part in what I'm writing now, in spite of his troll's name, because this is not a story, only life.

My mother had two miscarriages before she had me, so when I was born, in 1931, there must have been some satisfaction. But the times were getting less and less promising. The truth was that my father had got into the fur business just a little too late. The success he'd hoped for would have been more likely back in the mid-twenties, when furs were newly popular and people had money. But he had not got started then. Still, we survived, right up to and through the war, and even at the end of the war there must have been an encouraging flurry, because that was the summer my father fixed up the house, adding a layer of brown paint over the traditional redbrick. There was some problem with the way the bricks and boards were fitted; they did not keep out the cold as well as they were supposed to. It was thought that the coat of paint would help, though I can't recall that it ever did. Also, we got a bathroom, and the unused dumb-waiter became kitchen cupboards, and the big dining room with the open stairway changed into a regular room with enclosed stairs. That change comforted me in some unexamined way, because my father's beatings of me had taken place in the old room, with me wanting to die for the misery and shame of it all. Now the difference in the setting made it hard even to imagine such a thing happening. I was in high school and doing better every year, as activities like hemstitching and writing with a straight pen were left behind, and social studies became history and you could learn Latin.

After the optimism of that season of redecoration, however, our business dried up again, and this time it never came back. My father pelted all the foxes, then the mink, and got what shockingly little money he could for them, then he worked by day pulling down the sheds where that enterprise had been born and had died, before heading off to take the five-o'clock watch in the foundry. He would not come home until around midnight.

As soon as I got home from school, I went to work making my father's lunch. I fried two slices of cottage roll and put lots of ketchup on them. I filled his thermos with strong black tea. I put in a bran muffin with jam on it, or perhaps a heavy piece of homemade pie. Sometimes on Saturdays I made a pie, and sometimes my mother did, though her baking was getting to be unreliable.

Something had come upon us that was even more unexpected and would become more devastating than the loss of income, though we didn't know it yet. It was the early onset of Parkinson's disease, which showed up when my mother was in her forties.

At first, it was not too bad. Her eyes only rarely turned up into her head in a wandering way, and the soft down from an oversupply of saliva was just visible around her lips. She could get dressed in the mornings with some help, and she was able to do occasional chores around the house. She held on to some strength in herself for a surprisingly long time.

You would think that this was just too much. The business gone, my mother's health going. It wouldn't do in fiction. But the strange thing is that I don't remember that time as unhappy. There wasn't a particularly despairing mood around the house. Maybe it was not understood then that my mother wouldn't get any better, only worse. As for my father, he had his strength and would have it for a long time yet. He liked the men he worked with at the foundry, who were, for the most part, men like himself, who'd had some sort of downturn or extra burden added to their lives. He liked the challenging work he did in addition to being the early-night watchman. That work involved pouring molten metal into moulds. The foundry made old-fashioned stoves that were sold all over the world. It was a dangerous job, but it was up to you to look out, as my father said. And there was decent pay—a novelty for him.

I believe he was glad to get away, even to do this hard and risky work. To get out of the house and into the company of other men who had their own problems but made the best of things.

Once he was gone, I'd start on supper. I could make things that I thought were exotic, like spaghetti or omelettes, as long as they were cheap. And after the dishes were done—my sister had to dry them, and my brother had to be nagged into throwing the dishwater out over the dark field (I could do that myself but liked giving orders)—I sat down with my feet in the warming oven, which had lost its door, and read the big novels I borrowed from the town library: *Independent People,* which was about life in Iceland, harder than ours by far, but with a hopeless grandeur to it, or *Remembrance of Things Past,* which was about nothing I could understand at all but was not on that account to be given up on, or *The Magic Mountain,* about tuberculosis and containing a great argument between what on one side seemed to be a genial and progressive notion of life and, on the other, a dark and somehow thrilling despair. I never did homework in this precious time, but when exams came I buckled down and stayed up almost all night, cramming my head with whatever I was supposed to know. I had a prodigious short-term memory, and that worked quite well for what was required.

Against several odds, I believed myself a lucky person.

Sometimes my mother and I talked, mostly about her younger days. I seldom objected now to her way of looking at things.

Several times, she told me a story that had to do with the house that now belonged to the war veteran named Waitey Streets—the man who marvelled at the length of time it was taking me to get through school. The story was not about him but about someone who had lived in that house long before he did, a crazy old woman named Mrs. Netterfield. Mrs. Netterfield had had her groceries delivered, as we all did, after ordering them over the phone. One day, my mother said, the grocer forgot to put in her butter, or she forgot to order it, and when the delivery boy was opening the back of the truck she noticed the mistake and became upset. And she was prepared, in a way. She had her hatchet with her and she raised it as if to punish the grocery boy—though, of course, it wasn't his fault—and he ran up to the driver's seat and pulled off without even closing the back doors.

Some things about this story were puzzling, though I didn't think about them at the time and neither did my mother. How could the old woman have been sure already that the butter was missing in the load of groceries? And why would she have come equipped with a hatchet before she knew there was any fault to find? Did she carry it with her at all times, in case of provocations in general?

Mrs. Netterfield was said to have been quite a lady when she was younger.

There was another story about Mrs. Netterfield that had more interest because it featured me and took place around our house.

It was a beautiful day in the fall. I had been set out to sleep in my baby carriage on the little patch of new lawn. My father was away for the afternoon—perhaps helping out his father on the old farm, as he sometimes did—and my mother was doing some clothes-washing at the sink. For a first baby there was a celebratory load of knitwear, ribbons, things to be washed carefully by hand, in soft water. There was no window in front of my mother as she washed and wrung things out at the sink. To get a look outside, you had to cross the room to the north window. That gave you a view of the driveway, which led from the mailbox to the house.

Why did my mother decide to leave her washing and wringing out in order to look at the driveway? She was not expecting any company. My father wasn't late. Possibly she had asked him to get something at the grocery store, something she needed for whatever she was making for supper, and she was wondering if he would be home in time for her to make it. She was a fairly fancy cook in those days—more so, in fact, than her mother-in-law and the other women in my father's family thought necessary. When you looked at the cost, as they would say.

Or it may have had nothing to do with supper but have involved a clothes pattern he was picking up, or a piece of material for a new dress she wanted to make for herself.

She never said afterwards why she had done it.

Misgivings about my mother's cooking were not the only problem with my father's family. There must have been some discussion about her clothes too. I think of how she used to wear an afternoon dress, even if she was only washing things at the sink. She took a half-hour nap after the noon meal and always put on a different dress when she got up. When I looked at photographs later on, I thought that the fashions of the time had not been becoming to her, or to anybody. The dresses were shapeless, and bobbed hair did not suit my mother's full, soft face. But this would not have been the objection of my father's female relatives who lived close enough to keep tabs on her. Her fault was that she did not look like what she was. She did not look as if she had been brought up on a farm, or as if she intended to remain on one.

She did not see my father's car coming down the lane. Instead, she saw the old woman, Mrs. Netterfield. Mrs. Netterfield must have walked over from her own house. The same house where, much later on, I would see the one-armed man who teased me, and just the one time his bob-haired wife, at the pump. The house from which, long before I knew anything about her, the crazy woman had pursued the delivery boy with a hatchet, on account of butter.

My mother must have seen Mrs. Netterfield at various times before she saw her walking down our lane. Maybe they had never spoken. It's possible, though, that they had. My mother might have made a point of it, even if my father had told her that it was not necessary. It might even lead to trouble was what he probably would have said. My mother had sympathy for people who were like Mrs. Netterfield, as long as they were decent.

But now she was not thinking of friendliness or decency. Now she was running out the kitchen door to grab me out of my baby carriage. She left the carriage and the covers where they were and ran back into the house, attempting to lock the kitchen door behind her. The front door she did not need to worry about—it was always locked.

But there was a problem with the kitchen door. As far as I know, it never had a proper lock. There was just a custom, at night, of pushing one of the kitchen chairs against that door, and tilting it with the chair back under the doorknob in such a way that anybody pushing it to get in would have made a dreadful clatter. A fairly haphazard way of maintaining safety, it seems to me, and not in keeping, either, with the fact that my father had a revolver in the house, in a desk drawer. Also, as was natural in the house of a man who regularly had to shoot horses, there was a rifle and a couple of shotguns. Unloaded, of course.

Did my mother think of any weapon, once she had got the doorknob wedged in place? Had she ever picked up a gun, or loaded one, in her life?

Did it cross her mind that the old woman might just be paying a neighbourly visit? I don't think so. There must have been a difference in the walk, a determination in the approach of a woman who was not a visitor coming down the lane, not making a friendly approach down our road.

It is possible that my mother prayed, but never mentioned it.

She knew that there was an investigation of the blankets in the carriage, because, just before she pulled down the kitchen-door blind, she saw one of those blankets being flung out to land on the ground. After that, she did not try to get the blind down on any other window, but stayed with me in her arms in a corner where she could not be seen.

No decent knock on the door. But no pushing at the chair, either. No banging or rattling. My mother in the hiding place by the dumbwaiter, hoping against hope that the quiet meant the woman had changed her mind and gone home.

Not so. She was walking around the house, taking her time, and stopping at every downstairs window. The storm windows, of course, were not on now, in summer. She could press her face against every pane of glass. The blinds were all up as high as they could go, because of the fine day. The woman was not very tall, but she did not have to stretch to see inside.

How did my mother know this? It was not as if she were running around with me in her arms, hiding behind one piece of furniture after another, peering out, distraught with terror, to meet with the staring eyes and maybe a wild grin.

She stayed by the dumbwaiter. What else could she do?

There was the cellar, of course. The windows were too small for anybody to get through them. But there was no inside hook on the cellar door. And it would have been more horrible, somehow, to be trapped down there in the dark, if the woman did finally push her way into the house and came down the cellar steps.

There were also the rooms upstairs, but to get there my

mother would have had to cross the big main room—that room where the beatings would take place in the future, but which lost its malevolence after the stairs were closed in.

I don't know when my mother first told me this story, but it seems to me that that was where the earlier versions stopped—with Mrs. Netterfield pressing her face and hands against the glass while my mother hid. But in later versions there was an end to just looking. Impatience or anger took hold and then the rattling and the banging came. No mention of yelling. The old woman may not have had the breath to do it. Or perhaps she forgot what it was she'd come for, once her strength ran out.

Anyway, she gave up; that was all she did. After she had made her tour of all the windows and doors, she went away. My mother finally got the nerve to look around in the silence and concluded that Mrs. Netterfield had gone somewhere else.

She did not, however, take the chair away from the doorknob until my father came home.

I don't mean to imply that my mother spoke of this often. It was not part of the repertoire that I got to know and, for the most part, found interesting. Her struggle to get to high school. The school where she taught, in Alberta, and where the children arrived on horseback. The friends she had at normal school, the innocent tricks that were played.

I could always make out what she was saying, though often, after her voice got thick, other people couldn't. I was her interpreter, and sometimes I was full of misery when I had to repeat elaborate phrases or what she thought were jokes, and I could see that the nice people who stopped to talk were dying to get away.

The visitation of old Mrs. Netterfield, as she called it, was not something I was ever required to talk about. But I must have known about it for a long time. I remember asking her at some point if she knew what had become of the woman afterwards.

"They took her away," she said. "Oh, I think so. She wasn't left to die alone."

After I was married and had moved to Vancouver, I still got the weekly paper that was published in the town where I grew up. I think somebody, maybe my father and his second wife, made sure that I had a subscription. Often I barely looked at it, but one time, when I did, I saw the name Netterfield. It was not the name of someone who was living in the town at present but had apparently been the maiden name of a woman in Portland, Oregon, who had written a letter to the paper. This woman, like me, still had a subscription to her hometown paper, and she had written a poem about her childhood there.

> I know a grassy hillside
> Above a river clear
> A place of peace and pleasure
> A memory very dear—

There were several verses, and as I read I began to understand that she was talking about the same river flats that I had thought belonged to me.

"The lines I am enclosing were written from memories of that old hillside," she said. "If they are worthy of a little space in your time-honoured paper, I thank you."

The sun upon the river
With ceaseless sparkles play
And over on the other bank
Are blossoms wild and gay—

That was our bank. My bank. Another verse was about a stand of maples, but there I believe she was remembering it wrong—they were elms, which had all died of Dutch elm disease by now.

The rest of the letter made things clearer. The woman said that her father—his name had been Netterfield—had bought a piece of land from the government in 1883, in what was later called the Lower Town. The land ran down to the Maitland River.

Across the Iris-bordered stream
The shade of maples spread
And, on the river's watery field,
White geese, in flocks are fed

She had left out, just as I would have done, the way the spring got muddied up and soiled all around by horses' hooves. And of course left out the manure.

In fact, I had once made up some poems myself, of a very similar nature, though they were lost now, and maybe had never been written down. Verses that commended Nature, then were a bit hard to wind up. I would have composed them right around the time that I was being so intolerant of my mother, and my father was whaling the unkindness out of me. Or beating the tar out of me, as people would cheerfully say back then.

This woman said that she was born in 1876. She had spent her youth, until she was married, in her father's house. It was where the town ended and the open land began, and it had a sunset view.

Our house.

Is it possible that my mother never knew this, never knew that our house was where the Netterfield family had lived and that the old woman was looking in the windows of what had been her own home?

It is possible. In my old age, I have become interested enough to bother with records and the tedious business of looking things up, and I have found that several different families owned that house between the time that the Netterfields sold it and the time that my parents moved in. You might wonder why it had been disposed of when that woman still had years to live. Had she been left a widow, short of money? Who knows? And who was it who came and took her away, as my mother said? Perhaps it was her daughter, the same woman who wrote poems and lived in Oregon. Perhaps that daughter, grown and distant, was the one she was looking for in the baby carriage. Just after my mother had grabbed me up, as she said, for dear life.

The daughter lived not so far away from me for a while in my adult life. I could have written to her, maybe visited. If I had not been so busy with my own young family and my own invariably unsatisfactory writing. But the person I would really have liked to talk to then was my mother, who was no longer available.

———

I did not go home for my mother's last illness or for her funeral. I had two small children and nobody in Vancouver to leave them with. We could barely have afforded the trip, and my husband had a contempt for formal behaviour, but why blame it on him? I felt the same. We say of some things that they can't be forgiven, or that we will never forgive ourselves. But we do—we do it all the time.

A NOTE ABOUT THE AUTHOR

Alice Munro grew up in Wingham, Ontario, and attended the University of Western Ontario. She has published fifteen previous books – *Dance of the Happy Shades*; *Lives of Girls and Women*; *Something I've Been Meaning To Tell You*; *Who Do You Think You Are?*; *The Moons of Jupiter*; *The Progress of Love*; *Friend of My Youth*; *Open Secrets*; *Selected Stories*; *The Love of a Good Woman*; *Hateship, Friendship, Courtship, Loveship, Marriage*; *Runaway*; *The View from Castle Rock*; *Alice Munro's Best*; and *Too Much Happiness*.

During her remarkable career she has received many awards, including the WH Smith Award in the U.K. for the year's best book. In the U.S.A. she has won the National Book Critics Circle Award, the PEN/Malamud Award for Excellence in Short Fiction, and the U.S. National Arts Club Medal of Honor for Literature. Her stories appear in magazines such as *The New Yorker, The Atlantic Monthly,* and *The Paris Review,* and her work has been translated into thirteen languages. She is in demand to visit many countries, such as Italy, where she received the Flaiano Prize in 2008.

In Canada she has won too many prizes to list. They include three Governor General's Awards, several Libris Awards, and two Giller Prizes. In 2005, she was included in *Time* magazine's list of the world's one hundred most influential people, and in the summer of 2009 she won the Man Booker International

Prize for Lifetime Achievement. In 2001, *The Atlantic Monthly* called her "the living writer most likely to be read in a hundred years' time."

She lives in Clinton, Ontario, in what the literary world now calls "Alice Munro Country."